THE EAGER
APPRENTICE

A gift to Lady Combermere from

Chris Elgood

The Eager Apprentice
by
Chris Elgood

First published in 2011 by Chris Elgood

32 West Street, Tadley, Hampshire, RG26 3SX.
United Kingdom

www.chris@chris-elgood.co.uk

ISBN 978-0-9568948-2-3
Copyright © Chris Elgood

The right of Chris Elgood to be identified as the
author of the work has been asserted by him in accordance
with the Copyright, Designs and Patents Act 1988.

This is a work of fiction. Any resemblance to actual persons,
living or dead, or locations is entirely coincidental

Printed by CPI Antony Rowe, Eastbourne

Chapter One
The Overhearing

The conversation was still going on when Simon's mobile rang and he was summoned to the conference suite – the tiny receiver was still in business, quietly whispering secrets to the empty armchair and anybody near enough to hear. But enough had already come through for Simon to recognise its awfulness.

His mind brought up a childhood memory. He had been walking in a country lane with his uncle, who had suddenly raised his walking stick and slashed madly at something in the hedge. 'An adder,' his uncle had said, 'Very dangerous'. Simon had doubted his uncle's knowledge of snakes and had seen little reason for the savage attack. But now his subconscious had dredged up the appropriate response to perceived danger. Kill it. Kill it quickly. Even before he reached the conference room, Simon had identified assassination as a possible course of action. It was just a microsecond flash, like those used to advertise a coming television serial. Not enough time to show detail, enough only to grasp an image and an action. He saw a death. He knew he had seen it, and he knew it was completely at odds with his ordinary life, or with the life of his imagination. Shocked, he slammed a mental door. There had to be another way; nobody in his position could be so constrained that only an extreme course was possible. But he was disturbed. It was poor preparation for the conference.

For the first ten minutes Simon hardly followed the discussion at all. It mattered little, because he knew very well what his boss was going to say. Instead, he reflected on the unfairness of what seemed now to be thrust upon him. Am I the heroic type, he thought? Was I born with a silver spoon in my mouth and an arrogant confidence in my ability to shake the world? I was not. Simon Trent had no great talent, and was honest enough to face the facts. He had reached his present position as a junior government minister by learning how human systems worked – especially the system of the political party that he had joined. His first contact had been through the owner of the small engineering company to which his school sent him for work experience. Steve Sowerby had been a dedicated party member all his life and made his views obvious to all his staff. When Simon had difficulty finding a job, Steve got him taken on – at the minimum wage allowed – by the constituency office. Simon spent ten years making himself useful, graduating from tea-making to report-writing to minor speaking engagements. He also spent time at college, without much success. Finally, a candidate in a neighbouring constituency fell ill, and a body was needed quickly for a parliamentary seat that was thought impossible to win. Simon was chosen, and his party had a landslide victory. Unexpectedly, Simon found himself in the House of Commons.

In working his way up, he had learnt a great deal about his fellow members, both their good points and their weaknesses. Gradually he had built up a stock of people who felt some sort of debt to him and another stock of people who were slightly afraid of what he might reveal about them. He was a political fixer. He might not be able to move mountains himself, but he often knew somebody else who could.

Simon was not a bad person at all. He believed honestly in the moral objectives of his party, but had come to accept that the end sometimes justified the means. He had cut a few corners and done one or two shady deals. So had thousands of others. He was modestly proud to have found a form of behaviour that brought him a degree of advancement.

Physically, Simon was unremarkable. He was neither tall nor short: neither thin nor fat. His face would have been 'standard issue' if he had not decided to grow a moustache. This was neatly kept, but drooped a bit at the ends, giving him an appearance older than his thirty years. If he had been senior enough to feature in political cartoons, the moustache would have been the feature that cartoonists picked on to exaggerate. He also had ears a bit bigger than the norm. His eyes were his best feature: clear and blue and conveying an image of frankness.

When he had calmed down sufficiently to focus on the conference, he found it quite enjoyable. The issues were ones that he understood and the negotiating ploys subtle. For ninety minutes he concentrated, and his worries took a break. When the conference was over, he was like a patient after an operation – reorientation, the return of pain and a need for strong drugs. He was assailed by the memory of what he had heard and by a deeper realisation of where he stood. He managed to behave normally as he bade farewell to colleagues, collected his coat, passed through security, drove from the car park and showed his pass at the east gate. Then he turned left instead of right and lost himself in small country lanes. It didn't matter to him where he was going, provided nobody else knew. He had to be alone.

He was sufficiently aware of his environment to realise that while he was distraught, the natural world was relaxed and happy. It was a marvellous summer evening. Golden sunlight made the trees an extraordinary bright green, and their shadows a mysterious black. He drove past fields that contained cows and horses and sheep rather than mixed weeds or 'set-aside'. The birds were many and vocal. No hoardings advertised luxurious new developments. There was even a small river with a hump-backed bridge and an optimistic fisherman. 'Lucky man,' Simon thought.

A sign proclaimed Stanford Tump, and another identified The White Hart. 'How English,' he thought. ' How many hundreds of White Harts there must be, scattered around our different counties. Each publican probably thought he was a bit original in his choice of name. It's still a green and pleasant land'. Possibly a drink or two might improve his state of mind. It was a Tuesday, the inn had few customers, and most of those were in one corner, apparently conducting the Annual General Meeting of the District Darts Association. Simon sat on a bench outside the door and attempted logical thought. What had actually happened?

He had arrived early. His brother had persuaded him to try satellite navigation and it had just been installed in his car. Having heard horror stories about technological misdirection, he had allowed time for off-road adventures but experienced only one. He had extricated himself from a gypsy encampment near Slough and thereafter matched the girlish voice of the system quite easily to his perceived surroundings. When it was obvious that Thisbee Manor was only a mile away, he had considered how best to fill in half-an-hour. Stay in his car, smoke a cigarette (obviously impossible once he had arrived) and read the paper? Or arrive early and wait in some draughty entrance hall? Neither won. He was interested in historic buildings, and there was a chance he might be able to have a look round the place before the meeting started. He had driven round two sharp bends and glimpsed entrance gates as he left the second one. Stop! He had overshot. Backing up he had turned into the drive and passed up the typical tree-lined avenue of an aristocratic home. There was a croquet lawn on his left and a tennis court on his right.

As soon as he drew up, a security guard had opened the driver's door. When he stepped out, the guard had whisked the vehicle away to a secure area. He had climbed the imposing stone stairs and entered between the classical pillars, thinking that business high-flyers did themselves rather better than government employees. He had booked in at the reception area and asked for the toilets as a way to escape further directions. These turned out to be beyond a set of double doors. When he left the toilet, Simon realised from the directional signs that his employers had taken over only a part of the house. There were unlabelled doors that presumably led to private areas. He had felt unobserved and free to explore.

After a while, he had found himself in a small drawing room, furnished for after-dinner use. A portrait had attracted his attention: it looked like a Gainsborough, and he had been searching for a signature when he heard voices. He had called out, but heard no answer. Then he had noticed a small loudspeaker. It was on a table, beside a knitting bag, and close to a well-worn armchair. The chair must belong to the mistress of the house and the speaker must be linked to a nursery. It had accidentally been left on. He was hearing a live conversation from some room on an upper floor.

Turn off the speaker. That was the obvious and polite course of action. How Simon wished, now, that he had done so! But he had been slow to react and suddenly he had heard words to prevent him – and not the random mutterings of a sleepy child. Understanding had come to him in stages: first, realisation that this was a wholly adult conversation, next that there was something clandestine about it. Then he heard words like 'casualties' and 'destructive power', also 'storage' and 'concealment'. Simon had shaken his head: this was not possible; his mind was playing tricks – probably based on the present governmental paranoia about terrorism. It was not – not, repeat not, possible! It was a trick. He was hallucinating. Yet he listened very carefully. Five minutes later he knew the worst. He was listening to a plot: a terrorist plot. The talk was now about biological warfare and radiation poisoning and the choice of targets. Somewhere in this Elizabethan country house, conspirators were awaiting a visit from a senior man who was to hear their plans, and, perhaps pronounce upon them.

And then this person was named as 'The Prince'. He was referred to with some annoyance because he had designated this house as the meeting place, and done so with little notice. One of the conspirators was aggressive.

'It's always the same. His convenience is all that matters. He has a high level meeting scheduled here with the British, so we must accept the risk of gaining access illegally and hiding away in the attics.'

Another voice countered, 'You complain too much, Majid. We have a cause and a fine leader. That must outweigh any risk and discomfort.'

Simon remembered how, at the mention of the title, he had collapsed into the nearest chair – and broken a pair of spectacles that somebody had accidentally left there. The only Royal Arab due here for a meeting with the British was Prince Thaqib. He was the chief negotiator for his country in a controversial arms deal. So important was the deal, and so highly controversial that the meeting had been secretly arranged for an unexpected location. The present mansion was not government–owned but had been borrowed for a brief time from a rich industrialist. The British were to be represented by two Ministers of State, one of whom was Simon's boss. Simon was to be present, he had been told, to gain experience.

Surely there was some mistake. This situation was not credible. It was a hoax, maybe. Perhaps some pacifist pressure group had got wind of the arms deal and was mounting a campaign to discredit all those connected with it. Unlikely, Simon's mind told him. Perhaps the children of the house had been left behind and were up there rehearsing a play. Even more unlikely.

Then the child-minding system had delivered the sound of a door opening, chairs scraping as people stood up in respect, and various voices saying 'Good evening, Your Highness.'

A new and authoritative voice called the meeting to order. 'I don't have long. They will be looking for me downstairs in half-an-hour.'

Simon knew that voice. At least, he thought so. They had met often enough and he was 90% sure. But all electronic systems distort sound to a degree and part of him was hoping desperately that he was wrong. He listened eagerly for a longer sample.

'The big thing I have to tell you is that our operation will not take place quickly. There has been a death in our ranks, and I have now been put in charge of a wider campaign of which ours, here, is just one part. It gives us more preparation time, but less excuse for any errors.'

And then Simon's mobile had rung – the conference would start in ten minutes. He left the drawing room and heard no more.

During the meeting, Simon reflected, Prince Thaqib had been his normal self: competent , knowledgeable, decisive, courteous. He was very impressive.

Chapter Two

At The White Hart

The sign creaked loudly in the wind. Simon looked up, and his thoughts moved briefly into another channel. How perfectly, during the meeting, Prince Thaqib had maintained his standard pro-western image. Was it really possible to see him as a terrorist mastermind?

Simon realised that uncertainty had already caused him to compromise his position. He might have spoken out immediately. He could have forced an opportunity to speak to his minister before the meeting started and told of his discovery. He would have been ridiculed, but the world, later on, would have judged it as the natural, immediate response of an honest, if misguided man. He could still speak out now, but it would lack the conviction of a spontaneous action.

Yet surely he had to speak. Every further delay would make it worse. He took out his mobile to dial the minister's direct private line. 'It will end my career,' he reasoned, 'but there's no alternative.'

No signal! In an age when radio masts lurked beside every tree, Stanford Tump was not covered! And then the AGM of the Darts Association broke up and several of the members gathered at a table just inside the door. There was the sound of chairs scraping and pint mugs being placed on the table. Every word of their conversation carried to Simon.

'It's a compromise, of course, but we can make it work and there was no better option.'

'Stanford Dell won't like it, will they?'

'Of course not, but The Archers Butt is too far away in these days when you can't drink more than a pint before driving home.'

'Suppose they ask to have it at The Plover instead? That's closer than The Poachers Rest, which we have kept in the list.'

'Then we reconsider. But that's for the next AGM. Right now, we run with what we have decided.'

'Compromise.' It struck Simon as a word of extreme beauty. How wonderful it would be if he could find a compromise. Instead, it was a stark choice - speak out or keep quiet. Or, just possibly, that other frightful action. Work through the options, he told himself. Suppose he spoke out. What would happen?

Disaster. Consider the position and status of Prince Thaqib. He was adjudged to be very pro-western, and influential in strengthening ties between the UK and his own oil-rich country. He had a huge amount of money to spend – money that would keep thousands of UK workers in decent jobs for five years or more. He had been at Oxford with three current cabinet members and had played two seasons of cricket for a famous amateur club. When in the UK, he dined with all the most important people and attended all the right social events. He even hunted. He rode regularly with the Snargate Vale, despite the hunting laws.

Simon set the credibility of Prince Thaqib against his own status. Who would be believed? Who would people want to believe? The people in power, anyway? One of their own was being accused of an incredible, evil deceit by an upstart party schemer who had somehow landed a minor ministerial post. No contest.

Who was he, Simon Trent, anyway? A political activist who had worked his way up by manipulating things: by fixing people and events in such a way that those most likely to reward him in the future received recognition now. All the things that he wanted overlooked or forgotten would be dragged up. Like being the product of what his party leader called 'a bog-standard comprehensive' and a drop-out from an obscure university. Who would the hierarchy want to believe? Prince Thaqib. Who would be seen as victim rather than criminal? Prince Thaqib. Who would be discredited? Simon Trent. If his story was later proved to be true, would he be vindicated? No. The credit would go to more acceptable people and organisations.

What evidence did he have, anyway? An unsupported report of an overheard conversation – and not even an observed conversation. He had never seen the speakers and had placed his own interpretation on the words. Perhaps what he had heard was a group of actors rehearsing for a play, as he had himself imagined. Perhaps the radio link was not to a nursery at all. Perhaps it was linked to some distant location and the listener in the drawing room – briefly absent – had been a British agent bugging a suspected terrorist hide-out. Any intervention by Simon would blow the whole affair. He could imagine some nasty outcomes.

The evening sun went behind a cloud and Simon's mood slipped from the worried to the maudlin. Why me? He thought of other people who had found themselves in impossible positions. Hamlet. A man who believed his uncle had murdered his father, but was not quite certain and had delayed too long in the hope of finding proof. What a mess Hamlet had made of it! Better to think of a few people who had accepted an apparently impossible burden and yet succeeded. The shepherd boy David had made a good King of Israel, Simon reflected, and Frodo Baggins had carried the One Ring to the crack of doom, and what about Bruce and the spider? He, Simon Trent, had to do something constructive, but what?

Or did he? Nobody knew what he had overheard. He could keep the knowledge to himself. Perhaps the conspiracy would be abandoned, or frustrated by the security services. That would be great. But perhaps not. Maybe the plot would succeed and large numbers killed because of his inaction. He could never live with that. And he might himself be one of the victims – blown up or burnt to ashes or poisoned by drinking tap water.

Then he realised that he had a lesser but more immediate problem. He had drunk much more than he should and was stuck – with his car – in a remote rural district. He explained his problem to the landlord.

'Is there anybody local who could drive me to a mainline station? I could leave my car in your yard overnight and come back for it tomorrow.'

'It's not a good night for that. Jeff Watson does that sort of work, but he's away towards Wales on some journey for the horse racing set. I can't think of anybody else.'

Simon asked for a map, and began planning a route that would keep him away from major roads and police patrols. A conviction for drink-driving would be bad news for a junior minister. Looking up from the map, he noticed that the landlord's wife had joined him behind the bar and was whispering to him. Simon registered the fact that she was a very large woman – cheerful, smiling, rosy-complexioned, full-breasted, and showing brawny arms below a short-sleeved blouse. With only the landlord behind it, the bar had looked small but adequate: with both behind it there was a strong resemblance to a Punch and Judy box.

'Excuse me,' the landlord said, 'but my wife has just reminded me that we could offer you a room here, if you wished. You probably didn't see it, but our sign does say "accommodation". It's ages since we took anybody in, but the room is comfortable enough and it would solve your problem. We could do you an excellent breakfast, too.'

The last hour of Simon's day was improved by some humorous comparisons. He was accustomed to plastic modern hotels with en suite rooms, air conditioning, lifts, and television that offered several channels plus a choice of pay-to-view films. They usually had bathrooms designed for a contortionist. The White Hart was not in that league. His room was large. It was furnished with a double bedstead that had large brass knobs on the corner posts: the type that unscrew and can be used as a secret hiding place by small boys. Simon unscrewed one, and was rewarded by a cache of four old pennies carrying the image of Queen Victoria. The floors were oaken boards, uneven, and in some places having gaps that showed sections of the bar underneath. The stairs were narrow, and twisted, and they creaked. The bathroom was huge – presumably designed in the 17th Century as a bedroom – and was reached by two passages and three corners. The toilet stood on a raised platform in one corner – like a throne. It flushed by pulling on a chain that disappeared through the roof. The response to pulling was a volcanic explosion somewhere in the attic and a torrent reminiscent of Niagara. There was an old, faded notice beside the toilet;

'Do not flush unnecessarily. This drains into a septic tank. Size and location are unknown.'

Simon thought that the Ministry of Health might not like this.

The whole place had character, Simon felt, and individuality.

The bed was very comfortable, and Simon sank into it gratefully, wearing pyjamas loaned by the landlord's wife. They buttoned the wrong way and were too large. He watched the last of the twilight fading in the west and pondered a new thought. He could now, he realised, go back to the mansion early next day and look for clues that might affect his belief. That, at least, would be a constructive action. It was Hamlet-like, but reasonable. But just as he was dropping off another voice whispered to him, 'You will end up hiring an assassin.' Why would that thought never go away?

It was absent briefly when he woke up. His first feelings were of warmth and comfort. The first sounds he heard were birds chattering in the trees outside. The first sight he saw was a ripple of reflected sunlight as it sparkled on a pond in the pub garden and bounced back to hit the ceiling of his room. For a moment he believed he was back in the home of that country-dwelling uncle whose hospitality had made such a change from the two-up-two-down terrace house in Sunderland.

And then reality broke through. He was back in the real world.

Chapter Three

Irresolute and Uncertain

His breakfast was excellent, as promised. At 8.30am Simon was retracing the route to the mansion. He half expected that security staff would be on duty, but in fact all traces of governmental use had disappeared. The estate looked exactly what it was: the home of a rich industrialist, currently away on holiday with his family. The only activity Simon could see was a tractor pulling a gang-mower and describing huge circles around an area of parkland. As it passed him, Simon waved and shouted. The shout had no effect because the driver was wearing ear-defenders, nor did the waving for the driver was concentrating on holding his line. Simon waited out a circuit, and positioned himself where he must surely be seen. The equipage stopped. The driver cut the engine, removed his ear-defenders but remained in his seat and waited, looking faintly belligerent, for Simon to approach.

'What is it now? I thought your lot were all gone.'

'Good Morning. I was here last night for a meeting and I left an important document in the house. Can you help me?'

'Why would I do that, after all the trouble your people caused me? Most of yesterday gone in futile talks with security men. Officious types in some sort of uniform. How long had I worked here? Had I ever been a communist? Did I have a key to the house? Did I speak Arabic? When did I last travel overseas? Had I ever signed the Official Secrets Act? Who recommended me for this job? Had I seen any suspicious strangers around? I was totally pissed off with it all. Today the whole circus has moved on. Good riddance, I say.'

Simon tried his most conciliatory manner. 'I know what you mean. I've worked in the same building for three years and they still stop me sometimes to ask for my pass. If I ask why, it's

"Regulations, Sir. You might have forgotten it, and our job is to prevent anybody going in without one." It's crazy.'

He went on with his friendly act for a time. 'I must say, you're doing a very neat job, here, each cut lapping the last by the same amount. It must take serious concentration.'

The driver relaxed, climbed down from his perch, and leant against the massive rear wheel of the tractor.

'Concentration? I'll say it does. But I'm an old-fashioned fellow who takes pride in the work. Learnt it from my Granddad, I did. He worked an old horse-drawn plough like you see in story books. Straight furrows he ploughed. Straight and true like the strings of an 'arp. Me, I've got machinery instead, but there's still a huge difference between a good job and a bad one. Trouble is, they won't leave you alone to get on with it. Got to interfere, they 'ave.'

Here the driver pulled a mobile phone from his pocket and sneered at it. 'My Granddad, see, his missus gave him his lunch in a tin and off he went to the field to work all day, alone with his horses. Good company they were. Now one of those manager twits might ring me on this and say "Leave off that, Bert, and take Mr Baker to the station in the limo".'

'But don't you like company from time to time?'

'Company? Depends what you mean by company. Mostly it's half-wits sent from the exchange – or whatever they call it now. The last one didn't know the difference between a rose bush and a lilac – would you believe it! And the one before that! He turned up with a floosy in tow and asked, could she take a video of him driving this tractor. I nearly clobbered him with my wooden leg.'

Here the driver tapped his left leg with the mobile phone and produced a hollow sound like a badly-tuned drum. Simon was aware that his friendliness had worked too well: he had tapped into a garrulous old man. But he couldn't ignore the last comment.

'You're joking.'

'No, Sir. I done it. Just once, but I done it. Young man got me really angry and there was no weapon handy. Unstrapped my leg, I did, and hopped towards him waving it like one of those creatures you see in old, old books about unknown parts – people with heads underneath their arms and only one leg.. He ran, he did. Fast.'

'You're quite a character, aren't you? But look, Bert, can you help me?' Simon cast himself as the endangered subordinate. He had left this document behind, and would be in big trouble if he failed to recover it. Unwisely, he also passed a compliment upon a nearby bed of flowers, and got a five-minute lecture on soil conditioning. He listened patiently.

He was rewarded. It turned out that Bert was the head gardener and had a key to a side door. Ten minutes later, Simon was inside.

The nursery proved to be on the third floor and was clearly a 'working' nursery and not a relic. The thing bothering Simon most was that serious conspirators would surely have swept the place electronically to make sure there were no bugs. Just possibly the domestic scene and the late choice of venue had made them discount any danger. But these people were surely professionals: they were unlikely to make mistakes. Simon decided that either they had not found the child-minding system (which he could not at first see) or else they had found it and assumed there would be no listener.

What he did find was a large stuffed toy – a tiger. He rattled it. Inside, Simon found the microphone for the system. It would have been easy to overlook when searching for a physical object, but could the conspirators have missed it electronically? He didn't figure it out at the time, but learnt later that it operated on a different wavelength from modern surveillance equipment. State-of-the-art technology would never have noticed it.

The crunch point was a very familiar smell. Prince Thaqib was addicted to an expensive brand of cigar and Simon had been in meetings when he lit up. The smell was still strong in the nursery.

Finally, to kill one of the doubts that had attacked him last night, Simon found the nursery clock and set it beside the tiger. He went down to the drawing room, switched on the speaker and listened. 'Tick – Tick – Tick'. Yes, the link was certainly between this room and the nursery.

Without knowing his reasons, Simon looked briefly around the mansion. He was struck by the subtle differences between this place and the official residences of senior government ministers.

Those always reflected the taste of the current occupant – as if each incumbent found it necessary to remove all traces of his or her predecessor and to order up from the government stores a new set of pictures and furniture. This place, Simon realised, had continuity. If some ancestor had been very badly painted by a second-rate artist, that was no reason for banishing the portrait. If grandfather had spilt a bottle of port on the carpet, that was family history, not a cause for shame. Just re-position one of the chairs. The building declared that it was a family home.

For two weeks Simon refused to listen to the voice in his head. The whole affair had to be deniable. Perhaps he had suffered some temporary mental disturbance. Perhaps it was real, but the matter was already being dealt with. He even used his political contacts to ask if Prince Thaqib was in any way of interest to the security services. It appeared not. He was clean. The voice in his head became accusatory. 'This one has your name on it. People have to accept the responsibilities fate throws at them. It's a job for an assassin. Unilateral action is the only solution. Without its leader, the plot will collapse. Forget Hamlet – think Lady Macbeth. She saw her husband vacillating and took over. "Infirm of purpose – give me the dagger".'

Could he, Simon wondered, find an assassin, and pay one? He faced up to the questions in his bachelor flat. His sitting room looked out over Regents Park towards the zoo and the sight always had a calming effect. The second question – payment – was not too hard. Considerable responsibilities were delegated to him and his minister was not a strict supervisor. Using his manipulative skills, he could divert substantial amounts of public money. He could also offer rewards in terms of status and influence and prospects that would be exciting if the practitioner he found was already rich. He was a fixer. He could do it.

But how would he find the right man? At that time he was in close touch with his brother, who had no interest in public life and enjoyed the quiet respectability of a solicitor's life in Carlisle. His brother was having the most awful time finding a plumber, and an assassin might be even worse. Both tradesmen were in short supply, which meant that a host of cowboys were trying to get in on the act. In both trades there had been technical developments that were understood and applied by only the very best – who were, of course, so busy that they often ignored an enquiry. His brother had so far employed two men whose claims vastly exceeded their competence and now had problems with the system that had never existed before. Similar incompetence in an assassin would be disastrous. Yet it must be possible to find a good one. After all, thought Simon, it's no good being the best if customers don't know it. Such people must have methods of attracting clients: he just had to find out what they were.

There was also an up-side to a lengthy search time: something might turn up that solved the whole problem. 'I can explore the possibility without committing myself. I shall be taking action and it will stop me feeling guilty.' He argued the case in his mind. 'Finding an assassin and discussing contracts is not in itself a crime. I am not seriously at risk until I clinch the deal. I must take preliminary steps and learn as I go.'

So the enquiry process was tentatively and discreetly started. At that time the name Nshila Ileloka had no meaning for him. If he had known of her as Director of The Rain Consultancy, Non-executive Director of the Euro-African Charitable Trust, that would have had no significance. If he had known of her as the former pupil of the witchdoctor Kwaname, and expensive, choosy, semi-retired assassin, that might have been different.

Chapter Four

On The Downs

At the time Simon Trent reconciled himself to drastic action, Nshila Ileloka was not projecting a prestigious image. She was struggling – hot and sticky – up a footpath near Goring-on-Thames, attempting to keep pace with her brother, Masuko, and her close friend Mike Fanshawe. It was uncomfortable, and flies were buzzing about her.

She had developed a great love for her adopted country, and liked to explore it. Mike (Michael Henry Fanshawe) was English to the point of caricature and an excellent companion. They had made many expeditions together, and this time they were to walk part of The Ridgeway, up from the Thames at Goring, over the Berkshire Downs and down to Swindon. Nshila had been there once before, and appreciated the wide open spaces, but she had been too busy, then, to fully enjoy them. She had been struggling to transfer the body of Grant Toppley from the mortuary van into Tetherman's Volvo.

On this trip she also had a private agenda. But that was easy to reconcile with Mike's company. He was dimly aware of her occult interests, but quite prepared to ignore or deny them or shut his eyes to them. If she had tried to explain her agenda to him, he would have said quite clearly that he really did not want to know, and could they talk about sports cars instead. Their friendship had developed in a way that observed certain boundaries within which they were both perfectly happy.

But then her brother had telephoned from his school at Margate. He wanted a few days of her company. Never had that happened before. Masuko was her half-brother, about six years older, and relations between them were complex. She was in his debt, certainly. He had been selected for her country's top multi-racial secondary school and by participating, against all the rules, in the National

Lottery had won a huge prize. A side-effect of his win had been payment of school fees to allow Nshila to follow in his footsteps. None of the academic successes that she had achieved would have been possible without this start. She would not have had a First Class Degree from LSE, nor an MBA from The Open University.

But feelings of gratitude gave way, at times, to annoyance at his superior elder-brother attitude and his rooted objection to her occult activities. And it seemed to her that the methods he was using to achieve success in his adopted country were faintly ridiculous. Taking a job as a schoolteacher was understandable, and so was acceptance of a job in a fee-paying school once that was offered to him. But why did he have to pursue the correct image so hard? Why had he paid for elocution lessons so that, when he spoke to parents, they took him for a second-generation immigrant who had been to a school like theirs? Why did he have to wear tweed suits? Why did he have to learn the jargon of horse racing? Why did he have to smoke a pipe? So far as Nshila knew, the class of Englishman he wanted to emulate had given up smoking long ago. But Masuko had fixed ideas, and on the whole they seemed to work for him.

When he explained his unusual request to join their party, he told of a rare but unpleasant case of racial discrimination. A parent had asked for his son to be placed in a house with a white housemaster. It had affected Masuko seriously, and he talked about it quite a lot.

Nshila could not refuse the request. But it made pursuit of her private agenda much harder, because that objective was linked to her practice as a witchdoctor. It would produce an aggressive older-brother tirade, typical of Masuko ever since she had begun to visit Kwaname in the hut under the baobab tree. Her agenda was, as often before, the pursuit of knowledge. As a child in her remote village, she had gained basic skills. In England she had learnt how some of those skills could be supplemented by modern technology. She had also learnt about the magical traditions of old Europe. Just recently, she had become aware of Norse mythology. It was a rich field to explore, and Waylands Smithy, high upon the Downs, was a good place to start. Masuko would be quite capable of interfering physically with her plans. He would have to be deceived.

But as she climbed the path this worry took second place to another that she had not foreseen. It was the male bonding that took place between Mike and Masuko and effectively excluded her.

Mike was a product of traditional English private education and Masuko had bought into the system enthusiastically. They had much to talk about. They were also evenly matched physically and now they marched ahead of her discussing the intricacies of rugby football. This was something she watched avidly because of its violence and drama, but without much true knowledge. Any comment that she made was treated by the men as irrelevant and ignorant. It annoyed her.

She tried to bully herself into making an adult intervention that would change things. Maybe honesty would help. 'Look here, fellows, I don't like being ignored. If you two could remember your manners you could make space for me. If you think I don't know anything about the subject, then the polite option is to explain things. Why don't you give it a go?'

For a few moments it worked. They started with names and rules – scrums, rucks, line-outs and so on. But only seconds had passed before they were correcting each other and getting deep into technicalities. 'That's only true, Mike, if the side is deemed to be going forward.' 'Don't confuse the issue with detail, Masuko. We have to keep it simple for her.' So Nshila lost interest and lagged behind.

She twice made the effort to catch up. The third time she didn't bother. 'In time,' she thought, 'those stupid twits will notice my absence and come looking.' When it happened, they found her fifty yards up a lane, gazing at an empty and nearly derelict manor house.

'Isn't it marvellous? Did you ever see something so perfect? Whoever designed that was a real genius.'

'Then I'm glad he's not alive to see it now. What a decrepit dump. It would cost a fortune to repair.'

'Mike. Masuko. Just listen. One day that's going to be mine. I won't need the whole of it. I'll knock down the newer part, and put the rest in order bit by bit. I'm serious. That's my personal fragment of the English countryside. It's got my name on it.' She made a private resolution to follow up this desire. She would make time amongst her other activities to research this place.

They walked all day, gradually adjusting to the triangular relationship. The men were quite interested by Nshila's meteorological knowledge: what she could deduce from wind directions and cloud formations and changes of temperature. In the late afternoon her mind became more and more occupied by thoughts of the barrow – Waylands Smithy. That was what she had come to see.

Norse mythology! There was African witchcraft and European witchcraft, in both of which she had experience. Her recent reading had made her aware of this additional untapped reservoir of power. She had to learn about it. Wayland himself, she knew, had never lived in that Neolithic burial chamber high on the Downs above Ashbury. The legend had been attached to a convenient location. But power makes legends and legends can also make power. A concentration of thought can attract the power to any suitable location. Lack of a physical connection is no bar to spiritual colonisation. Something of Wayland and his magic might well be found by an honest enquirer listening carefully in the mind.

In the evening they struck a main road and walked down into Ashbury, Masuko and Mike already speculating on the quality of food and beer they might find. Nshila was determined to spend part of the night at Waylands Smithy and was prepared to spike their drinks if necessary. If they knew her intention, they would unite to prevent her. She didn't have to bother. After dinner they became deeply involved in an argument with some locals about sport and business and politics. When she pleaded tiredness and the need for an early night, they almost ignored her.

She was at the door of the hotel when it struck her that it might be cold upon the Downs at night. Should she go back to her room and find a coat? No need to bother. Hanging on a peg inside the hotel door was her brother's safari jacket, which he had been carrying rather than wearing for most of the day. It was not thick, and was certainly too big for her, but it promised a little extra warmth.

It was a long walk up the hill. If she had missed a bus and needed a lift, nobody would have stopped. Wanting solitude, she had to offer polite refusals to three kindly drivers. Where the path left the road, she sat on a stone and did deep-breathing exercises for five minutes. Then she walked on. She had no special plan in mind, but she knew that an experience awaited her. She walked around the barrow several times and then lay down on top gazing at the moon. Sometimes it was brilliant, sometimes hidden by fast-moving clouds. She heard cars and lorries on the road, but she also heard the wind, blowing from the west. Gradually she was able to tune out the sounds of human origin and concentrate on natural ones. She heard the rustling of the trees more clearly and could distinguish between the sounds each made as a gust caught it. She heard animals. She heard an owl calling. She heard, remotely, the chime of a village church clock. Most of all she heard the changing notes of the wind as the strength varied. Almost she caught words in it. She lay so still that a passing rabbit brushed against her leg.

She thought about the legend. She thought about Wayland the Smith – a name that went back for centuries. He was supposed to have made Beowulf's chain mail, and Beowulf was way back in the first millennium. Before that the barrow-owner had been Welan and before then the Norse Volundr from Iceland. She thought of him as the immensely skilled young metalworker who outshone his teachers. (Would she herself ever have an apprentice?) She thought of the marvellous things he had created and the desire of Niduth, King of Sweden, to imprison him and obtain a monopoly on his services. She thought of his escape – on wings manufactured from bird's feathers by his brother Egil. She thought of his long flight to England, his discovery of this barrow and his constant dedication to his craft in this very place where she now lay. She slept.

There were no startling dreams – at least not to begin with. Instead, she experienced comfort and reassurance. 'You're doing right,' she was told. 'The craft is all. Your craft and mine. Extend your craft. Grow in it. Look at what you did today and resolve to do better still tomorrow. Work for the craft and the craft will work for you. It will strengthen you and empower you'. She felt exalted, spiritually at one with all those who had fought to excel.

And then a dream did come. Muddled, as dreams are. First The Moon Stallion, fire flashing from his newly shod feet as they struck the stone. Then a tinker, leaving his horse beside the smithy with a coin and returning at daybreak to examine the smith's magic handiwork. Then, somehow, the traveller was Elijah from the Christian Bible. He put down a coin, but instead of leaving his horse, he left a small round earthenware pot and spoke to a woman who stood nearby. Nshila was frightened, then, because she knew no Hebrew and would look an idiot if he addressed her. And then the waking process began and she realised that her lack of Hebrew didn't matter. She did not need to make polite conversation with the prophet.

Was there anything she had to do? Something in her mind said 'Yes'. Why had Elijah appeared with his empty pot? Something to do with a widow's cruse – but what was a cruse? It came back to her – a small pot of oil. In the Bible story it was perpetually refilled by God so that the widow could go on cooking dinner for Elijah. She realised that she had to leave some offering for the god, and she had to leave a signal about her own needs. Yet she didn't quite know what her needs were. As she moved, the pocket of Masuko's safari jacket fell against a stone and there was a muted metallic sound. Investigating, she found a round tin, half-full of pipe tobacco. Good enough. She could put a payment in the empty tin, and if the god was moved to make her some gift, he could put it in or under the tin. How about money? In another pocket of the jacket she found five two-pound coins. Briefly she hesitated. Gods were unpredictable and maybe this one liked pipe tobacco. No, that was not credible. She threw the tobacco into the wind and left the coins in the tin.

She walked down the hill. As she entered the hotel the clock behind the reception desk showed 3.00am. There was a night porter asleep behind the desk. Awakened, he responded poorly to her request for five two-pound coins in exchange for notes. But eventually he scrabbled around in a drawer and succeeded. Nshila put the coins in the pocket of the safari jacket and hung it back on the hook. The tobacco tin, she decided, could be written off as lost. Masuko had been carrying the jacket and it must have fallen out.

Breakfast was normal. Mike and Masuko asked if she had slept well and were happy with the conventional answer. Obviously she didn't look especially tired. In any case they were both more interested in the food and consumed, she thought, far more than was good for them. 'Gives you an appetite, all this walking,' said Masuko. Eventually they were off up the hill again.

'Let's have a quick look at Waylands Smithy,' said Masuko.

They looked, but neither Mike nor Masuko were very impressed. They were busy exchanging critical comments and failed to notice as Nshila stooped down and picked up the tobacco tin. It seemed empty. The bottom was clearly visible. But as she lifted it, she felt weight. She looked more closely. There was some clear substance in it. Not a liquid, obviously, or it would have spilt over the edge when she moved the tin. Carefully, she turned the tin upside down over her left palm and some clear round discs fell out. Ten of them. They were transparent, and so clear that if she dropped one on the ground it was almost invisible. Each had a hole in the middle. If they had been a bit larger, and opaque, they might have been CDs for a computer.

She picked one up and looked through the hole. Nothing: just the normal world. There was no obvious magical significance. And then she noticed another oddity. Close beside the spot where the tin had rested were two more of the discs, as if the god had wanted to give her more than the tin would hold. She put them all loose into her handbag. The tin she threw away, not wanting any argument with Masuko if he saw it.

An odd thought drifted into her mind. Back at LSE, when she was doing her first degree, she had learnt that one of the functions of money was to be 'a store of value'. Wayland, she thought, must have been paid in all sorts of currency over the years. How did her two-pound coins compare in his view with their Anglo-Saxon equivalent? What did he think he had been given in terms of value? Perhaps it didn't matter. Perhaps what the god assessed was the degree of sacrifice made by the giver, or the degree of need, or the power that his gift would bring in the hands of the right person. And what value did this particular gift have? What would it enable her to do? She was puzzled. But she was convinced that the capability of the discs would be revealed to her in time. The gods were always purposeful.

They all enjoyed the next two days, and Masuko seemed to have got the monkey off his back. He had got over the insulting parent who had preferred a white house master. 'My house is going to win every school competition next year. Applications will shoot upwards.'

Nshila went back to work with her stock of discs. They must have power and purpose, but power of what sort and when should they be used? Time would tell. She also carried in her mind the image of a small red-brick manor house – now, in her dreams, perfectly repaired and surrounded by green lawns. There had been no 'For Sale' board outside the ruin. But a call to any local estate agent would get the facts for her.

Chapter Five
Honing Skills

She had become an assassin partly by accident, partly through love of experiment and partly through her inability to refuse a challenge. It had certainly been an accident that led to her friendship with old Kwaname and her acquisition of witchdoctoring skills. Small requests had then come her way, and most of them she had been able to discharge – sometimes by unaided witchcraft and sometimes by the admixture of technology. The first death had been an inter-tribal affair in which the needs of her people had made other considerations irrelevant. She had killed since, but had always been convinced that the targets were totally evil and that the world would be better without them. There were times when she asked herself whether the excitement of the contract made her too ready to believe in the evil-doing of the target. It was a question she dismissed; she relished the self-image of a gardener – one who destroys weeds in order that flowers can flourish.

As she moved into her thirties she had become more discriminating than ever, getting more satisfaction from status and success as a businesswoman in her adopted country. But witchcraft still interested her, and the relationship that might or might not exist between witchcraft and science. On many occasions she had planned to achieve her goal by physical means, which were still subject to chance. They might work or they might not. She had tried to improve the odds by occult means. When the outcome was successful, which method had the credit? At thirty-five, she was no nearer a conclusion than she had been at eighteen. But she worked hard to maintain her skill levels in both areas – and to enhance them when opportunity came along. That was why, when her reading made her aware of Norse mythology, she had manufactured the chance to visit Waylands Smithy. That was also why she agreed to fix Gillian's wedding. It was a zero-risk development opportunity and in no way criminal.

Gillian was one of her two employees at The Rain Consultancy, the meteorological business that occupied the attic floor of an old building in Eastcheap and was the perfect cover for other activities. It was 100% genuine and legitimate and profitable. Gillian Harker and Peter Grace both worked there, and neither was involved in witchcraft or assassination. But they had been there a long time and knew Nshila as a friend as well as an employer. It was unlikely that they had no suspicions at all. Conversation with Gillian about her wedding more or less proved it.

Nshila was happy about the marriage. It had to happen some time, and she was relieved that the man was not going to be the creature Albert who Gillian had been attached to a few years back. This man was a well-educated Pakistani, permanently settled in England and possessed of a rather sexy black beard. Nshila liked him, and Gillian made it clear that she was not giving up work straightaway. Then came Gillian's request about her wedding day.

'Nshila, I have been with you long enough to know that you have some strange powers. I've never said anything because it was none of my business, but I know you grew up in a remote part of Africa, and I know that witchdoctors can make it rain. Sometimes it has suited us, for the business, that it should rain in a location that ought, according to meteorological science to have wall-to-wall sunshine all day. And despite that, it has rained. I have wondered whether you fixed it.'

'Wedding nerves are scrambling your brain, Gillian. I'm no magician. I agree that there have been one or two surprises in the past, but they were pure coincidence.'

Gillian looked unimpressed.

'If you say so, then I have to believe you. But just in case this is something that exists and yet can't be acknowledged, can I just tell you what I want?'

'I'm listening.'

'If you have any power along those lines, then I want a fine day for the wedding. The place is not far from Cambridge, on the edge of The Fens, and East Anglia is the driest part of the country, so it ought not to be too hard."

It was a challenge! Different, novel and exciting! Naturally, she told Gillian that it was impossible and advised her to check past data so that she could do the sensible thing and choose the most promising date. Gillian was a fully qualified and very experienced meteorologist, and knew exactly what to do. But in Nshila's mind the problem took root.

'Do I know about rain-making?' She asked herself. 'Of course I do. I learnt a great deal from old Kwaname. I can make rain with some success, though not always to the extent I want. Sometimes I have got drizzle when I wanted a flood, and sometimes the reverse. Sometimes I have got the location wrong. There was that grim time when I wanted a thunderstorm in Upper Bullfield and Lower Bullfield got it instead. But mostly I have succeeded. But how about preventing rain? It could be harder.'

Later that evening she was in the private flat that formed part of the attic floor rented by The Rain Consultancy. She was searching in a cupboard for an old DVD. She found it hidden underneath some forgotten files: relics from her time at the Open University. They brought back memories of a long-haired, unwashed, rather smelly tutor who was always promoting 'lateral thinking'. What did it mean? Nshila tried to recall some of the examples used, and as she did so the answer to Gillian's problem hit her. They had called it 'thinking outside the box'. She had forgotten why. But she thought that if she made it rain really hard for the three days before Gillian's wedding then there would be an increased chance of fine weather when it stopped. The enthusiastic, experimental risk-taking fellow who occupied one half of her skull got excited. 'Give it a go, girl,' he said, 'If it works, you will have opened up a whole new field of indirect witchcraft. It's a fabulous opportunity. You can call it "reverse magic" – like "reverse swing" in cricket.' She ignored the cautious sober fellow who owned the other half of her skull. Useful at times, she deemed him, but boring.

She found it really hard work. Rain-making features in many African adventure stories, and the witchdoctor does the job by mumbling a few spells and casting a few bones. Whether that is true or not, rain-making in Europe is more demanding. The practitioner needs the old methods, but much more is required: more concentration and mental effort. He must picture the wind currents, and the areas of high and low pressure, and the temperature, and the nature of the clouds. He must visualise the torrent of water falling just where he wants it. It's a little like sport psychology. The coaches teach their performers to picture in their minds the various movements that they have to make. They sometimes call it 'imaging'. It's supposed to ensure that when the moment of truth arrives the athlete does exactly the right thing. Nshila did that for three days in a row.

It worked. But there were variations, such as the spirits love using to prevent the witchdoctor getting conceited. East Anglia is mostly flat, with what the locals call 'hills' being minor bumps. The church stood on one of these bumps. When the wedding day dawned (wall-to-wall sunshine) the church stood in the middle of a lake and was inaccessible except by boat! Initially, panic! Then everybody combined to produce a very British solution. Gillian's father was a fellow of a Cambridge college and he hired twelve of the flat-bottomed punts that the colleges keep on the river Cam. The best man had a brother who was a transport contractor. He loaded the punts onto a lorry and brought them ten miles to the waterside. Bride, bridegroom and guests, all in their wedding finery, were punted to the church by volunteers from the Parochial Church Council. The Vicar, a sailing enthusiast, kept a Mirror dinghy on the river beside his home and attempted to sail to the church. He grounded a hundred yards out and had to wade the remaining distance. Luckily, he kept a change of clothes in the vestry. The Best Man reproved him. 'Pity you can't walk on water, Vicar. You should pay more attention to your boss.'

It was not the wedding Nshila had planned or Gillian expected, but the novelty was a terrific success. Naturally, the wilder young men managed to lose their punt poles and fall in. The bride walked up the aisle to the standard music, but had to avoid the puddles on the floor.

Nshila enjoyed the event. The punt to which she had been

assigned had been poled by a highly competent young man and she loved to watch anything being done well. His pole seemed to find a firm bottom whenever he lowered it; he leant on it without visible effort, yet the punt moved fast through the water. He moved a few steps back along the deck to get maximum value from every dip of the pole. He knew exactly when to lift the pole and start the process again. There were no splashes and no abrupt changes of direction. He projected an image of controlled and economically applied strength. She found it sexy.

Just before the service, an announcement was made about changing one of the hymns. Because of the strange weather they were now to sing the one that says 'God moves in a mysterious way, his wonders to perform'. When they came to those words Gillian turned from facing the minister and stared at Nshila.

There was one other unexpected event. Many Fenland churches have small quirky features, and this one had an imp carved into the stone high up on a pillar at the front of the chancel. He had a glass eye that seemed to wink at whoever sat in a certain pew. By luck, Nshila was in the favoured place; small movements of her head caused him to wink. She winked back – and some sort of spiritual link was established. He started to wink at her spontaneously. Scared, for a moment, she shifted her position and then looked rigidly at the imp for what she deemed to be five minutes. He winked at her. Not regularly, in a manner that might have some scientific explanation, but erratically and personally. Across several hundred years there was a link between her and the long-dead mason. Had he told anybody what he had done? Had he been admired for his individuality or sacked for sacrilege? Had he just hugged his secret to himself and imagined the interest he would arouse down the years?

Nshila regarded the wedding as a useful developmental experience: by maximising one thing beyond its normal strength, she had provoked the reverse. Perhaps the principle could be applied elsewhere. Certainly she could count it an increase of professional skill. The Open University MBA course had been very heavy about the pace of change, and the rapid arrival of new methods, and how the businessman who failed to move forward would soon lose customers.

But she still didn't know what those discs were for – the ones given to her at Waylands Smithy. Nor did she know, at that moment, that Simon Trent had started fumbling attempts to find an assassin.

Chapter Six
Fred Seeks His Idol

Fred Mbwele, five thousand miles away, also knew nothing of Simon Trent. He did know something about Nshila, though under a different name. He had worked for her on a two-week assignment. He had also stumbled across records of her activity in a way that might have been pure chance but might also have been intended by some higher power. There was a mystery about her, and a hint of supernatural capability. He thought about her from time to time and wondered if he could tap into whatever special skill she possessed.

He was not thinking of her on the day his final exam results were due: he was pre-occupied with visions of a large, white crested envelope and the news it would contain. The results in his first and second years had not impressed his father, who had made pointed comments about the expense of it all and the headway Fred might have made in The National Progressive Party if he had started straight away in politics. Fred's belated response had been to work much harder than ever before, but he had felt unable to withdraw from a football team that seemed to need him, and he had also lost two weeks through illness. He believed he had done well in the exams. He was not certain. Had he, perhaps, missed the point of some questions and given an answer that was only regurgitated facts and had no original thought?

He woke early that morning and sneaked out of the house without breakfast and without speaking to anybody. There was no chance that the post would have been sorted yet, and placed in the boxes, so he filled in time by walking to the railway station to watch the arrival and departure of the northbound and southbound trains. He had no deep knowledge of railways, but one of his lecturers had started his working life as a fireman on the huge long-distance steam trains that were still used whenever one of the diesels broke down.

That morning he was lucky. The line from the south climbed up a valley towards the city and was visible sometimes where the trees were thin or the ground fell away. Fred saw the cloud of smoke, and then glimpsed the long dark shape of the engine. Through another gap he saw the bright yellow livery of the first class carriages and then the mountain of rooftop baggage on the third class. For the last two miles of its journey the train was invisible, and it seemed ages to Fred before it rounded the final corner and drew majestically into the station. It dwarfed and upstaged the modern, uninspired diesel standing on the other track. Fred watched the passengers moving to the exit or to the restaurant, and noticed with sympathy the third class travellers who looked stiff and tired and spattered with soot. He had experienced that himself. Then he saw the fireman, standing beside the engine, smoking. A large man, and obviously very strong. He must have shovelled a lot of coal on the journey.

Soon he judged that enough time had passed for the staff to sort incoming mail into the post office boxes. He walked into town and put his key into Box 224. Some bills, a small packet addressed to his sister, two foreign letters and a nasty brown one addressed to his father that said 'Income Tax' in large black letters. Nothing yet from the university. But Fred could hear movement on the other side of the battery of boxes and knew that the sorting process was still going on. He decided to walk three times round the block and try again. During his second circuit he had a great idea about the tax bill. This was not a day for having his father in a bad mood; when he took the mail from the box he would re-post that item and ensure a day's delay.

He made his three circuits, and then another three to make sure. And there it was: one large white envelope. Fred crossed the road to a café, and looked for an empty table in an obscure corner. There was only one. He had just sat down when he saw a smear of grease on the table and a not-quite-dry spot of spilt soft drink. If the contents of the envelope were good news he would have to show it around – maybe even frame it. He signalled for a waiter, who performed with a damp rag. Not satisfied, Fred improved things with his own handkerchief. Then he drew out the letter and it slid onto the table face down. He paused, and rehearsed strategies for alternative outcomes. A Third, perhaps? Go out and get sufficiently drunk to face his father. A Second, perhaps? Accept family congratulations and express disappointment that it had not been better. A First, perhaps? Somehow he couldn't see it happening. Well, nothing would change it now. He turned over the paper.

His shout startled the other customers. It also caused a passer-by to stop and stare into the café. Bliss! Triumph! Heaven! Success! Contrary to his own expectations and those of his tutors, he had managed a First Class Degree. He closed his eyes and opened them again. The paper still had that magic word 'First'. He did it again. No change! It was true!

The next step was a short walk to The Black Flag Saloon on Cross Street. Fred and five others had agreed to meet there on degree day, about the middle of the morning. They were to compare results and congratulate or commiserate as appropriate. Whatever happened, they had agreed, there was to be no change in their friendship. A better or worse degree – or none at all – made no difference to your value as an individual.

Aaron Mutale was already at the bar. 'Hi, Fred. I had you tagged for an Upper Second. Was I right?'

'You were wrong, Aaron. You underestimated the Mbwele genius. I got a First.'

'I don't believe you. What are degrees worth if a dope like you is going to walk away with a First?'

'It's true. But I never expected it. If they were marking high then you must have got an Upper Second yourself'.

'Right, for once. And I'm pleased to have it. I don't want your First: people would expect too much of me. You'll find it's a hard reputation to sustain. Whenever you get something wrong, people will feel you have let them down.'

The other expected friends arrived, and were generally content with their results. Quantities of beer were consumed. The last arrival was Michael Maputo – already more famous as an international athletics star than an academic could ever hope to be. He had only taken the exam because it was a condition of his sports scholarship.

Everybody expected him to fail.

He arrived slightly drunk and wearing a tracksuit that bulged in a strange manner round his shoulders. He made no reply to the greetings, but removed the top of his track suit slowly and with great drama in the manner of a stripper removing veils. Draped over his neck was an academic hood. Apparently he had been out for early training, had then gone to the post office, and then on to a friend who had graduated the previous year. He had since been weaving his way from bar to bar and boasting about his prowess. 'I did it! I did it! I did it!'

He was loudly applauded.

Fred reached home in the early evening. Lunch had finished about 3.00pm, and on his way home Fred had passed an abandoned building site where he had played as a boy. He had often lain down, in those days, in a left-over section of a huge sewer pipe. Was it still there? He needed sleep badly. Amazingly it was. Fred gathered a few handfuls of grass to serve as a pillow and collapsed, grasping his precious envelope. Four hours passed pleasantly.

His father already knew. A colleague had come to him at work and described the scene in The Black Flag Saloon. He forgave the fact that Fred was unsteady, and smelly.

'Fred, I am pleased with you. I really am. I never thought you would apply yourself sufficiently to get a First. You were always bright enough, but I thought you were too adventurous and impatient and easily bored.'

'I'm still like that, father, but obviously they never saw all the faults. I'm glad I have pleased you. I know that educating children is tough and expensive. I'm grateful.'

The education isn't quite over, Fred. There is one more thing that I want you to do.'

'Not another exam, father. That's too much.'

'No. This is different. I want you to spend a year in England to gain cultural and political awareness. I will fix up a job with our embassy in London - I have enough influence for that. You may be given some pretty low-grade tasks, and you may have to work hard sometimes. But it won't be like that every day. There will be plenty of time for recreation. I hope some of it will be educational and cultural, of course, not all sport and girls and gambling.'

Fred was over the moon. He had no doubt that he could please his father and still find time for those other delights. He had friends who had spent time in London, and all their reports said that once you had become used to the foul climate you could have a magnificent time. Fred spent some hours on the telephone, talking to those friends. He recorded the names of clubs, and girls, and sporting events, and eating houses, and various beers. And then, staring out of his window at a magnificent African sunset, he had an idea of much greater significance. 'That woman!' – Nshila, whom he had first known under her cover name of Isabel Ngombi – 'I could meet her again. That would be a real experience.'

During the next days, academic worries behind him, Fred thought more about Nshila and her activities. They had met her, he and Abel Mubala, the day after they had left school. They had just lost out on a lucrative holiday job and the Headmaster had fixed them up instead as assistants to a former pupil. She was into meteorology and was arriving from England to set up weather recording stations in the bush. The Headmaster knew little about it himself: he merely told Fred and Abel to get some kit together and meet her at the airport.

It had been a great time. She had turned out to be black and smart and very intelligent, and a good payer. Neither Fred nor Abel had possessed any knowledge of meteorology, so they had cheerfully and uncritically done whatever she told them, setting up monitoring stations at various places on the route to the western borders. The things had looked rather like dog kennels on sticks, but had been stuffed with fancy recording gear. A few strange things had happened during the assignment and Fred had begun to suspect that his employer had an objective of her own for which the trip was just an elaborate cover. In particular, Fred had observed – unseen – an appointment she kept in the middle of the night outside a remote village. She had met just one figure – but sometimes it was solid and sometimes he had been able to see through it. The feet had never seemed quite to touch the ground and it had slithered rather than walked. Scary.

Fred had never asked her about it. It was not his business, and trafficking with the unseen world is more common in Africa than Europe. It doesn't stigmatise a person as evil. Fred saw it as no more blameworthy than telling beads or kissing the feet of an image – actions sometimes performed by a Roman Catholic friend of his mother. And his overall impression of Isabel – as he then knew her – was highly favourable. They had been to the same school, and several times during that journey they had talked quietly under the starlit African sky. Fred's memories centred on the way she had put her education to use: how it had opened her eyes to opportunities and given her the self-confidence to grasp them. 'You are what you have done, Fred.' She had told him that many times. 'Nothing develops you more than having an experience and learning from it. No experience – no learning. Grab your opportunities, Fred.'

It was her influence that had made him enrol at university. He had not been an academic star at school, and until that time the prospect of three more years learning had been unattractive. Isabel changed his mind. She had shown him how empowering knowledge could be. He was accepted at the country's one university for a degree course called Biological Systems.

The course had proved excellent. The core of it had been biology, but there had also been a strong emphasis on how different life forms solved common problems. Fred learnt a great deal about alternative adaptations and about the properties and capabilities that arose from that. Naturally, there was a tendency to judge everything African in a favourable light and to portray European science as simply one approach out of many. Fred remembered a discussion about how chemicals derived from certain plants and animals had beneficial effects on humans. An exchange student from England had scorned the idea and been quite rude to the professor.

'That's just homeopathy. It's all a fairy tale. It's no different from witchcraft.'

'What's wrong with witchcraft, young man? Come to my tribal area with me for a few months and your opinions will alter somewhat.' The professor referred him to a website on which a renowned local expert had recorded his views.

'There is no witchcraft in Africa. There is African Science, which the West has never understood, and instead considers it witchcraft.'

Recalling the event, Fred conjured up the image of Isabel and her ghost-like contact. Had he been associated with a witchdoctor? Had her influence conditioned him to pick up on any subjects that had an occult connection? Or was it quite normal for him to notice them. After all, witchcraft was a recognised source of power in most African societies. Whatever educated people might say, no national football team would take the field without invoking spells against the opposing goalkeeper.

Half-way through his university course Fred had attended an alumni dinner at his old school, St Albans, and spent some idle moments looking at past photographs. In one of them he recognised Isabel Ngombi and learnt her real name. Another alumnus, rather older than Fred, had seen his interest.

'That's one alumnus you want to steer clear of, my boy.'

'Why is that?'

'Sorcery, witchcraft and the black arts. Do not, my boy, put her on your visiting list. Erase her number from your stock of girls worth phoning.'

It turned out that the informer, named Patrick Quinn, had been a contemporary of Nshila. He had various stories about her schooldays, suggesting that she had some sort of supernatural power derived, Patrick believed, from association with a witchdoctor in her tribal homeland.

'I never quite worked out if it was real magic or just instinctive knowledge of human nature and manipulative skill. I paid her money to get Mary Zonde into my bed, and it worked. But I think I could have done it on my own, anyway. Look at me as I was in that photograph. Quite a heartthrob I was.'

Fred remembered that the Patrick Quinn of the photograph and the Patrick Quinn standing beside him had been different. Time had spread the once-slender figure into a pear-shape and the expression suggesting youthful adventurousness had become an obscene leer. There were indications that Patrick might not always be reliable. He was now, it seemed, a lecturer at a little-known English Polytechnic.

Fred had learnt more again when he got a vacation job assisting with the national census. Was it chance, or was it some sort of guidance directing him towards sources of power? His team covered an area that included the village of the ghost-like encounter. Knowing Nshila's name, he was able to ask discreet questions. Yes, she had been born in the village. Yes, she had been befriended by the local witchdoctor (now dead). Yes, she had gone away to school at St Alban's. While she was away, the witchdoctor had died and a tribal crisis had arisen concerning cattle-theft. Nshila had been brought home from school and had somehow managed to identify the thief and arrange his death. Soon afterwards she had left again, for which the villagers were very glad. They had had no idea how to treat a female witchdoctor who was also a schoolgirl. The dignity of the tribal males had been threatened. Fred had asked whether anybody knew what had happened to her. No. Nobody knew anything for certain, but it was believed that she had gone to Europe. She had sent money to her mother for a while, but her mother was now dead.

Ten days after hearing about his degree, Fred set out to trace Patrick Quinn and soon located him as Professor (now) of Sociology at Hungerbridge Polytechnic. It had a website, and e-mail addresses for all the staff. Fred fired off an e-mail reminding him of their meeting and their discussion of Nshila Ileloka. Could he tell him more about her? Could he help with an introduction? There was no reply to his first two e-mails, but the third one must have caught Patrick at the right moment and the reply told Fred a lot.

The strongest part of it had been a warning. Patrick was long-winded and often irrelevant, but, translated into direct speech, his message read, 'Don't mess with this woman. She is dangerous and unpredictable. Keep well clear.' There was some explanatory stuff, saying that although she could be a good friend she possessed genuine psychic power and could do very nasty things to people she was against. At the end there was an address, and full contact details. Patrick wrote, 'This is the address of The Rain Consultancy, a business concerned with meteorology which she runs in London. It is completely legitimate, but I'm sure she uses it as a cover for less respectable activities. Keep clear.'

'That,' Fred decided, 'is one piece of advice I am going to ignore.'

Chapter Seven

Arrival

Fred was reluctant to use the national airline, which seemed to survive more by luck and government subsidy than by any skill in its ground-staff or aircrew. However, he was now on the embassy staff and had no option. He arrived safely, despite his fears. He found the London Underground most confusing (such a lot of it seemed to be overground) but eventually he reached the embassy on Ludgate Hill. Who was he? Why was he here? The paperwork had been mislaid and two hours passed before the situation could be put right. Lodgings were arranged for him, but embassy funds were stretched and he rated only a top floor attic with disastrous plumbing. It was cold. The living room had a single radiator that became lukewarm at unpredictable intervals. The bathroom was quite large but heated only by a wall-mounted electric fire just above the door. It was switched on by a short, dirty piece of string that somebody had lengthened by knotting on a bootlace. The heat it produced could hardly be felt. How Fred longed for the old pit latrine in the village of his boyhood, the comfortable wooden seat, the warmth of the sun, the friendly spiders on the wall and the distant view of the river.

He settled in at the embassy and made no complaint about the low-grade tasks that were assigned to him. He knew that it would change once people got used to him, or somebody more important fell sick. He enjoyed being sent on errands, because these gave him a chance to explore London, plus the perfect excuse for diversions. It was so easy to say that he had got lost, or gone the wrong way on the tube. One grey, overcast day he ventured eastwards into The City of London, past Mansion House, down Cannon Street and past Monument tube station. With little warning, a heavy storm broke and Fred could see no shelter on his side of the road. On the other side were several office buildings with open doors into reception areas that already sheltered passers-by. Fred ran across the road, narrowly avoiding death, and entered the least crowded.

After shaking water from his clothes, and getting his breath back, Fred looked around to see where he was. Amazing. And a bit scary. What force had brought him here? The building had a street number locating it in Eastcheap. There was a board on the wall listing the firms that rented different floors, or parts of floors. To Fred's eyes the last name on that board seemed to him to be written in all the colours of the rainbow glittering and flashing and expanding and contracting. Could nobody else see it? Apparently not: they all looked gloomily at the wet street outside.

The Rain Consultancy. Fourth Floor and Stairs.

Fred experienced a feeling of being driven, of being influenced by an external force so powerful that only one course of action was possible. But it was also a pleasant feeling. The way he was being directed was the way he wanted to go. No decisions had to be made. The stairs, when he reached them, were rather narrow, but carpeted in rich crimson. The door at the top was made of a light oak and instead of a bell-push there was an ornate cord with a brass ring at the end and a notice saying 'Pull'.

He pulled. And felt another shock, for the noise of the bell was the noise of the bell on the lead cow when he had been a herd boy. Various images shot through his mind and he was mentally absent when the door opened and a pleasant, blond girl said 'Good Morning' – and then 'Good Morning' again when he seemed not to have heard her. Dangling behind her was the bell. It had made the same noise as the one on the lead cow because it was the same sort of bell. Fred recovered.

'Excuse me, but I believe this firm is owned by Nshila Ileloka. Is that true?'

'Yes, certainly. What is your business with us?'

'Look, I know this sounds strange, but it's more of a social visit than a business one. I worked for Nshila for a few weeks when she handled a project in my country. My name is Fred Mbwele. I'm now in London for a while and I saw the name of the firm on the list of tenants. I really came up to see if she was here and if she remembered me at all.'

'Come in, then. You can join us for morning coffee. Sit down for a moment while I check with Nshila.'

The girl disappeared through a half-open door that was two steps up from the main room. Fred was on his own. Were there only two people here? Surely not. There must be somebody else around. His immediate impression of the place was emotional. It felt a happy place, where people were sure of themselves and their work and had no need to pretend to each other. He took in the physical environment, without at that time knowing the history.

It had been, he learnt later, the private flat of the housekeeper in the days when office buildings employed such people. It had been a generous space, about half the floor area of the lower storeys, with the missing half given over to a water tank, various service installations, and a roof garden. The size of the flat could not be judged, but the rest of the layout still seemed quite large. It easily accepted the three work-stations set against the walls, despite the fact that those had extensive state-of-the-art computer equipment all around them. It also accepted a few tables and chairs and a large global world atlas on a stand. The latest modernisation had pre-dated the time of permanently sealed windows and universal air-conditioning. So the top part of each window could be opened, and through one of them came the sounds of traffic in the street below. Several pigeons were pecking away at scraps on the parapet. Running past two of the windows was an ugly iron fire escape.

Fred heard footsteps running up the stairs and the door burst open. In came a dark thickset man with an aggressive face and short, black curly hair that made him look like a prize-fighter.

'Hullo! Good morning. Who are you?'

Fred stood up to introduce himself, but simultaneously the fair-haired girl emerged from the flat. Fred was seeing the employed staff of The Rain Consultancy.

Gillian Harker, who had opened the door to him, was a very pretty girl in classic English Rose style. She had the trusting air of a person who expects and offers friendship. She was dressed that day in a high-necked candy-striped cotton blouse and a straight white skirt that fell to calf level and stopped just short of white ankle-boots. Peter Grace wore a business suit, but managed to make it seem totally wrong for his personality. The gear ought, in Fred's view, to convey an image of formality and convention. On Peter, it failed. Both pockets of the jacket were bulging, and one of them had the flap of the pocket turned in. The crotch of the trousers was an inch lower than a tailor would have wished. The legs of the trousers, which a tailor would have expected to break neatly over the laces of smart black shoes, ended half an inch too high and offered a glimpse of garish pink socks. This was the sort of person, Fred guessed, who poked fun at conventions and gave full rein to his own individuality. Business suits were clearly not his best thing.

A strange feeling in the back of his neck made Fred turn round. It was not another person he encountered: it was a presence and a personality. A large black cat sat beside the coffee machine, quite motionless, with green eyes that never blinked and never left his. In an extraordinary way it seemed to grow larger as he watched – like a man drawing himself up to his full height and throwing his chest out. It also exuded a controlled malevolence that seemed to be saying, 'One false move from you, just one, and……' Fred moved a step backward before common sense told him that it was only a cat. Gillian explained. 'That's Rasputin. He's Nshila's cat. Most of the time he's normal and friendly, but for new people he puts on that dangerous-to-know performance. How he manages the transformation act I'll never know. He tolerates Peter and me because he knows we are her friends, but Nshila is the only one he really loves. Just don't touch him till she has told him that you are OK.'

And then Nshila herself stepped into the room. She was not wearing the khaki blouse and slacks that he remembered from the bush, nor the flowing African robes she had flaunted in the airport hotel the evening of their first meeting. But nothing obscured her personality. Today she seemed taller than he remembered because her hair was dressed high on her head. She was wearing a black long-sleeved pullover and a mid-length skirt in the brightest of greens, slightly flared. She had a black patent leather belt and matching shoes with a medium heel. As the memories flooded back, Fred became confused and unable to find the right words.

'Hullo Isa......' and then, hurriedly, 'Remember me? Fred Mbwele? Your driver?'

Nshila was equally at a loss. This man was not supposed to know her real name, and certainly not supposed to appear unannounced at her business address in London. Was there danger here? Perhaps the name part was not serious: they had been to the same school and she had once written an article for the school magazine under her own name. The fact that he had connected Isabel Ngombi with Nshila Ileloka was not seriously suspicious. But finding where she worked and turning up on the doorstep implied effort and research.

Thoughts happen fast, but there was still a significant pause before she replied: long enough for Gillian and Peter to sense a mystery and make eye-contact with each other. Something new about their employer was coming out.

'Yes, Fred, I remember you well. But I had forgotten that I was using a different name during that trip. What brings you here? It's good to see you, but it must be three years or so since we parted at the airport.'

'Just under three years. Partly because of meeting you, I changed my mind about further education and went off to university. You are looking at Fred Mbwele, newly qualified Bachelor of Arts. And I am attached to our embassy here in London. Look, what do I call you? Out in the bush it was all first names, you and me and Abel. Here you are obviously the boss.'

'You might not think it from the way Gillian and Peter treat me. Nshila will do. It's my true birth name, in case you had doubts.'

Nshila was uncertain about how to handle the meeting. Gillian, on the other hand, was quite sure what she wanted. She soon had all four people sitting around the conference table, with coffee and biscuits. Her suspicions about Nshila had been enhanced by the drama of her wedding and here was somebody from the past who might have tales to tell. She started boldly.

'Was it you, then, that took part in that journey to establish weather recording stations? We get regular data from them, but so far we have done nothing very positive with it.'

'Yes. But I can't say that Abel and I were more than unskilled labourers. Nshila told us about data being sent up to a satellite and down to London. It didn't seem a big deal to us. I mean, what would people in Britain care about storms brewing up in Central Africa?'

'Not a lot, I agree, but there is technical knowledge to be gained by studying the forces that influence the weather and how important they are in different places. I have played about with the data from those stations you set up, and there are fascinating ideas in it. For instance, ground temperature is much more important with you than it is with us.'

'Why don't you show him a few sequences on your computer, Gillian?' Nshila felt she could use time on her own to figure out a strategy.

'Over here, then. Peter, are you coming, too?'

'Might as well, I suppose.' Peter sometimes felt mildly deprived of male company and enjoyed the freshness of Fred's approach.

That left Nshila isolated. She made one or two routine phone calls and then interrupted the threesome around Gillian's workstation.

'Fred, don't you have to get back to the embassy, some time? I mean, it's great to meet you again but we don't want you to get into trouble.'

'Oh, no! That won't happen. My duties are very vague and flexible. Sometimes I don't think they really know quite what to do with me. And what you do here is really interesting. I wish I could be involved in some way.'

The comment re-ignited Nshila's concern. What did the man want? Was he trying to work himself into her organisation? Peter Grace didn't help, either.

'How are you finding London, Fred? Are you into culture, or sport, or entertainment? There's masses of opportunity, but it can be quite hard to know where to start.'

'So far I have just gone to shows and cinemas and drunk more than is good for me. What I need most is exercise. At university I played squash every week and it kept me fit. Since I hit London I have put on four pounds, and today the waistband button on my trousers gave way.'

'Squash,' said Peter, 'I can help you there. I belong to a club, and new members are always welcome. Would you like to come along?'

'I'd like that very much. Thank you. Coming in here was a happy chance. But for the rain coming down just when it did, I would have been in another part of London, and never met you. But I wish I could learn a bit more about your work. You don't use casual staff, I suppose?'

'We don't,' said Nshila. 'You are welcome to drop in from time to time, and maybe Gillian and Peter can help you a bit socially. But that's all we can offer.'

The off-putting strategy didn't work. Gillian had other ideas. 'Nshila, you remember that conference you booked Peter onto?'

'Yes. It's nothing special, but one of the speakers is very good on technical terms: what they mean and how they came into use. Peter gets on well with some clients, talking his racy, down to earth language and using common sense illustrations – but he could do with a bit more professionalism.'

'I heard you telling him. But look, the firm doing that conference are making a push to interest beginners and amateurs. They have a free 'taster course' going on at the same time and it's open to any firm sending a fee-paying delegate to the main conference. Fred could go along. It would cost us nothing, and it would be company for Peter – a drinking partner in the evening – and Fred would learn a bit about what we do. We can fairly claim that he has a connection with our sort of business because of that fortnight in the bush.'

'Good idea,' said Peter.' It would be fun to have company.'

None of this pleased Nshila. Yet nothing had happened to which she could object, and sounding ungracious would make things worse. So, with a few admonitions about proper behaviour and heavy words to Peter about the responsibility, she agreed.

Time had passed and there seemed little point in resuming work for twenty minutes or so. An early pub lunch was indicated. At Peter's request, Fred was included. The two seemed to be drawn to each other despite their different backgrounds. Lunch was a noisy affair, Peter and Gillian arguing about a current London musical, and trying to explain to Fred why it was both funny and beautiful. Fred did his best to appear intelligent, but was not sufficiently familiar with British humour to grasp all the details. One thing that he did notice was that Nshila took little part in the discussion and seemed at times to be away in some realm of her own. Several times Peter or Gillian sought her opinion and she had to be dragged back into their world, often asking for the question to be repeated. In the afternoon, Grace and Peter played catch-up with all the work they had neglected in the morning and Nshila took Fred into her private flat to grill him.

The results were reassuring, for everything he said was logical and believable. He could very easily have learnt her true name at an Alumni event, and his description of Patrick Quinn was accurate. He had even identified some of Patrick's strengths and weaknesses. He could well have had a vacation job with the census department – they often used undergraduates to supplement their own staff, and the country had certainly carried out a census in the year he mentioned. It was strange that he had been assigned to the area that included Nshila's village, but there were only six provincial areas and one in six was hardly extreme odds.

Also in his favour was Nshila's memory of him and Abel Mubala during their weather station assignment in Africa. That whole thing had been an elaborate cover allowing her to return unknown to her village, meet with the spirit of Kwaname and retrieve the tin box. For an intelligent boy there must have been a few suspicious signs. And Fred was highly intelligent. Yes, it was possible to imagine Fred becoming interested in her and wanting to know more. During the conversation he said nothing at all that suggested other people in the background directing him. It seemed better to let Peter and Gillian have their way and to keep an eye on Fred by proxy.

Chapter Eight

Rowan Hall

'Rowan Hall? It's unsaleable. Ask any estate agent based near here, Madam, and you'll get the same story again and again. The people who own it have been arguing with the planning authority for ages and made no progress at all. My bet is that it will sit there until it's just a heap of rubble.'

'What do the owners want to do with it?'

'First of all, they want to demolish it. If and when they finally get permission then they will review their options. They might go into the development business themselves and build expensive housing or they might sell to a supermarket firm, or perhaps start a business park or even an entertainment centre. Anything to bring profit from the land. But it's a listed building - has been so for a very long time - and they are stuck with the situation.'

This was not the response that Nshila had wanted when she began enquiring about her dream home one Saturday morning. The feeling of frustration in the agent came over the line strongly. It sounded as if he had been through such conversations before, and already knew exactly where this one would end. Yet he needed to go through with the tale because the caller might later get interested in another of the properties on his books.

'I can understand that it's a listed building. It's so beautiful. I need to know what's wrong with it. Is the price ridiculous?'

'Yes. It's ridiculous. It's ridiculously low.'

'You're not being very clear.'

'That's because I am ashamed of what I have to say about the hall. It's haunted.'

'I don't believe you. This is the twenty first century, in a rich, very sophisticated country, and you tell me about a house being haunted! Tell me the truth, Mr Scanlon.'

Slowly, Nshila got the information. The story began twenty years before when the last member of a well-known, respected family had died tragically in his early forties. Rowan Hall had then been sold three times in the next six years, the sellers taking a loss each time. It had now been empty fourteen years and the stories about it had grown with time. Several buyers had viewed it. All had decided it was not for them, but been unable to say exactly why. The most common comment had been: 'There's something odd about it. We could never be comfortable there.'

'Haunted how?' Nshila wanted to know. 'You're not going to tell me about headless white ladies and clanking chains?' She stretched in her chair and put the phone to her other ear.

'No. It's not like that. It's just that somebody lives there.'

Colin Scanlon felt that he was making an idiot of himself. He tried to change the conversation. If he got off the phone, that smart couple looking at the properties in his window might see that he was available and come in. 'Can I interest you in another local property, Ms. Ileloka? I could give you all the details about Rowan Hall but I know how you would respond.'

'No. Tell me about the haunting. The idea is so ridiculous that it can't affect my attitude.'

'Very well. The people who lived there all reported that some other unseen presence was sharing the house with them. There was no malignancy: only a constant presence. They would go downstairs in the morning and find that somebody had apparently eaten a meal at the kitchen table and then washed up the dishes. Flowers would appear in rooms where none had been placed. Pictures on the wall would have been changed. They heard the toilet flushing when there was nobody present. New cosmetics would appear in the bathroom. Extra pairs of ladies' shoes would be found in the cupboard. None of it was physically harmful. All of it was frightening.'

At that point, Nshila thanked him and rang off. Colin Scanlon was grateful for the escape. Nshila pondered ways to learn more. The County library provided a list of local societies, and amongst them was a history society based in Pangbourne. A phone call to the secretary took her further, providing the name of a retired solicitor who was deeply interested in the supernatural and had studied Rowan Hall exhaustively. 'But do be warned, Ms. Ileloka,' she was told, 'George Wakeham is old now, and not very well. He has good days and bad days. Sometimes he's morose and surly. At other times he talks too much and embroiders his stories. You have to be a bit sceptical.'

'Where does he live?'

'In an old house that he inherited from his mother. It's remote and decrepit but it seems to suit his reclusive life style. By the way, I think he used to be Edwina Awford's solicitor – she was the last real owner of Rowan Hall. Don't try using that connection to get him talking: he's still quite professional in some ways. But if you lead in with your interest in the paranormal, he'll be unstoppable. And he has a drink problem, of course.'

'If Rowan Hall is haunted, what about this place?' Nshila asked herself as she left the dirt track and pushed through the bushes on her left to enter a small clearing. She had left the car on the verge of a small country lane above Pangbourne allowing, she hoped, enough room for a normal vehicle to pass. The track had looked rutted and overgrown and muddy: not a place where she wanted to scratch the paintwork or get bogged down.

She was looking at a large cottage, not a Dracula-type castle or a moated grange. It was the sort of cottage that might shelter a witch. It had a thatched roof, in poor repair, and small windows with shutters folded back against the walls. Those walls were plaster over brick, and had at some time been painted camouflage green – the shade once favoured by government offices. Weeds grew all round it, except on the path Nshila was treading and another path leading to a shed. Smoke came from a chimney and the door was open. But there was neither sight nor sound of life.

And then the door of the shed opened. The illusion was destroyed by an utterly normal and non-threatening figure. George Wakeham was dressed in a tweed suit that was old but clean. He was slightly below average height but held himself upright and hardly seemed to need the stick that he carried.

'Ms. Ileloka? I knew you were here because of that branch just behind you. All my callers have to push it aside and I know the sound exactly. It gives me an extra minute to prepare myself.'

Inside the house he adopted a proper host-like role. 'Whisky? Retired people can make their own rules and mine say alcohol is OK any time after 10.00am.'

It looked as if this was one of George's good days, so Nshila accepted whisky, wondering whether all retired solicitors favoured ten-year-old malt and left a large pile of empty bottles in the grate. She took advantage of his apparent goodwill to raise the object of her visit immediately. He responded willingly.

'Yes. I know a lot about Rowan Hall and it's all completely understandable if you're bright enough to believe in a spirit world.'

'Can you tell me the story?'

'Easily. Ned Awford was a soldier. He was a Captain in a famous cavalry regiment and he was killed in one of those stupid minor skirmishes that our politicians got us into in those days. It was all about keeping two bunches of savages from killing each other. Stupid and pointless. They should have been left alone to get on with the job.'

'Did he own Rowan Hall, then?'

'He did. His wife, Edwina, came from an old, inbred family. She was nervous and highly-strung. Ned's death was a terrible blow to her and she gradually lost her grip on reality. She surrounded herself with things he had owned and loved, imagining that he was there to enjoy them with her. Sometimes she would say that he wanted her to retrieve an item for him: something he had left behind on a visit or lent to a friend. And when she had a visitor, she often spoke about Ned as if he was present, or addressed him rhetorically. She would say things like "Of course, Ned, here, was dead against it" or "You love this colour I'm wearing, don't you, Ned?" You know how some children invent an imaginary friend, and can involve him so thoroughly in their lives that the parents call in a psychiatrist? It was like that.'

'Pretty scary for the visitors, I suppose.'

'Yes. Naturally, her relatives wanted her to go into a home. She took no notice at all, and she wasn't quite mad enough to be committed. I mean, she looked after herself perfectly well and was no danger to anyone else.'

At that point George Wakeham realised that the bottle of whisky was empty. He threw it into the grate, stood up, and asked Nshila to choose between ten expensive brands, all of which he had in his wine cellar. Being ignorant about whisky, she told him that the one he had just finished – and of which she had drunk one small tot – had been quite wonderful.

She expected him to disappear down a staircase. Instead he walked out of the door and turned towards the shed from which he had first emerged to greet her. Nshila followed, curiosity overcoming politeness. George left the door open while he rummaged around. It was obvious that his shed was not devoted to carpentry or gardening but was completely filled with bottles. Filled, that is, except for a work bench supporting wine-making equipment. It seemed that George was both producer and consumer. While George was still searching, Nshila turned back to the cottage. How long would she have, she wondered, to extract information from George, sober? George drunk might be unreliable. She took a direct line.

'So Edwina died while she was still living in Rowan Hall, did she?'

'Yes, and that's where she's living now.'

'You're being too mysterious, Mr Wakeham. Explain it to me, please.'

'I was her solicitor at the time, and her relatives asked me to put it to her that she would be better off in Rollo's Rest Residence up at Cholsey. I knew it was quite pointless, but the argument was probably true and I promised I would raise the subject. I did so, and it was at a time when she was searching desperately for some item connected with Ned. She never said what it was, just using the word "it" over and over again. As she left my office she said very firmly, "I'm not leaving Rowan Hall until I've found it." She died a week later without finding it, and she's still there looking.'

'She sounds a harmless ghost. What form do her activities take?'

'Two main forms. There are signs of searching, such as things being moved about in order to look behind them or underneath them.

I am talking now about the earlier times when people lived there and had furniture and fittings in place. Now, when it's empty, there are sounds that reflect the ordinary business of living. For instance, Ned Awford had an old grandfather clock that had to be wound every day by pulling the chain. There's no clock now, but if you're in the house just before bedtime you will hear in being wound up. If you're there on a Saturday morning, you'll hear the washing machine going – but there's no washing machine. One of the steps on the staircase squeaks loudly when you tread on it. Sometimes it will squeak when there's nobody there. The same thing goes for the cellar door. Edwina's there, alright: you just can't see her.'

'Have you been there yourself, and heard these things?'

'Oh, yes. I'm very interested in the paranormal and, like I said, there's nothing malignant about Edwina. I've been there overnight about ten times.'

'Do you have a theory about it?'

'Certainly. It's simple. She'll go on living there, and go on looking until she finds this unidentified object. Then she'll leave, just as she said in my office.'

Nshila wondered what the thing sought for might be.

'Have you ever tried any experiments? Like taking objects with you to see if they arouse interest?'

'Yes. I've asked myself what mementoes of a dead husband a woman might treasure. I've taken cufflinks with me, and medals and a hairbrush and a Coronation Mug from the Queen's accession. Nothing happened, except that the medals had been sorted through. The order in which I left them had been changed. It was pretty hopeless, of course, because whatever I took it was mine, and therefore different from the thing she wanted.'

'Do you believe that the thing she wants – whatever it is – is still there, and might one day be found?'

'I do. But it's only a personal belief and I've no logic to support it. I've told you that she was pretty weird towards the end. She might have found it and forgotten she had done so, or it might never have existed at all.'

'Oh! I forgot,' said George. 'There's one other very odd thing.

Not many people know, but she's buried on her own estate.'

'How on earth can that happen? Surely there are laws about burial?'

'Indeed there are, but she was a smart woman in her own weird way. The churchyard is an odd shape, and at one point it adjoins the Rowan Hall grounds for about fifteen yards. When she knew she was dying, she got the vicar to promise to bury her as near as possible to her own territory. He agreed that the grave should be dug right up against the fence.'

'How did that help her?'

'She had a workman move the fence two yards into her land. The sexton dug 'close to the fence' as he had been told, and her physical remains are within the legal boundaries of Rowan Hall. The fence is in the wrong position, but nobody realises it. I only know because the workman once did a job at my place and let it out by mistake.'

'Do you think it helps her to stay anchored to the Hall?'

'Maybe. Who knows?'

That was all Nshila was able to get from George Wakeham, and she was unsure whether she could make any use of it. She returned to her car and was pleased to find it had suffered no worse fate than being splashed with mud where a tractor had passed.

Chapter Nine

Elusive Tradesmen

Simon Trent had never thought it would be easy to find an assassin. But he knew he had to start somewhere, and maybe one thing would lead to another. He began in his constituency. It was where he had grown up and been to school. The man who had captained the football team when Simon had been a rather ordinary goalkeeper was now a Chief Inspector in the local CID. As the sitting MP, Simon had official dealings with the police and it was not hard to arrange meetings nor to improve on their old acquaintanceship. Jack Hammond was politically opposed to Simon, and had the occasional dig at him.

'How's the scene looking to you, now, Simon? The polls are moving against your lot and there have been a few major foul-ups recently. How big was your majority, last time?'

'Not enough to make me safe if there's a big swing. But all governments are unpopular mid-term. It's nothing I worry about at nights.'

'Be odd, wouldn't it, if two years on I was sitting comfortably in a Superintendent's chair and you were on the street? Have you got various irons in the fire? Journalism, maybe? I remember you wrote stories for the school magazine, and you even had a few published in the local rag.'

That was the cue Simon needed. It was true. He had done those things. And writing was an activity he considered when politics seemed too grim. He steered the conversation towards a writer's need for sources, and suggested that Jack would be an excellent one for facts and figures about crime.

'What could you tell me, for instance, about assassins and hit men?'

Over three meetings, in the Police Club and The Red Lion, and without arousing suspicion, Simon learnt a lot. Sadly, most of it was inappropriate. He found that there was a hierarchy of practitioners, not just the top-flight internationals that featured in books and films. There were far more of the really crude, low-life types: the sort of people who operated by sitting in a car outside a pub where the target was drinking, and spraying the door with automatic fire when he emerged. These tended to call themselves hit men rather than assassins. Jack Hammond had met three of these during his career. One was dead, one was inside and one had disappeared. Simon heard of others who were a bit more competent, but hardly capable of taking on a high-profile target like the Prince.

It was common for middle-grade practitioners to rely on their underworld reputation for safety, rather than any skill in concealing their identity or making death look like an accident. They were known to the police, but nobody was going to provide evidence that would convict them. That sort of widespread mutual awareness was utterly impossible from Simon's point of view. Nobody must ever suspect that he had commissioned a death. He was coming to believe that Jack had no more to offer, when a third pint of Newcastle Brown triggered a memory.

'The top people are a whole lot more sophisticated and almost impossible to identify. The nearest I have come to an encounter was meeting a stuffy, ultra-respectable local politician from Dusseldorf. He visited here five years ago and two German detectives came to our division at the same time. Their force had picked up a hint that the politician had been targeted by a contract killer and they had been briefed to mind him. They talked about the situation, but they never found any evidence, then or later.'

Simon's strategy was successful insofar as it pointed to other lines of enquiry. He read several works of fiction, believing that the authors must have done a degree of research to make their stories credible. He read autobiographies of retired spies. He studied back numbers of newspapers. He traced, and talked with an investigative television reporter who had been mysteriously sacked and had his film destroyed.

From all that, he learnt that he must look in more exalted circles and must convey his needs in an oblique manner. He must never say that he wanted an assassin. He must talk about terrible personal problems that beset him and how he had no idea how to cope. He must show interest in assassination only as an abstract subject. He must convey the idea that he was rich enough and powerful enough and unscrupulous enough to use drastic means to get his way. He must wait patiently, for somebody to say 'There are ways to solve your problem, Simon, if you are not too squeamish.'

It was all very ambiguous and uncertain, he realised. At school he had learnt about Henry II and his troubles with Archbishop Thomas à Becket. 'Who will rid me of this turbulent priest?' That's what Henry is supposed to have said. Was that really an order for assassination or was it only an expression of frustration with no serious intent? Perhaps it all depended on the type of person you were talking to: some would interpret your words one way and some would read them differently. You didn't know which was which. Did Henry really want what he got, or was he totally shocked?

The missing element, for Simon, was that he had to make these subtle moves in an environment where they would be noticed and picked up. King Henry, of course, was surrounded by knightly courtiers, some of whom would do anything to earn favour with the king. Simon was not so well placed. But he tried. He manoeuvred skilfully for invitations and attended at least ten parties at which suitable people might be present. In quiet moments he pictured himself as a fly fisherman, seeking out promising reaches of a river, and promising pools, and casting his fly in hope. For a long time no fish was tempted.

And then it happened. He was at a party given by a professor at the School of Oriental and African Studies that forms part of London University. The talk in one group drifted onto the subject of witchcraft: to what extent was it real and to what extent fiction. One of the 'believers' was a little drunk, and said that the top practitioners were likely to mix witchcraft and science in their activities. He said that there was one person operating in London as an assassin who had caused deaths by just such a mixture. Simon said, in a joking tone, 'I could use somebody like that.' But he said it with a dead serious face, staring fixedly into the other's eyes.

Before he left Simon gave this person a business card – carrying fictional details but making contact possible. On the back he had written, 'Cost not an issue.'

And he waited.

While he waited, and unknown to him, various intermediaries were speaking quietly to each other and saying 'There might be business here!'

Chapter Ten

Risk Assessment

Nshila was still concerned about Fred. Security is vital to an assassin: the concealment of identity behind a respectable, and genuine persona. Anybody capable of linking the two was dangerous. What did Fred know? What might he suspect? Nshila reviewed what he had said, and speculated on what he might have omitted.

The tin box. In that box, retrieved from burial in the hut under the baobab tree, had been witchcraft-related items that had since increased her power. It was possible that he had seen the box. Was it even possible that he had opened the box and seen what was inside it? That seemed unlikely. Kwaname would have arranged protection for the contents, and Fred would have suffered.

He had explained his discovery of her true name and place of work. But it was an astonishing coincidence that he had taken shelter from the rain in the one building that housed her office. If that story were true, then sight of the company name on the display board and memory of their earlier contact were quite enough to justify his arrival upstairs. But had somebody directed him to the building? Had somebody led him there, and Fred just followed that person across the street? He had spoken of visiting her village, but he had said nothing about her elimination of the cattle thief – a story that he must have heard. There were missing pieces in the puzzle. She must watch and wait.

She considered, briefly, that he might be an admirer, in a sexual sense. It's quite common, she reflected, for young men to fixate on competent, sophisticated older women. Perhaps, in those late night talks under the wide African sky, he had been secretly lusting after her. That she could cope with, and even enjoy.

She extended her security review. It seemed a good time to do so because word had reached her about a possible new target. This was apparently a very high-profile foreigner whose elimination must be handled with the utmost discretion. The more important a target was, the greater the security risk.

Was she dangerously exposed in any way? What did the world know about her? Security lay in the fact that different people knew different things and had no reason to compare notes. A biographer might do it at some future time, but that was all. Mentally, she ran through the people and activities that might spell danger.

The Rain Consultancy. What did that say about her? Just that she was a successful businesswoman and a good employer. The data available at Companies House would show that she paid herself quite well, but would say nothing about the Swiss Bank accounts into which assassination fees were paid. Could her employees give her away? Gillian must surely have suspicions about the rain-making issue and must have wondered what else Nshila could do. But she could prove nothing and was fiercely loyal anyway. Peter Grace was a deep one, and might have made some good guesses. One of her targets had died in a burnt-out car, and a week or so before the event Peter Grace had been with her at a meeting when such accidents were discussed. But Peter was an ex-criminal and regarded 'grassing' as unforgivable.

Her brother. He knew plenty about the witchcraft activity and missed no chance to condemn it in a heavy older-sibling manner. But he had no knowledge of how she used her skills. He was also family, and he was now so respectable that he would resist any questioning about his sister. He wanted to be a good advertisement for the school, and impress the fee-paying parents.

Mike Fanshawe could put enough facts together to construct a hazy picture of illegal activities. But Mike made a conscious effort never to do so. He simply didn't want to know. Their friendship was so valuable that they built a firewall around it.

Zach Kawero was the person who knew most. Zach had been present with her that night in the derelict cricket pavilion where they had seen the questions for the examination paper in her cauldron. He knew for sure that she was into witchcraft. He had also suffered from it when she lost her temper with him and set The Companion to persecute him. That incident had only ended when she burnt out the 'target' mark on his shoulder with one of his own foul cigars. Zach was not going to forget it! Zach had also hacked into the computer of a target and posted seductive images that lured the target to the place from which he fell to his death. Zach was also aware that she had used the Hand of Glory to immobilise Maud Franklin while Zach worked electronic magic with her PC. But Zach liked her, and Zach was loyal, and Zach knew that all her victims improved the world by their dying. And Zach owed her. He owed her for the MBA exam and the Mercedes his father had given him for passing.

Patrick Quinn knew something, of course. He knew about the love potion business at school. But would anybody take Patrick seriously? Nshila thought not.

Jessop. What about him? He was the man at the top of her supply chain. The only man who could make contact with her directly. He knew what a contract was all about, and could, if he wanted, use his knowledge of the communicative procedures to trace her identity. Would he ever do so? It seemed very unlikely, for he served other operators as well and exposing her would make him an immediate target for one or all of the others.

So none of the potential threats seemed abnormally severe, and for none of them was there an obvious neutralising strategy. She could live with them, and if the new contract came alive, she would probably take it.

Lying on the table beside her – carried through from the office by accident – was a publication headed 'Health and Safety Executive'. She remembered how she and Gillian and Peter had laughed together about it's ultra-cautious demands.

'Have you done your risk-assessment?' That had been Peter's question to Gillian before she switched on the coffee machine. 'And be careful not to sneeze within ten feet of me, won't you!'

Nshila felt she had done her own risk-assessment and was satisfied.

Chapter Eleven
Articles Of Apprenticeship

Fred Mbwele entered the circle as an acquaintance and progressed towards being a friend. He met Mike Fanshawe and he met Zach Kawero. Both of them liked Fred, and Peter Grace soon introduced him to the squash club. He would sometimes come to the office just before the end of the working day and wait for Peter so that they could go off together. One day he turned up while Peter and Gillian were both out, and asked if he could speak with Nshila about something serious. She took him into the private flat.

'Nshila, do you remember that evening when we set up the last of the weather stations and were about to turn back towards the city?'

Nshila, slowly and with growing concern, 'Yes, I remember that evening.'

'I did not sleep very well that night.'

She stared into his eyes and threw the words back at him. 'You did not sleep very well that night. Go on, but be very careful.'

'I woke in the middle of the night and went outside the tent.'

'You woke in the middle of the night and went outside the tent. You're on dangerous ground, Fred.'

'I looked down into the valley where we had set up the station and I saw…..'

'Stop, Fred. If you go on with this tale you won't be able to unsay it.'

He didn't stop. He wanted something badly, and he was willing to take risks.

'I saw you down there.'

'You saw me down there. What was I doing?'

'It seemed to me as if you were meeting somebody, but I couldn't tell if it was a living person or a spirit. Sometimes it looked solid and sometimes I could see right through. I think you bowed to it. It gave you some sort of box. I know that for sure, because you had a tin box with you on the journey home. You kept it concealed most of the time, but once or twice I saw it.'

'So what do you make of it all?'

'I think you have some sort of spiritual or magical power. I think you have some skill at witchcraft or sorcery. I think you were meeting some older or more powerful spirit and gaining strength from it.'

'And why are you following up this suspicion? Are you aiming to expose me or blackmail me? If I really am the sort of person you describe then you ought to be very much afraid of me.'

Fred hesitated – and plunged.

'I know it. Yes, I do feel scared. But there is something I want and I want it really badly. I think you might be willing to give me what I want because it would be good for you, too.'

'Go on, Fred. I'm listening.'

'I want to be your apprentice.'

Wow! That shook her to the core. There had been moments in her life when she had wished for somebody to share secrets with, but never had she seriously thought of taking on an apprentice. And if she had ever thought along those lines, how on earth could she have followed it up? One can't put an advertisement in the national press asking for a trainee witchdoctor and assassin. All the cranks in the world will apply. You may even get a visit from the Special Branch to make sure it is only a joke and to warn you against 'inciting crime'.

Still, there had been those moments of longing. There is something attractive about passing on knowledge to a pupil who really wants to learn. It's nice to be sought after as a teacher of valued skills. Suddenly she wondered how Kwaname had felt that day when a terrified girl collapsed on the floor of the hut under the baobab tree. Had he seen the chance of teaching once again? Had he realised that this child might help to preserve a store of knowledge?

Thoughts are secret. It is a fiction to say that a person can 'read another's mind'. What Fred actually saw was evidence of shock and surprise as Nshila rocked back in her chair and almost overbalanced. What he actually heard, a moment later, was delighted, spontaneous laughter. He was hurt.

'What's funny about it? You are an expert and I want to learn.'

'I'm sorry, Fred. I just had some hilarious scenes running through my mind. Do you know much about apprenticeship as it used to be in this country?'

'No. Just that it was a way of learning a craft from an established master. I think you're one of those, and can teach me.'

'An apprentice had to serve his master for five years, Fred, under a contract that demanded full obedience. 'Articles of Apprenticeship', the document was called. When his 'articles' were over he was subjected to a 'passing out' ritual. If he were a cooper, for instance – a man who made wooden barrels – his mates used to roll him around inside one. I was imagining what sort of ritual might be suitable for a witchdoctor. And then the young man would put in a few years as a 'journeyman'. That meant travelling from place to place, using his skill to meet all sorts of local needs. I was imagining you turning up at an English pub and asking "Do you people need any witchdoctoring?" I couldn't help laughing.'

'Very funny, for you. But I'm serious. I really do want to be your apprentice. I want it more than I have ever wanted anything.'

It was time for quick thinking. If Fred were sent away with a flea in his ear, he might become dangerous. He knew, or had guessed, too much. Perhaps he should be neutralised. No. An immediate negative to that one. She had never assassinated anybody who didn't thoroughly deserve it. And Fred was close to being a friend. The other option was to accept him, and get him so deeply involved that he could not betray her without betraying himself. He also had to be very, very frightened of her. That, she could start on straightaway.

On her coffee table stood a round silver ashtray, highly polished. From a shelf beside her, Nshila took a small bottle of Indian ink. She poured some into the ashtray, bent her head over it, concentrated, and spoke a few words of power. Then she replaced it on the table and said, 'Look hard into that, Fred.' He did.

Crash! Thump! Fred's chair was on its back and Fred was backed up against the wall with his hand out in a protective gesture and his face contorted with fear. The graduation picture behind him was crooked and a small piece of plaster had fallen from the wall.

Nshila waited thirty seconds, and then – slowly – poured the ink back into the bottle. As she did so she could see Fred relax. The fear went from his face and he moved back to the table, picking up his chair and sitting down. But there was sweat on his face and his hands were unsteady. Nshila spoke.

'Do you really want to be my apprentice? It could be tough at times.'

'Yes. Yes, I do. It's scary, but I want it. And what was that you did? It was ghastly.'

'I call it the Emotional Intensifier. It's something I picked up from one of those old books of magic in the British Library. By concentrating my own emotions I can project them into the mind of the next person to look into the ink. I just thought of everything that terrifies me most and put out a huge dose of naked terror. When you looked into the ink, you saw whatever it is that most terrifies you, personally. Did you enjoy it?'

'Don't ask. You saw well enough. But can I be your apprentice?'

She thought, 'He's got determination, at least. And he recovered quickly. Two good signs'.

'Well, Fred, the other alternative I have is to kill you quickly and use my Voodoo skills to make a Zombie of you. Zombies are rather boring creatures, so my answer is Yes. It will be a strange experience for both of us, but maybe we can make it work.'

'That's great. Absolutely great. I feel marvellous. Thank you. Thank you. Thank you.'

'Fred, there will be times when you feel quite the reverse, I promise you. For a start, the apprentice has to do exactly what the master says, all the time. And some of the tasks that fall to an apprentice are unexciting, low grade ones.'

'I can take it. Give me a start.'

'Here you are, then. The root of all witchcraft and sorcery is knowledge: knowing about the people and things around you in a way that other people don't. You can then make things happen which seem to others like magic but are really the outcome of manipulation by you. Go back to the embassy, and return to me a week from now with a list of twenty things about the staff that you know, but nobody else knows. Now get out. This has been as stressful for me as it has for you, and I still have work to do.'

Chapter Twelve

Straws In The Wind

She was in no state after that interview to make big decisions. But she could complete simple administrative tasks. She rang Jessop, who had passed on rumours about a possible contract. It turned out that he wanted to send a written summary. That archaic method was their response to the lack of security characteristic of the electronic world. Nshila had once asked Zach if he could provide total electronic security. He had replied that it was impossible. 'The field changes so fast,' he said, 'that what looks completely safe one day gets broken into tomorrow. Look on your computer as a potential traitor and don't tell it too much.'

Nshila and Jessop had fallen back on yesterday's technology. If he wanted to pass serious and secret information, he wrote one original text in his own vile handwriting. He sealed it in wax with his signet ring and sent it to her by courier. Nshila read it, memorised the details, and destroyed it. This time, Jessop said that he had only just started writing and the job would take about four hours.

'What am I going to do for four hours?' She asked Rasputin, who was dozing on the bed. The answer was a wide yawn and silence.

'Rubbish, Rasputin. I can't sleep away the day like you. It's not in my nature.'

This time she got a long hard stare that seemed to convey contempt for all humans. Rasputin seemed to be saying they were incapable of assessing priorities correctly. The eyes closed again.

There were, of course, plenty of useful tasks she could do around the flat. Nshila mostly did the housework herself, because of the materials and artefacts and books and tools that she wanted nobody to see. There was much that could be done, little she wanted to do.

Company, that's what she needed. Company, with unimportant talk, and arguments about trivia. Things to rest the brain. It was

Friday, and with luck she might find Mike Fanshawe winding down with his friends in one of their favourite watering holes in Fenchurch Street. She put on a lightweight coat and set off. The crowds, of course, were moving west towards Monument, Bank, Cannon Street or London Bridge. Progress was slow, with much sidestepping and a few apologies.

How young some of the faces were! Apprentices, she thought, with Fred Mbwele still on her mind. Apprentice financial wizards destined to guard and increase the wealth of the nation. And behind each of them, a master. A master, she reflected, who must have taken them on for good reason. He wanted something, he felt a need. A need to ensure that his mystery was not lost. That motive she could share. Was there another motive? Perhaps an awareness of waning powers? Perhaps even the most skilful professional realised that changing times demanded new ideas. Perhaps he developed a fear of becoming locked into old habits and incapable of new thinking. Those were less welcome thoughts when applied to herself. 'Not true!' Her mind rejected them. 'I'm still learning, still growing. Look how I handled Gillian's wedding. And the gods must have confidence in me since they gave me those magic discs. They gave them when I had no idea what to do with them (I still don't) so they must have anticipated that I would grow further.'

'...I'm so sorry. I was miles away. Let me help pick it all up.' She found herself apologising profusely to a middle-aged lady with a stick whose carrier bag had shed its load on the pavement when Nshila walked into her.

'You should look where you are going, young lady.'

Slightly chastened, Nshila walked on. Her thoughts also took a downward turn. Yes. The spirits had sent her the discs, but was the fact that she could not use them indicative of lessening intuitive powers? Ten years ago, would she have seen their meaning immediately? Suddenly she saw the arrival of Fred in a different light. He might himself be a gift from the spirits. The message might be that she was now to extend her powers by finding and developing and using the skills of her apprentice. Another reversal of mood! This was a door opening before her! A step upwards! A promotion!

Suddenly she realised that she had passed the first of the bars where Mike might have been found. Had she gone in? Had she checked it? Or had she ignored it? Should she go back?

She was outside the second pub on the search list. As soon as she opened the door she heard known voices. No need to go back. Mike was there – welcoming and reliable as always – and three colleagues. Two men and a woman. Vince Mallon she knew well, because he and Mike formed one of those double acts in which complete opposites strike sparks off each other. Like Laurel and Hardy or Morecambe and Wise. Mike was Old Etonian – an extreme version. Vince was the child of immigrants from Lithuania, small, wiry, state-educated. His mind was so quick and sharp that one had hardly formulated a point before he had grasped it and jumped two steps ahead. The other man was Ray Leverton, an Australian working an exchange tour and possessed of the strongest accent Nshila had ever heard. He was thin and tall, crowned with a mass of unruly near-white hair. The woman, Nshila had never met. Her name turned out to be Elaine Manners. She was a bit shorter than Nshila, with a full figure, an olive complexion, curly black hair and a rather sultry look. Her voice was soft and very sexy. Mike greeted Nshila with an inquisitive smile.

'What brings you here? You don't often seek us out like this.'

'I was bored, Mike. I've got a few hours with nothing to do except wait, and I thought you might be somewhere round here burbling on about the mysteries of finance. It's interesting sometimes.'

That was true. Nshila always found it amazing how complex the affairs of other specialists could be – how often there were parallels to her own activity as a meteorologist. She was not unique in trying to judge the strength of different forces and predict how they would combine if and when they met. Mike's skill had similarities to her own: it was just applied to different data and used different language.

'Anyway, you're very welcome. Elaine has just been moaning at us about barriers thrown up against women. Maybe you can support her. She is trying to convince a client that this is not the right time to go for a public flotation. She's right, but they won't listen to her. But you need a drink first. What shall I get you?'

Just then a party moved out and a corner table became vacant. They made themselves comfortable.

There were times when Nshila liked being on the fringes of a conversation, and just listening to other people. This time it was a bit different from the usual Friday evening winding down session. More often than not the talk was about sport, especially motor racing, with long arguments about wet-weather tyres and pit stops and late braking, etc. Today it was about their profession. Elaine was making her case powerfully and with some indignation. Nshila, knowing nothing about the facts, found herself drawn into the issue through the behaviour Elaine had encountered from the client representatives. She could see that Elaine had been answered less than logically. There had been prejudice, she sensed, and a lack of openness. Mike and Ray could see nothing wrong. It was Vince who foresaw a gender-based conflict and changed the subject.

He turned it to globalisation and inter-cultural relations and immigration. Nshila got heavily involved, being originally from a very different culture and an immigrant, though a fully integrated one. Mike, of course, knew that she had an MBE for contributions to inter-cultural relations. The thing that struck her most forcefully was Mike's fear for his national identity. He was the ultimate patriotic Englishman and seemed to be saying that immigration, and the transfer of values across national boundaries through the internet, was likely to destroy the concept of Englishness – whatever that might be. He was quite paranoid about the English Cricket Team. He believed that talent should always be recognised, but was very unhappy about the small number of genuine home-grown people in the national team. Ray was deliberately provocative.

'That's because you belong to a nation in decline, Mike. You are all so obsessed by fairness and equality that the idea of winning has been forgotten. You're dependent on immigrants from more virile countries like Australia and South Africa.'

Knowing Mike's likely response, Nshila tried to divert him by kicking him under the table. She missed – only managing to dislodge

Elaine's handbag, which was wedged between her chair and Mike's. All five of them grubbed around to retrieve the contents. Everything visible was gathered up, but Elaine was seriously distressed by her failure to find a ring. It seemed odd. This competent, sophisticated woman was suddenly close to panic. Nshila found herself wishing she could remember an effective finding spell – and annoyed that one seemed to be lurking at the back of her mind, yet not emerging. The ring finally turned up; it had rolled towards the bar and was hidden behind one of the brackets holding the foot-rail. Greatly relieved, Elaine apologised for her anxiety. Later, she explained privately to Nshila.

'I was married, once. It was a genuine love-match and we were very happy. He was killed in a traffic accident when he was twenty-four and I was a year younger. That ring was my wedding ring and it has huge sentimental value for me. Losing it would be a big psychological blow.'

'Why did you have it in your handbag, then?'

'I don't normally, but I had to get it valued for insurance. Don't tell Mike and Ray, please. I don't want any chauvinist comments about female sentimentality.'

Nshila promised, though she was a little surprised at the strength of Elaine's feeling. It threw new light on the story of Edwina Awford, staying on year after year at Rowan Hall, forever searching. The idea of a woman haunting a house to search for some sentimental token had seemed feeble. Perhaps it was possible after all. The finding of Elaine's ring might be a clue to the cleansing of Rowan Hall.

'Elaine, thanks for a marvelous idea.' She almost spoke it aloud.

Soon after the handbag incident, Vince had to leave, being scheduled to address a stamp-collecting club. It was his main hobby, and he was something of an expert on Russia and Eastern Europe. That left a party of two men and two women. The mood favoured a trip down-river by water-taxi and dinner on one of the floating restaurants moored off Canary Wharf – locations familiar to Mike. Nshila got back to Eastcheap very late and slightly drunk, knowing that Jessop's courier had missed her and that the vital document would lie in a carrier bag overnight.

But she felt relaxed and happy. There was nothing like stepping into a completely different world for a time. Both Fred and Jessop would have to wait till morning and it worried her not at all.

Rasputin was still asleep on the bed.

Chapter Thirteen
Delegation

Nshila valued Jessop highly as the person nearest to her in the 'supply chain' through which business came. But his literary skills were minimal and she hated wading through masses of verbiage to get at the meaning. He had once been a policeman and his reports were reminiscent of, 'I was proceeding down Buckingham Palace Road at approximately 09.43am etc. etc.' The morning after her down-river excursion she was confronted by a lengthy text.

> This contract opportunity has been discussed in circles known to me for at least a month and, in my judgement, it is the same contract rather than several similar ones.
>
> During the years we have been associated (to our mutual benefit), you will, I am sure, have gathered that I possess extensive contacts across the murky world in which clients grope around for professionals such as yourself. There are always intermediaries, people of greater or lesser competence and discretion. Some of these I know only by hearsay: with others I have limited personal interaction. I never know anything about the principals for whom they work. They are scrupulous about that, just as I am extremely careful to protect your identity.
>
> At least four such intermediaries have been approached by what I believe to be the same individual. The name given was always different – as you would expect – and the appearance altered in minor ways. But basic physical details like height and weight have been similar, and when negotiations have broken down it seems always to have been for the same reason. I suspect an extreme degree of secrecy and deduce that the client is himself (or herself) acting as an individual rather than the representative of an organisation. I have the impression that the plan, whatever it may be, is known in very general terms to two people only, and the name of the target to only one. Since services such as yours are extremely expensive, I deduce that this client is either a rich philanthropist or so highly placed in an

organisation that he (or she) can easily divert large sums of money without suspicion. That person might be, I judge, the chairman of a blue-chip company or even a cabinet minister.

When the client's emissary made himself known to me, it was obvious that his previous enquiries had foundered on what I may call the crudity of the solutions offered by other professionals. The emissary described them as lacking in subtlety, and when I pressed him I learnt that the ideal solution would be a death showing no signs at all of 'foul play'. It would be perfect if the target appeared to die from natural causes or from a freak accident that could not possibly have been engineered. When I said, 'You seem to be asking for witchcraft or sorcery or an Act of God,' the emissary responded, 'That would be perfect.' I can't account for what I am now going to say, but I had the oddest feeling that there was some moral or messianic motive in the background: something like 'The health of the nation is at stake and nobody except me can recognise the danger.' As regards the presumption of natural causes or an Act of God, I indicated that your talents were exceptionally broad and included that option.

As regards the fee, I believe we are talking about a very large sum of money – so large that I may even be able to retire on my commission and buy a farm in Provence. But the client's desire for secrecy is so obsessive that he (or she) won't accept your preferred type of meeting . He realises that you will use a trusted intermediary, but he wants to meet that person at a place and time of his own choosing. He promises privacy and security, promising further that he will then reveal data, him as much at risk from exposure as you are.

The proposal is that, your representative should walk across the footbridge that links Waterloo East railway station with Waterloo proper on Friday next week. He should start from Waterloo East at 3.25pm exactly, taking the time from the clock on the departure board just before the passage slopes down to the platforms. He should carry a green and gold golfing umbrella, loosely furled. Before he he reaches Waterloo proper, somebody will accidentally collide with him and say 'Watch yourself, mate'. Your colleague will be making a train journey and will be away for several hours.

Jessop wrote that he saw no great risks. He favoured acceptance.

That was the text that Nshila read, and re-read before she burnt it. She did not intend to accept Jessop's comments without a lot of careful thought. Was the farm in Provence causing a tiny bias in his mind? Allowing space in her head for that idea soon made her feel guilt: he had always been loyal. Forget it! He would recognise the temptation and reject it.

She was still left with a major deviation from her normal mode of operating - which was to choose a meeting place herself, a spot that was safe from human or electronic intrusion. She was now in danger of doing something entirely new. It might open the door to unexpected hazards.

What was she going to do? The normal procedure was to act as her own representative, adopting a suitable disguise. This she did because a personal assessment of the client was much better than second-hand data. She used various disguises, her favourite being the spinster schoolteacher, insistent on precision and accuracy. It was an act that was apt to annoy clients but provoked informative responses.

This was a situation where the sole operator was handicapped. She had nobody who could meet the other party without learning what that party wanted and, therefore, how she could help him.

What were the options? She could have Jessop reject the terms that had been suggested and make a counter-proposal more in line with her own needs. Or she could reject the contract absolutely: a decision that might be wise, but rather offended her ego. She was moving towards the second option, when a third possibility struck her. Send the apprentice! Wow! The novel idea caused her to pour herself a vodka. Send the apprentice! It might be just the task that would involve him and test his skills. The more she thought about the idea, the more she liked it. He was due to report in a few days. If he wasn't serious about working with her, this would make him chicken out. If he welcomed the task, he would be committed.

Before briefing Fred for his task she read and re-read his paper about the embassy staff. It was good. He had observed his targets carefully and noticed what was significant and what mattered less. With practice, he would see those characteristics of individuals that made them vulnerable and accident-prone. Nshila showed him how a misfortune happening to one person might be seen as an understandable accident while the same thing happening to another would arouse the deepest suspicion. What he told her about the First Secretary fitted neatly with facts already known to her, and would have enabled her to have him sent home in disgrace.

She would use him. She told him selected details of the possible contract and explained his role.

'Your only duty, Fred, is to hear what the potential client wants, and report that accurately to me. The big prohibition is that you must never give any clue at all to my identity. Present yourself as an underling who gets instructions from an unseen source. You must be seen as a safe and reliable way to communicate with me. That's important to all clients, because they have a serious need for something that I can provide. Work hard at presenting yourself as a unique channel.'

'What sort of thing might they want? Might they want you to kill somebody? Would you do it?'

'Curb your imagination, Fred. Am I a killer? There may be other options. We have to test for them'

Alright, but, I know you have killed. When I was in your village they told me about the cattle thief. They said that they had found and buried the body.'

'Fred, I never touched that man. He fell down a slope into a muddy creek, bashed his head on a stone and drowned. I never touched him.'

'Maybe, but why did he fall down that slope? It could have been your witchcraft. And, while we're talking about death, will I be in any danger on this trip?'

'I don't think there's any risk at this stage. Just act out your role honestly and bring back the information. If they ask questions about my professional competence, you can tell them whatever you already know or guess. If you are in doubt about whether I can do something, tell them "Yes" and I'll figure out a way to make it come true. I'll also watch you from time to time.'

'Can you do that? How does it work?'

'Remember that biscuit tin that you saw me pick up? One of the things inside it was a small quantity of powder that Kwaname used to burn over a smoking fire. If I stare into that smoke and concentrate hard on the person I want to observe, then something will appear. It's not always crystal-clear and sometimes I can't see much of the background.'

She could see Fred's mind assimilating the possible meanings.

'Could you watch me anytime, whatever I was doing?'

'If I really wanted to, then probably Yes. I could watch you finding yourself a woman, and see exactly what you did together. But don't worry. There are three good reasons why I shan't do so.'

'Like what?'

'First, it takes extreme concentration and I can't keep it up for long. Second, you are not important enough to justify the effort – except for quick snapshots when you are doing a job for me. Third, I don't have a big stock of powder.'

'Why? Is it hard to get?'

'So far, I have found it impossible. All I have got came in that biscuit tin you saw Kwaname give me. Chemical laboratories here in London have so far failed to discover exactly what it is, let alone create it. It bugs me considerably.'

During this conversation Nshila realised that smart apprentices have an up side and a down side. One part of the latter is that they are continually asking questions: questions that you don't want to spend time answering, or which challenge your assumptions. Her mind called up the image of The Elephant's Child in the Just So Stories, where inquisitiveness got him into big trouble. Had Kwaname, she wondered, sometimes got utterly fed up with her questions? Was Fred going to be as inquisitive as she had been? Fred was still wanting answers.

'If you can see things in the smoke, like that, why didn't you know that I was coming? When I walked in through the door a few weeks ago you were clearly surprised.'

'Because until you appeared, I had forgotten you. You just didn't have any space in my mind.'

'But I have space now, haven't I? I'm your apprentice.'

'Get out of here, Fred, and don't let me down.'

Chapter Fourteen

Suburban Encounter

Fred didn't turn up in Eastcheap on the evening of his adventure. Nshila viewed him vacillating between bus and taxi outside Waterloo station, and deciding on the bus that would take him to his lodgings. She went to bed early.

The alarm had only just gone off next morning when she had a phone call from an excited Fred asking for the earliest possible meeting. It didn't suit her to have events driven by her apprentice, so she told him that whatever he had to say couldn't be desperately important and he could come at 4.30 in the afternoon. Discipline, she thought. It has to be obvious who is the master and who is the apprentice.

She also took a firm line when he appeared – still in an excited state and bursting to share news. 'I want an orderly report,' she said. 'Just calm down and tell me what happened from beginning to end. And why did you not come back here last night? You were at Waterloo at 8.15 and could have been here by taxi in fifteen minutes.'

'You watched me! Well, I thought about coming but decided that you might not want to be bothered at that time in the evening. And you might have been out, or had a visitor. It was too uncertain, so I went home. What else did you see?'

'Nothing, beyond you deciding between bus and taxi. Remember, I told you I would watch infrequently, and that's true. But you will never know when I watch and when I don't. Anyway, get on with your story. But keep it accurate and logical and don't get overexcited.'

'It was fun. I've never done anything like it before and I think I did quite well. I was early at Waterloo East and I filled in time with coffee and a bun in the coffee shop on Platform C. Before that, of course, I checked my watch against the clock so that I could pass the start point at exactly the right moment. I almost failed, for a huge man, clutching a brief case, knocked me into the wall, as he ran for a train. But I got myself up and hurried. Nothing happened as I covered the first part of the bridge, to the point where you can see ahead to the escalator that goes down to the main station. Then I could see about twenty people walking towards me and I was hoping the contact would be the tall, smart girl in the red, military-cut overcoat. She was quite something. In fact, I was still looking at her when a fat, unshaven labourer in a boiler suit bumped into me and said "Watch yourself, mate". When I recovered I realised that I had a train ticket stuck to my hand with a post-it note.'

They were talking in the flat, and at that moment Peter Grace put his head round the door to ask Fred whether he was OK for a doubles match at the squash club that evening. He obviously didn't know the answer. Nshila said 'Yes' for him.

'Go on, Fred.'

'The ticket was a return to Virginia Water, and I thought the intention must be for me to take the first train. I found one scheduled for 4.05pm. and took it. Nothing happened during the journey. I got out at Virginia Water and was looking around vaguely when a middle-aged lady who looked like somebody's housekeeper walked up to me and said "Welcome, young man! I've been waiting for you. The car's outside".'

He broke off there, and asked, 'How did they work the timing and the recognition? The labourer type can't have known exactly when I started over the bridge. I mean, I might have been delayed. They couldn't have relied on the time specification alone. And the housekeeper type must have known who I was.'

'There's no magic in that, Fred. They had mobiles. Somebody behind you at Waterloo East sent the labourer a signal. And the labourer took a picture of you to send ahead to Virginia Water. Go on.'

'Here's where it gets mysterious. The car drove through a maze of country lanes so that I was unable to remember the route. I could tell you where it turned off the main road, and I would recognise one or two places that we passed, if I saw them again. One of those was very unusual: the road crossed a 'restored' railway track and there was an old notice advertising their Midsummer Romantic Revel. The barrier came down and we had to wait while a tiny, antiquated steam engine crossed, hauling two restaurant cars – both empty. I would recognise that place easily. But the rest of the route was obviously intended to confuse me, and I think we passed some places more than once. We finally went through the back gates of a substantial country house and stopped close to a side door. I was led inside, and only got the vaguest impression of a huge ivy-covered building. The housekeeper opened the first door on the left and asked me to wait a few moments. The room surprised me. What do you think it was?'

'I don't want guessing games. Get on with it.'

'Well, don't you want clues? It was a billiards room. There was only one window, which looked out onto a paved yard. The scoreboard had the names of Bartholomew and Percy on it. The ceiling was painted, and had a whole herd of angels blowing trumpets. Don't you want to identify the place?'

'I may need to later, but maybe we shall find out who the client is without that. What happened when you actually met him?'

'Here's the bad news, then. I was called into the next room, and as the door opened a spotlight came on, shining straight into my eyes so that I could see nothing. Then the door closed, the spotlight went out, and I could still see nothing because the room was totally dark. Black dark, I mean, like a photographic dark room, not just dim. A male voice told me that there was a chair just in front of me, and I should grope for it. There was something unnatural about the voice: it was blurred and indistinct as if the speaker had had a stroke, or had got a marble in his mouth. Disguise, I suppose. I sat down and he got started.'

'Give me the sense of what he said. I don't need it verbatim.'

'First of all, he told me that I was not the person he expected, and that he had expected a meeting with someone close to my principal. I acted humble on that one. I explained that you were very security-conscious and there was no way you would attend a meeting personally unless you controlled the conditions. I said that you had planned, as a big concession, to send your closest colleague but that he had been in an accident. I was a poor substitute.

'I got an angry response, saying that his need for security was every bit as great as yours and that one party or the other had to compromise, or there was no deal. I said nothing, and there was a long silence. I was getting worried before he spoke again. Then he said that he was going to make the first move and wait for your response. I'll have to give you his own words as near as I can. He wanted it that way.'

Here Fred lost control of himself and actually bounced in his chair. 'This is the crunch, Mistress. This is the bit you really need to hear.'

'I won't know that till you tell me, will I? Just report his words.'

'Tell your principal five things, and get these right:

I have special, privileged knowledge that identifies a man as an enemy of our country – extremely dangerous – so much so that he ought to be eliminated.
The man is above suspicion and to deal with him by legitimate means is impossible.
I have the power to offer very substantial rewards of almost any type.
My position and my whole career would be lost if any word of this contract was leaked.
The target is Prince Thaqib.'

'He made me repeat his points twice over,' said Fred. 'This is a big one, Mistress - big - big - big. He is asking us to knock off an Arab Prince. Will we do it? When? How? What will we be paid?'

'What makes you think that a recently accepted apprentice will have any role in such an activity - if it ever takes place?'

'Oh! You have to include me - you must. There are bound to be ways I can help. I'll do anything. Just give me a part in the project.'

She loved his enthusiasm but was reluctant to make promises;

'Maybe. Maybe. Right now, get back to the story.' Fred settled down again and resumed.

'Although my head was still in a whirl, I did remember to tell him how determined you always are to make your own assessment of people. I emphasised that if you were to get involved in his project (and I told him it was a very big 'if') then you would have to be satisfied that the act was necessary. He would have to convince you.

'That upset him a bit. He seemed to think it was a bit arrogant in a tradesman to question the client's decision. But he calmed down.

'That's it. I was taken back to the station with the same precautions and had just ten minutes to wait for a train. Did I do OK?'

'As an untrained observer, you were average. As an apprentice witchdoctor you were poor.'

Fred shrank. It was almost as dramatic as the bursting of a balloon. One moment he was cocky and up-beat, the next he was disoriented and lost. Nshila had to reconstruct his ego.

'Fred, think of this as your first real lesson in witchcraft. I'm not teaching you spells and incantations and conjuring tricks because the true basis of witchcraft is knowledge – and knowledge comes from watching and thinking and reflection. Yesterday afternoon you saw and heard a great deal, but your mind only attached significance to a tiny proportion of what your senses noticed. If you ask "why", then my answer is that you mentally filtered out everything that was not, according to your preconceptions, relevant.'

'You mean I saw things and blanked them out?'

'Yes. And I'll prove it to you. Let's start with the labourer-type who gave you the ticket. What sort of work did he labour at?'

'No idea!' Fred groaned and shifted in his seat and bent down to touch Rasputin, who was passing. Rasputin hissed at him.

'Yes, you have. Most labourers have some indication of their trade in tools that they carry around with them, or variations of dress, or give-away traces on their hands or faces. This man who accosted you was wearing a boiler suit. What was he wearing it for?'

'You're right. Now I come to think of it he was also wearing some sort of safety belt like you see people wearing when they climb telegraph poles. And there were a few tools stuck to it. I saw a hammer and a pair of pliers. So he could have been a telephone engineer.'

'The ticket that he gave you. When did he buy it?'

'How on earth would I know that?'

'By looking at it. Rail tickets are machine-made at the point of issue. They carry the time of printing on them. Have you still got yours? Sometimes they don't take them at the barrier.'

Fred dug around in his pockets and produced the return section. It had been printed at 6.45am the previous day at Woking.

'Does that tell us anything, Fred?'

'Perhaps. It may mean that whoever bought it was coming into London to work. He may be a commuter. And Woking may be his home station, and we may be able to deduce what train he usually catches.'

'So now you know what I mean by watching and listening and reflecting – as a serious exercise and not just a figure of speech. You're going to stay here in my flat, Fred, and re-live yesterday's experience in your own mind. You're going to write down all the new ideas that come to you, and then you're going to talk me through them. I'll see you in about an hour.'

He did well. When Nshila came back he had recalled significant facts about the 'housekeeper type' and about the car journey and the vehicle they travelled in. But the best bit was his enhanced feeling for the man talking in the dark.

'I think I must have been too much influenced by the status differential. I knew I was just a low-grade messenger, and he was obviously a man of position and power. And he had total control of the physical conditions in which we met. Yet on reflection, I think he sounded nervous and uncertain. He was angry at not meeting somebody more important, but I think the anger was not personal affront. It was worry about the set-back to his plans. He took quite a time to decide on his course of action – starting to speak two or three times and then breaking off to make a fresh start. It wasn't the performance of somebody who knew exactly what to do –

more that of a beginner who was feeling his way. Yet I felt he was very sincere. He came across as somebody who had started on a difficult and unfamiliar activity, but one that he felt compelled to carry through. I think he is in earnest about wanting contact with somebody like you. He is certainly in a position of power, but I think perhaps he operates in a very competitive world with frequent conflict and back-stabbing. At times he seemed almost afraid.'

'Not bad, Fred. Fairly soon now I'll let you start on the smells and spells that you crave.'

When Fred had gone, Nshila faced up to the full shock of his report. Prince Thaqib! Here was a very high-profile target, with maximum danger and uncertainty. She could certainly not contribute to his elimination just because one powerful client wanted it. Personally she was not surprised by the allegation. Major plots, in her experience, demanded major players and she found it quite credible that the tortuous politics of the Middle East had led Prince Thaqib into some secret, death-deserving action. But she would need more evidence. Even if she came to believe that elimination was right, could she achieve it? 'Give this one a miss,' said her reasonable cautious self. 'However big the fee, this one can never be worth it. Send a refusal right now and forget it.'

She knew that to be the sensible course and sat down to choose the right words for the refusal. But they never came. After ten minutes she found that she had written a 'holding' response that talked about 'extensive, time-consuming target research and costly choices of method'. But she had failed to say 'No'.

Tear it up and start again? No. The spirits had worked their magic on her and the outright rejection seemed cowardly. She could always cry off later. She called Jessop and told him what to say. Then she sent for Fred and told him what she had done. If he really wanted to be her apprentice, he could take the risks she took.

Chapter Fifteen

Peter Shadows The Prince

'What's got into you, Peter?' Gillian was nagging Peter one morning. She had developed quite a nice line in short snappy jokes and Peter normally obliged by laughing. Some of them she had picked up from her Pakistani husband and they had an inverted racism that made them very funny. On the morning concerned, Peter was sunk in gloom and offered zero response. Nshila took a hand herself.

'Come on, Peter, something is bugging you. The first three days of the week you were bright and lively. Now it's disappeared. I'll listen if it will help.' He was slow to start, but gradually found relief in sharing his worries.

His happy state, he explained, had been due to him and Fred getting through to the third round of their club championship. Peter had never got that far before, but it seemed that he and Fred combined well together. They had defeated a technically better pair in an exhausting second-round match and were pleased with themselves. They had been looking forward to the next match, which had taken place the previous evening.

'What we really hoped for, I suppose, was a rather cheap class triumph. One of the opposing pair was a rich Old Harrovian called Archie, and his partner was a foreigner: a Prince, no less! Fred was very impressed by the Prince and curious about him - so much so that I thought his behaviour a bit odd. Myself, I just thought what fun it would be if those two were beaten by an ex-convict and a young black immigrant.'

'Did it happen?'

'No. We played well – gave them a bit of a fright – but lost narrowly in the end. It's not the result that bugs me, but what happened afterwards.'

'Tell me.'

'We all showered and changed, then met in the bar. They were very pleasant and polite, seeming to enjoy our company despite the obvious differences. You know how it is. People like that talk as if they had a plum in the mouth, while my speech has a hint of Silly Suffolk and Fred's English lets him down at times. They tried hard not to patronise us. It was an enjoyable interlude. They even let us buy a round of drinks. Then I heard Archie ask the Prince whether he was going on to "the Moffat Street party" and, if he was, should they share a taxi. The Prince said "No". He had to get back to his embassy to take a conference call. We all went down to the entrance. Fred walked off towards the tube station and Archie flagged a passing taxi. I suppose he went to Moffat Street. The Prince was waiting for another taxi to show up and I went briefly back inside to check a date on the notice board. I came out again just in time to see the Prince getting into a taxi and hear him giving the driver the address. It was not the embassy. It was the Goat and Ghost club in Pear Street, off Goswell Road.

'Now, The Goat and Ghost club is not the sort of place where respectable diplomats go. I went there sometimes when I was active in the criminal world, and I was always happy to get out of it. The people who use it are a different class of evildoer altogether. As a mere thief, without any injuries or deaths to my credit, I was right at the bottom of the totem pole. There were men there who were known to have killed more than once. I've not been there since my spell in Parkhurst, but I hear things from people who did time with me and befriended me. They still go there. I hear it has got even worse over the past three years. It was raided a month ago by the police anti-terrorist unit and they arrested six men on suspicion of terrorist activity. They failed to get a conviction because some of their evidence was judged inadmissible.

Peter stopped abruptly. The Rain Consultancy was disturbed by the insistent clamour of the fire alarm. In many London offices the first reaction to the sound is inertia. Everyone assumes it is a false alarm and awaits the apology. If it never comes the conscientious employees leave their work stations in a shamefaced way and walk to the stairs. Others follow reluctantly when they have finished the telephone call they were on or their coffee. Not so in the Eastcheap building where The Rain Consultancy rented offices. The owners of the building had recently had a property burnt out and had been very dissatisfied with the way the insurance company had tried to reduce the pay-out - alleging breaches of regulations by the tenants. All tenants were required to respond quickly by evacuating the building. Nshila, Gillian and Peter dutifully went downstairs, after opening the door to the roof garden so that Rasputin could escape if necessary. Down on the street chaos reigned as the designated 'Fire Officer' of each tenant tried to account for the employees before reporting to the 'Chief Fire Officer'. He was himself the 'Fire Officer' for the largest tenant and was too busy counting his own sheep to listen to the reports offered to him. Gillian was the 'Fire Officer' for The Rain Consultancy – a conscientious one who regularly filled buckets of sand and tested fire extinguishers. She shouted to the 'Chief Fire Officer'. 'We are all here! All three of us!' Optimistically she asked 'Can we go back now?' She received a stern refusal.

When they finally returned to their top-floor eyrie, Nshila took Peter into her flat, gave him a beer and encouraged him to go on with his story.

'When I heard the Prince give that address it really shook me. He had lied to his friend about going back to the embassy and was off to some suspicious encounter. Naturally, I thought I might have misheard, and naturally part of me said that it was none of my business anyway. But I was worried enough to grab the next cab and follow. I felt I had to know more. I didn't ask my driver to follow the Prince's cab, but I asked him to drive me to The Goat and Ghost as quickly as he could, and to approach from the Central Street end. That way there was no chance of my cab drawing up directly behind the other.

'My driver was good, and we came down Pear Street in time to see the Prince's cab arriving. A man got out, paid the driver, and entered The Goat and Ghost. He wasn't dressed like the Prince had been, but the build and shape and bearing were right. He had switched his appearance. I was confident about it because I remembered the number of the cab the Prince had taken. Just to be sure, I asked my driver to find out where the other man had picked up the fare. "Outside Broadwick Street Squash Club."'

'I have seen something very suspicious and worrying. I don't know how to handle it. Worse, I saw two men watching the club who were obviously police or security service. There's an outside chance I might have been recognised and connected with the place.'

Nshila thought that some of this was indeed worrying, but she did not want him getting upset over something he could never influence. She made light of it.

'How can a bright character like you miss something so obvious? When a young man from a foreign country visits a murky part of London in disguise, he's after one thing only.'

'You mean prostitutes and sex?'

'Of course. Your Prince Whoever has done nothing worse than satisfy his sexual appetite and spend a small bundle of cash. He is probably doing his job better than ever because of the relief he feels.'

'I'd love to think you were right, Nshila, but it won't stand up. For one thing, that place has no connection with the sex trade at all. You don't find many women using it, and pimps are actively discouraged. If the Prince wanted down-market sex he would have gone north into the Kings Cross area.'

'Maybe he didn't know. Maybe some poorly informed person had just given him a name.'

'Not likely, is it? A man like that must have good sources of information. He's not going to choose a poor adviser. And, anyway, a person of his quality would never go slumming. He would use some high quality escort agency, meeting up for dinner at the Dorchester and moving on to a luxury flat in, say, the Barbican.'

'How do you know he wasn't excited by the other end of the market? Perhaps he wanted some rough trade, found it novel and exciting?'

'It still doesn't stand up. I saw him enter The Goat and Ghost, and it's far more likely that he did so for a heavy criminal reason than for sex. I know the place and the area. I saw an "above-suspicion" foreign diplomat getting involved with some very nasty people.'

So Nshila's efforts to kill his worries failed. The most she could do was kill the idea that he was in danger himself or that he had any obligation. She used his belief that there had been police or security people on the scene.

'Peter, there's no chance at all that people like that are going to be interested in a minor thief like you who has been straight for two years. Those men would never have heard your name. If they were real – and not just ordinary people transformed by your imagination – then they were keeping observation on The Goat and Ghost. And that means that third-party intervention is the last thing they want. There's nothing you can do. Just keep your mouth shut and forget it.'

'OK. But look, I might easily meet the Prince again at the squash club – Fred might do, too – if I see anything else suspicious, will you listen to me?'

'I will, but it won't happen. And I don't want you saying anything about this to Fred. In his country, plots and counter-plots are happening all the time. He'll get excited about it and give me more grief than you will.' But she resolved that she herself would ask Fred what he had thought of Prince Thaqib.

Chapter Sixteen

The Client And The Target

Jessop made contact a few days later asking if Nshila would offer a meeting with an 'intimate colleague' and negotiate a place and time that would give adequate security for both parties. It was unlike Jessop to take that sort of initiative. She wondered again whether he might not have been influenced by the size of his likely commission and that dream home in Provence. In the end she agreed, and Jessop fixed the meeting for a place known to him but not to her or to the client.

It was a decrepit corrugated iron hut, one wall open to the wind and the rain. It stood beside a rifle range. Jessop had explained it.

'Rifle shooting is a weekend sport. But it needs a huge area of open land, and in the middle of the week a rifle range is totally deserted. Nobody goes there, nobody overlooks it, nobody takes the slightest interest in it. The biggest range in the country is only fifteen miles out from London and few people outside the sport even know it exists.'

So Nshila found herself approaching this hut across flat boggy ground that was interrupted at intervals by long, raised sections studded with little wooden markers that carried numbers. She learnt later that these ridges were firing points on which competitors stood or knelt or lay down to shoot off their bullets. The numbers indicated the target each firer was supposed to aim at – but she saw no targets and wondered which way the bullets were supposed to go.

Some distance across the bog, she saw two men who seemed also to be aiming for the hut. She knew there would be two of them because the negotiations had specified that the client would be accompanied by his security man, or minder. There are a number of organizations in which senior figures are never allowed out without such an escort and escaping from the minder is frowned on The best strategy when the VIP wants a meeting to be private is to post the minder some distance away, but in a place where he can see his charge, and anybody who approaches. In this case the minder had been told that the VIP was going to meet an old and eccentric family friend to whom he felt an obligation and whom he had neglected for too long. This friend was an extremely keen bird-watcher, and the birds to be observed were frequent visitors to this deserted (on weekdays) stretch of boggy land.

The minder might have doubted that story, but he would have been reassured by the woman he saw walking towards the hut. Nshila was near-perfect as the late middle-aged spinster stomping through the mud in her Wellington boots, made fat by several woolly cardigans and made conspicuous by a bright yellow plastic mackintosh. Binoculars were slung around her neck and she carried a shooting stick. As she approached the hut she waved the stick and shouted 'Yoo Hoo, Bernard!' in a loud, aunt-like voice. The minder stopped at one of the ridges, and she discovered from 'Bernard' that this meant he was at least one hundred yards away.

The hut was awful: a dirt floor; empty coca-cola cans; discarded cardboard boxes that had once held ammunition; tree branches that scraped against the corrugated iron roof; wooden slats for seats, precariously balanced on concrete supports. But she did feel that anybody positioned to overhear the talk must have been extremely persevering.

The man she met denied that he was himself the client, speaking as if he were telling a story that happened to somebody else. But this was a thin pretence, since the presence of the minder accorded with the status of the person he described as 'my friend'. The story he told had, he claimed, already been written down and lodged with a solicitor. It was that of a rising politician who held a minor ministerial post and had overheard by accident the fabrication of a terrorist plot. The plot was being master-minded by a foreign diplomat of high status who was trusted and liked by the British establishment. The name? He had already given it to her messenger: Prince Thaqib.

Having already called out to him as 'Bernard', Nshila stuck with the name.

'Bernard, my principal won't like the sketchy evidence about his evil intentions. I don't either. Theoretically, I can believe any degree of evil in people who hold power – we all know that it corrupts. But that's not enough to prove a specific case. Are there any supporting facts you can provide?' She did not reveal that the name of Prince Thaqib had come to her notice already through his visit to The Goat and Ghost as told by Peter Grace. That knowledge, however, biased her towards belief in the client's story.

The answer was negative. The client had no absolute proof. What Nshila then said was that the actions of the client – the risks he had taken so far – were enough to make her principal take an interest, but that commitment would depend on investigations he would make himself.

Suddenly the external environment intruded. There was a gust of wind, the rubbish swirled around inside the hut, and a pennant-shaped flag flashed out to its full extent. Looking around, Nshila saw several other flags streaming from poles she had barely noticed. Had it any significance? Was it a signal that enemies had arrived – a visual equivalent of the music heralding the entry of the arch evil-doer in a film? No. The client knew enough about shooting to explain that the flags existed to show shooters the strength of the wind. The shooters could then allow for it.

Nshila turned to another issue.

'Bernard, through the earlier contact I learnt that you had other things you could offer as a fee besides cash. Things like position or appointments or a whole new identity. Is that true? I doubt if my principal would be interested, because such things would make it hard to conceal his identity. But my job is to report back with full details, leaving nothing out.'

'Certainly. Opportunities for patronage abound in politics and government. The real reasons why X gets preferment and Y is ignored have little relationship to what is given out publicly. And my position is a unique one in that respect. I could get more or less whatever your principal wanted. I mean, short of something ridiculous like marrying into the Royal family.'

Back in Eastcheap, she called Snakesmith and Co, private

enquiry agents. She commissioned a watch on The Goat and Ghost, and on two of the people who had been arrested there by the anti-terrorist squad. She got these names with some difficulty by asking Peter to tap into the old-lags network. If Prince Thaqib was seen, the watchers were to switch their focus and take him as their first concern.

Could she do anything else? Yes, she could redeem her promise to give the apprentice some practical experience and perhaps get useful data at the same time. If this contract really came to life, any limited skill she could impart to him might be useful. She told him to come to the flat late one evening and explained that he was due for some training in mental concentration. She put him through some basic exercises and then said:

'You have played squash against Prince Thaqib, and had a few drinks with him afterwards. Can you call up a clear mental image of what he was like?'

'That's easy. He has a distinctive appearance, and one or two peculiar mannerisms. And remember, you had set me that exercise about observing the staff in my own embassy. I can close my eyes and call up a very good picture.'

'Good. We are now going to burn a little of my powder, and you are going to watch in the smoke to see if there is any clue as to what he is doing now. The time of day is good: conspiring is mainly an after-dark activity. Statistically, of course, the odds are against us, but it's worth trying. From your point of view, if you can observe anything at all it will be a big skill gain.

Nshila put out all the lights except a small spotlight that would illumine the cloud of smoke above the small metal pan that held the powder. She lit the Bunsen burner underneath. Rasputin assumed his preferred position on the edge of the kitchen table. At the last minute, Fred had a question.

'Will you be watching, too?'

'No. I don't know the man and am less qualified here than you are. I will be mentally supporting you and forcing you to concentrate harder than you have ever done before.'

There was dead silence for three minutes. The powder smoked, there was a grey cloud above the pan, Fred was utterly still, Rasputin began to purr. Then Nshila sensed Fred's concentration beginning to slip. She put her hand on his neck. 'Focus. Concentrate. You can do it. You must. That's an order.'

Fifty seconds later he sprang to his feet with a yell. The powder and the pan and the burner were swept to the floor as he waved his arms. Rasputin howled and shot away into the bedroom.

'I saw him! I saw him! I saw him!'

'Calm down, Fred. You did well to see him at all, but it will be more use if you can provide some indication of what he was doing.'

'I don't know. Except that he was sitting at a table, reading. Getting through was just so great that everything else went out of my head.'

'Well, now it is going to come back. You'll sit here on your own with this mild hallucinatory drink that I'm going to give you. You'll re-live the experience mentally and write down whatever comes to you. I'm going to have a bath, and when I come back I expect a few positive results.'

One of Nshila's greatest pleasures was that she could open the skylights in the bathroom of her rooftop flat. The high-rise offices on each side blocked out much of the urban glow and on clear nights the stars were visible. This was such a night. She lay there with the glorious soapy, scented bubbles floating up to the rim of the bath and traced the constellations – Orion was just visible at one corner of the skylight. She thought of the brighter stars of the southern hemisphere. She thought of the Southern Cross. She thought of Kwaname. She thought of her brother in the school at Margate. She thought of Waylands Smithy and the mysterious discs.

She fell asleep.

The water was still warm when she woke up, but her watch said she had lost three quarters of the hour specified to Fred. Where was he? Had he gone home? What mischief had he got up to? She dried herself quickly, put on a heavy black dressing gown and went to look.

'Stop it! Stop! Crazy fool!'

Had she ever been as meddlesome and inquisitive when she was pupil to old Kwaname in the hut under the baobab tree? She didn't think so. But, of course, she had been a girl of nine years old and accustomed to obeying the authorities. Fred was a young man of twenty-two, with a university degree and relatively wide experience. But what he had done was still dangerous to any but the most advanced practitioner. There were several sheets of paper on the table, so he must have made a serious attempt at his 'homework', but then he had pulled back the carpet and drawn a pentagram on the floor. He had got a book in his hand and was trying out the pronunciation of various obscure spells.

Nshila snatched the book out of his hand, slapped him across the face, and rubbed out the most critical lines of the pentagram with her slippers. She shook the book at him, 'Where did you get this garbage?'

'From the public library. They did not have very much about witchcraft. This looked the most interesting one. I love these weird signs and symbols in Chapter Five.'

It took her a moment to control her anger. Finally she managed to achieve a manner that was tough and authoritative without displaying irrational rage.

'Fred. You wanted to be my apprentice. I didn't ask you. If you want to learn from me you have to accept my schedule for the learning process and do exactly what I tell you all the time. You do not – repeat not – take initiatives of your own. If you mess me around you may still get turned into a Zombie.'

'I'm sorry. I finished what you asked me to do, and I didn't want to disturb you in the bathroom, and I had this book in my briefcase. This thing on the floor was going to be the Pentagram of Solomon and the book says that it is a way to access wisdom.'

'We're starting from African witchcraft, and pentagrams have no part in that. I don't have extensive knowledge of them myself, but I know enough to realise that high levels of power are attached to them and the procedures are very precise. If you tangle with them from a position of ignorance there is a risk of unleashing quite devastating forces. What you did was extremely stupid and dangerous.'

'Yes, Nshila.'

She told him to get on the internet and identify the four most readable texts about Quantum Physics. She wanted these because the latest thinking – so her brother informed her – had similarities to basic witchcraft concepts. But the immediate reason for her choice was that the work would take him some time as he struggled with obscure scientific terminology. And while he was doing it he would not be conducting illegal experiments.

While he researched, she read his notes about the Thaqib observation and was pleased with them. He had recalled the appearance of the paper that Thaqib had been studying and described it as 'more like a letter than a copy from some text book'. There were diagrams on it, he had recorded, and a name – perhaps the name of the provider of the paper, or of the person whose knowledge it contained. She recognised it as one of the names Peter Grace had been given by his underworld contacts. Fred had also remembered seeing several books on the table, one of them having a bright yellow cover. Part of the title had been obscured by the book on top, but Fred had written down the words 'fragmentation' and 'sources'. That was enough to identify it as a text found in an IRA safe house when it was raided by police and publicised on television. Evidence against Thaqib was building up.

Nshila needed time to think about the project, and felt she had done enough to educate the apprentice. She didn't want him to monopolise her attention. It was the right moment to send him off on an educational attachment.

'You have had your first personal experience as an operator. You have done well, but I won't allow you to forget that it is all based on knowledge. That knowledge can be found in all sorts of places, because it derives from the human need to understand the world around us. People have constantly asked: "What's it all about?" They have tried to identify and influence the forces that control us. Their attempts often go under the name of religion. People postulate an external power, and give it a name, and seek for ways to make it do what they want. If they think they have had any success, they record what they have done and pass it on as some sort of spell.'

'I understand that. What knowledge do you want me to acquire now, and will it be impossibly boring? It's action I want.'

'Are you going to obey me, or not?'

'Yes, I will. But I can't take too much boredom.'

'This assignment may not be all boring. I will arrange an attachment that allows you to make a serious study of one religion – Christianity. It will be a good start. They make a big thing about influencing God through prayer. Come back and tell me whether it works and why.'

Nshila fixed it up through Mike Fanshawe. He had old school friends in all sorts of obscure posts and he came up with Squiggers Bromley who was the principal of a 'progressive' theological college preparing men and women for the ministry of the Church of England. Part of the 'progressiveness' was offering temporary attachments to people of other faiths and beliefs and disciplines. 'Squiggers will take him if I ask it,' said Mike. 'Fred might even find out where the name 'Squiggers' came from. I have never known'.

Chapter Seventeen

The Ordinand

Alice Abigail Fordcombe was a student – one of the brightest – at Hedgewood Theological College. It was situated in Bradford, West Yorkshire and it was there that she met Fred Mbwele.

Abigail was a woman keen to storm male bastions, and her chosen target was The Church of England. She had found the selection board an aggravating experience. On her board there had been three members.

One of them was known to have opposed the idea of women priests. Another was neutral. The third – a sort of twenty-first century John Donne – had repented of a rakish past but never escaped from the attitudes that lay behind it. He failed to conceal his attraction to Abigail – it was in his eyes all the time. There were many probing questions as to whether she had truly been 'called by God to the ministry', and whether her dedication would last, and whether she would not be better suited to one of the caring professions. Yet she was the daughter of a missionary, had a good educational record, and splendid character references. In the end she was accepted. Abigail privately thought that her intelligence had been the deciding factor. The Church of England was recruiting too many people of average ability and when they found an obvious high-flyer they were not going to miss out.

As a human being, she sympathised with the John Donne fellow. He had probably thought, 'This is a lively, attractive woman. Here's trouble in the making'. If so, he was right. She aimed to end up as Bishop Abigail Fordcombe and intended to use whatever skills were needed to get there.

Hedgewood Theological College had been exclusively male, but numbers were falling, and when women priests became a reality the principal had decided to open its doors. The reason was 100% financial, and it worked brilliantly. By another standard it was poorly conceived and worked badly. Many of the staff were opposed to it. At least half the students felt the same way: facilities for women were non-existent and the course of study included no references to female contributions. Abigail once asked a professor for his views on Dame Julian of Norwich. He had never heard of her. Amongst the students there were frequent battles conducted along gender lines.

The architecture was schizophrenic. When the college was started, the founders had bought land on the outskirts of a town and built what looked very much like a village church. In fact they must have used one as a model. It was light and airy and beautifully proportioned. Most of the windows were clear glass, but the limited number of stained glass ones had clear bright colours depicting simple biblical scenes. Abigail's favourite was the story of Balaam's ass from the Book of Judges. Balaam is going on a journey that God disapproves of, and God sends an angel with a flaming sword to stand in the way. Balaam can't see the angel, but the ass he is riding on can see it very clearly and gets the message. He refuses to move, Balaam gets angry. The window perfectly illustrated Balaam's frustration and the determined obstinacy of the ass. The church also had a small gallery at the west end that was actually an extension of the ringing chamber for the bells. They were well known locally and a bell-ringing society had an arrangement with the principal allowing them to practise there, and to ring peals for special events. Abigail loved sitting in the gallery when the fellow who pulled the tenor bell was bending and stretching his well-muscled body a few feet behind her. He always gave a tiny, gruff grunt as he started the downward pull. She found it sexy.

The other buildings, teaching blocks and residential blocks and so on, were built at different periods and not matched up at all. The worst one was the dining hall. The site was on a hillside, and part of the hall was built on stilts, where the ground fell away sharply. The position invited a newcomer to expect the vista from Keats' poem:

'*Magic casements opening on the foam*
Of perilous seas in faery lands forlorn'

Not so. The casements open on a disused factory site frequented by vandals and vagrants and drug-dealers. At remote intervals the scene was enlivened by a police raid, but mostly the view was static, boring and revolting.

The college estate – as opposed to the buildings – was pleasing. It straggled down the hill in a glorious muddle. There were numerous paths, joining each other and separating again for no logical reason. At each level there were small lawns of neatly tended grass, and flower beds re-planted each season. There were handrails at the steeper parts, mostly done in attractive wrought iron patterns – and very useful in wintry conditions. There were several large, old trees, and students spent summer afternoons relaxing below them. There were two gardeners, who pushed wheelbarrows before them like figures in old-fashioned children's books – reminiscent of Mr McGregor in Peter Rabbit. At noon every day, they disappeared into the 'Potting Shed' – a glory hole where they kept all sorts of serviceable and unserviceable garden tools and spread out their lunch packs on a prehistoric boiler that had once heated greenhouses.

That was the environment in which Fred Mbwele and Alice Abigail Forcombe began their friendship. The principal of the college believed strongly that religions should be 'inter-conscious'. By that he meant that each should have a sympathetic understanding of the others' theology. The course the students followed was restricted by the requirements of the final exam, but the principal fought his corner by introducing 'guest students' from diverse faiths and backgrounds. They stayed for as little as two weeks or as long as three months. Buddhists arrived, and Muslims and Animists and Sun Worshippers. With all of these the students were expected to discuss 'the God concept'. They had a Zoroastrian visitor and, once, a self-proclaimed fakir. He did not actually sleep on a bed of nails, but it was at least hard and rough – rather like a gravel path. Abigail turned it over once when he was away in the bathroom and found that it had been made by Mubunda Religious Supplies of Calcutta.

Abigail soon learnt that Fred Mbwele had been sent to Hedgewood by his boss to find out for himself 'whether religion actually worked'. He was black and good-looking and great fun to talk with, but his ideas were extremely confused and it took Abigail ages to understand what he meant by 'working'. Was he asking 'Can you alter physical things by prayer?' Or was he asking 'Does religion help you to live a better life?' He was interested in miracles and spiritual manifestations and dreams and portents. He wanted to know about the bells and smells aspects of Christianity. He wanted to know the significance of the bell. Why was it rung, and when? What was supposed to happen or not happen when it was rung? When incense was burned (only when the bishop came), what powder was used, what did it smell of, and where did it come from? Did it have any hallucinatory effect? He asked Abigail whether she had ever had a vision. What happened when she was really concentrating on God in the chapel services? Did she have out-of-the-body experiences? She said that if the bell-ringer was there, then it was very much an in-body experience.

It seemed to Abigail that Fred was unconcerned about the moral content of religion. For him it was the presence or absence of a causative chain that mattered – or perhaps that was what his boss had sent him to study.

'What is the 'how' of it, Abby? What mechanism is involved? Is it physical or psychological in some way, or is there a supernatural being? If the latter, is it your Christian God or the spirit of the trees to whom my witchdoctor appeals? Which is stronger? How does one access him?'

He was extremely persistent. Abigail often broke off the argument because it seemed unrelated to her own needs. She was going to succeed by intelligence and application and exploiting powerful men. She was never going to experiment with burning incense to Ashtaroth. But she got the feeling that Fred would try anything and everything to see if it worked and whether it might be useful to him. He was interested in means, not objectives.

She once accused him of being amoral and cynical. That was a mistake. He fastened on her unscrupulous ambition and said she should concentrate on serving her God. Preferment would then take care of itself. She lost her cool, and revealed things that would have been better kept under wraps.

'Look, Fred. God has nothing to do with preferment. The Church is an organisation like any other one. It has a hierarchy, and a language, and customs and procedures. Above all, it has human, fallible, men and women. Learn the jargon, pay homage to the received wisdom, cuddle up to the right people, and you'll get promoted. What you need is intelligence, sensitivity, guile and manipulative skill. I've got all those, and I'm a sexually attractive woman. I'll be a bishop, and I'll have a seat in The House of Lords.'

'What's that?'

'The House of Lords, you ignorant foreigner, is the upper chamber of our parliament.'

'Oh! Yes! I've heard of it. But surely that is the place full of hereditary incompetents that is going to be abolished? Anyway, I didn't know that bishops were part of it.'

'They were, and at the moment they still are, because The Church once had a great deal of power and influence. Bishops were important people. The reforms, when they come, will cause a different set of people to be appointed to the Lords, but it will be done in a very British way. The major powers and interests will all have representation. Candidates nominated by them will be elected or appointed. There will be bishops in there, you mark my words. I'll be one.'

'Good luck to you then. Remember me when it happens. I suppose your first step will be when you become The Reverend Alice Abigail Fordham next month.'

'It will, and my first job is already in place. I have got myself fixed up as curate in a fashionable London parish. I'm going to meet some highly influential men and women.'

Both of them enjoyed their arguments and became good friends. Three times they hired bicycles and rode out into the dales. Once they came upon the Meet of a small local hunt, and Abigail insisted on following it, to the extent that the bicycles and their knowledge of the terrain allowed. When Fred asked why she was so keen, he learnt to his surprise that Abigail was a competent horsewoman and hunted when the opportunity offered.

'Are you hoping, then, to get hunting invitations from some of those rich aristocrats you will meet in your parish?'

'I hope so. I don't see why not. And you can make all sorts of new contacts through the hunting fraternity.'

Fred's attachment came to an end. They didn't want to lose touch. Abigail said 'Let's arrange to meet some time in London. And I'd like to meet your boss. She sounds interesting.'

Chapter Eighteen
Dithering

Contracts like the elimination of a high-profile foreign national are not arranged and executed overnight. A typical time scale is several months, and there are times when the participants can do no more than think and plan and wait on events. At other times, there can be rapid and unexpected developments.

Nshila saw Fred off to his Hedgewood attachment with relief. She felt he could do little harm up in the north, and she would gain three weeks of peace. It worried her that she had not been a very good master. There were excuses, of course, because she had never planned on an apprentice and was unprepared. Another excuse was that she, in her time, had been a very young, docile and impressionable pupil. Fred was a lively and enthusiastic adult. She was not finding it easy to maintain the authority of the master. She had power to make Fred properly scared of her, but it never seemed to last long. She did something nasty to him and thought, 'That'll keep you in line for a while', but in a few days he had forgotten all about it and was demanding that she unfold more mysteries – or experimenting dangerously to see what he could find out for himself. She liked his spirit and resilience. He must have realised this, because he was obviously confident that she would never seriously harm him. It reduced the element of respect that a pupil should feel. Nshila was annoyed that, though she was qualified to be an excellent tutor, she was not doing as well as she would like. She sat down to prepare a credible summary of her craft so that she could put some order into his learning process. So far it seemed to have been driven by accident and Fred's impatience. Her text rambled erratically and often read as if she was talking to herself.

She gave up. She decided that the idea of a text book was impossible when the subject was so full of uncertainty. It was possible to describe methods and spells and procedures, but so often there had to be a caveat: if you do such-and-such then the following might – just might – happen. She asked herself whether there was ever any certainty at all. Is there anything I do which infallibly works reliably and in the expected manner every time? The answer was negative. The emotional intensifier with which she had terrified Fred worked almost every time, but there had been exceptions. Jeremy Judd had only seen images of himself in exciting sexual encounters. Martin Clarke had seen nothing at all. Yet the point of a text book was supposed to be that a reader could follow the instructions exactly and get exactly the result predicted. Perhaps the whole idea was stupid. After all, a person apprenticed to a mediaeval stonemason was never given a book, was he? He just worked alongside the master and learnt, for example, by handing him the tools that he asked for and by watching what the master did with them. He would have tried to do the same, and got imperfect results. Then the master would have shown him what he had done wrong. There would have been words like, 'You hold the chisel this way, and use short, sharp blows with the hammer'. And he must also have watched the master mason experiencing failure – like the stone splitting the wrong way. He would have learnt whether the stone was poor or whether the master had made a mistake – and, if the latter, what sort of mistake it was, and how it could be avoided next time. Her feelings of inadequacy might not be justified.

Suddenly it struck her that she was personally involved in the relationship. What she was doing to Fred was the flip side of what Fred was doing to her. Was she changing because she was now a tutor and teacher and in some sense responsible for the well-being of another? Had she changed because of the responsibility? Had she become more cautious and careful in order to counter-balance Fred's impatience? Without Fred, would she already have accepted the Thaqib contract and been half-way to a solution? Was it because of Fred that she was still ambivalent about it?

Worse still, was she being distracted by the issue of 'prestige rewards' and how these might be handled? If nothing except cash was involved, would she have accepted or rejected the contract long ago? These were disturbing thoughts.

She was in a confused mental state when she received the report that she had commissioned from Snakesmith and Co. Good! This would turn her mind in another direction.

They had carried out the surveillance thoroughly, and quite early on Prince Thaqib had appeared on the scene. As ordered, they had taken him as their main target. However, they had been hindered by the fact that some other organisation was also at work. Snakesmith's people had encountered other watchers who might, they thought, be employed by a government department. They reasoned in that way because competitors often shared information in order to reduce costs, and none had admitted an interest. They also knew that the security services commonly operate low level, intermittent surveillance on high-profile foreigners.

Snakesmith and Co were scathing about the competence of these observers, suggesting that some were too young to have the necessary experience and others were so old and decrepit that they must have been brought out of retirement. One of them seemed to be in need of an artificial hip: as soon as somebody he was watching moved at more than a slow walk, he lost contact. That also pointed towards a government department – too many demands made upon them and too few resources provided.

'The surveillance carried out by "the opposition" was less effective than ours.' Thus boasted Snakesmith & Co in their report. They justified the comment, too, because they had been close to the Prince many different times and in many different places. They had travelled with him, and a visit that he had paid to Leeds had proved highly informative. He had been met at the station by two young men who looked like university students from overseas. One of them was far too keen and eager to make a good plotter; while the three were waiting for a taxi the Snakesmith man overheard the words, 'It works, Prince – really effective – everything within fifty yards. We have got a projector set up to show you the sequence.' The Snakesmith man was able to follow them to a disused warehouse in which they remained for half an hour before returning to the station. When the Prince had left, the two boys turned into the nearest pub. It took the watcher some time to get a seat close by, but when he managed it they were obviously talking about the Prince.

'Not somebody you want to cross, is he?'

'Far from it. OK if he's on your side, but a cruel, ruthless enemy. He's a man of great power in his country and renowned for enforcing extreme punishments when people break the law.'

'In his country, extreme punishment means physical mutilation, doesn't it? An eye for an eye and all that stuff?'

'It certainly does. A fair number of people in his country are physically incomplete because the Prince was involved.'

Snakesmith had also investigated the Prince's personal life, and discovered that he lived in an expensive block of service apartments. The rental included use of a cleaning service that was under contract to the owners of the building. Tenants were not obliged to use this service, but since it had a good reputation and the rent reduction for not using them was small, most tenants did so. The Prince used them. Snakesmith and Company were able to get an operative taken on as cover for a sick employee and this woman struck lucky with the contents of the Prince's waste-paper basket. She found hard copy of some e-mails. These suggested contact with criminal elements, both in the Prince's home country and in England. They also found materials that could be used to make explosives and poisons. None of these were themselves illegal and all could easily be bought. Yet their normal purposes were far removed from the Prince's known interests, and what were these individually harmless items doing in a collection?

Did she have enough evidence? Nshila was still doubtful, and annoyed with herself for being so.

Chapter Nineteen

A Big Shake-Up

'Have you seen today's *Daily Topic* or any other broadsheet? No? Then go out and buy one and ring me back later.'

It was odd for Jessop to phone her in an excited manner and with that sort of message – not directly required by the needs of a project. But she did as he suggested.

ARAB PRINCE ESCAPES DEATH AT SOCIETY WEDDING. The story related how a friend of Prince Thaqib, attending a society wedding in his company, had noticed an object hanging loose from the back crease of his sponge-bag trousers. It had proved to be a feathered dart of the sort that can be fired from a powerful air gun or air pistol. Security staff attached to the Prince's embassy had insisted on forensic examination and the point of the dart had been found to carry a lethal poison. This had been an attempt at assassination – foiled by the poor aim of the would-be assassin or the thickness of this old-fashioned clothing. The point of the dart had not pierced the skin. The Prince was said to be relaxed about the event and contemptuous about further danger. He had said:

'Public figures from the Middle East are always in some degree of danger. One can't allow it to constrain one's activity. And I feel I have a mission in life that won't be allowed to fail. I judge that I shall be safeguarded until my mission is accomplished.' He didn't say what this mission was.

An hour after reading the paper, Nshila phoned Jessop. What was his angle on the story?

'It's obvious that somebody else is after Prince Thaqib, and I have picked up hints on the grapevine that the operative who has been hired is Jilly Jordan. What do you make of that?'

'I thought he was dead – or nearly so. The word was that he had retired through ill-health and returned to his village on the upper Amazon. Apparently he gave all his money to a fund dedicated to preserving the rainforest.'

'All that was true, but his death has never been reported and you do hear of remarkable successes achieved in remote areas by herbal medicine. Anyway, this attempt has his fingerprints all over it. How much do you know about him?'

'I have quite a lot on my database. I will study it and get back to you.'

It took a while for Nshila to get into the right section of her database, for there was a password (forgotten) into the 'Competitors' section and another one (also forgotten) into the file labelled G.Z.Jordan. She tried to recall the words she might have used, and where she might have written them down – if she had written them down at all. Rasputin walked past, and she remembered using the underside of his bowl as a secret place. Were they still there? Yes – but faded and hard to read. She finally got into the data.

NAME	Gilbert Zebedee Jordan. Known professionally as Jilly.
BORN	Un-named village on upper Amazon.
DESCENT	Son of a lapsed Christian missionary (Welsh) and a native girl.
EDUCATED	Local primary school. Then self-educated through evening classes and correspondence schools.
APPEARANCE	Slight, almost girlish build. Coffee coloured skin. Very regular features that allow him to escape notice. Subservient manner that allows him to masquerade as a harmless lower class employee, e.g. doorman, waiter, cleaner, cloakroom attendant, street-sweeper refuse-collector, etc. Has been known to dress as a woman. It is known that he once disguised himself as an air hostess. Of seventy passengers on a flight, sixty-eight walked off. Two - identical twins - were dead in their seats.

HEALTH	*Jilly suffers from an inherited disease that is likely to restrict his life expectancy. This has made him less concerned about the dangers of his profession and sometimes careless.*
RECORD	*Started with minor killings in Buenos Aires that were poorly rewarded. He might have progressed no further if Alfonso Grule had not fallen sick in the later stages of a contract. He sub-contracted to Jilly. The affair was a success and it enabled Jilly to win bigger contracts at a better price. Much of his recent work has been done for governments in the Middle East. His low profile and lack of charisma are an advantage when seeking to avoid the appearance of complicity.*
MOTIVE	*Jilly is thought to have no political or moral or religious motivation. But he is paranoid about the threat to his home environment and spends most of his money protecting it from exploitation. He is credited with killing the leaders of two ground clearance teams. This obsession means that Jilly is financially motivated and will accept new contracts readily. He spend less time 'resting' than other assassins and has been known to complete assignments on different sides of the Atlantic in the same week. He is a volatile character, quick to change his mind.*
METHOD	*In terms of method, there is none. While other operators acquire great skill with a particular weapon (bomb, knife, gun, poison, etc,), Jilly uses them all. He has no 'signature' by which his work can be recognised. His equipment is*

whatever comes to hand. Often he carries out only the slightest investigation or research or planning, but places himself close to the target and takes advantage of any circumstance that offers. This means that failure is quite common, but since there was no preparation, there are few clues to follow. Jilly disappears and has another try later. It bothers him very little, because he is persistent, and success is achieved sooner or later. Clients have become aware of this, and he is trusted to deliver, provided death is not considered urgent.

As Nshila read her notes, the moment of writing came back to her. She remembered the disgust she had felt about the double killing on the aircraft. Obviously Jilly had not known of the identical twins and faced a real dilemma. 'One of the two who are sitting there, but which of the two it's not quite clear'. Where did that jingle come from? She could not remember. What would she have done in such a case? Certainly she would have aborted the hit.

What she did in the present time was to phone Jessop, thank him for the 'Heads up' and tell him to take no action for the present.

Chapter Twenty
Revisions

Fred returned from his trip to the north and had to be debriefed.

'What did you learn, Fred?'

'You gave me very vague instructions, didn't you? But what I thought you wanted was for me to assess some religions, especially Christianity, in terms of their practical usefulness to people like us. Crudely, was there anything there that would help us to manipulate the world around us.'

'Not bad, Fred. Was there?'

'Not directly. Christians believe that prayer can influence their God to act in the desired way, but so do the adherents of many other religions. There is never any proof. People point to the dedicated use of prayer, and sometimes the thing prayed for actually happens. Then they say, "It happened because God heard our prayers". But it might have happened anyway, for quite different reasons.'

'You could say that about my rain-making,' Nshila replied. 'Maybe it was going to rain anyway and I had nothing to do with it.'

'Yes. But your rain-making activities are constant and consistent. You are always asking for the same thing and you have built up a track record. It's not a scientific test, but it's more nearly so than the huge variety of things Christians pray for. In your case the observer thinks, "ten times she asked for it, and nine times it happened. There must be something in it."'

'So you think that Christianity has nothing to offer us?'

'Not quite. I think that prayer has an effect on the people praying. It makes the issue seem important to them, and they are therefore more inclined to act in a way that will fulfil the prayer. In that sense you can argue that prayer has an indirect effect.'

'Go on.'

'The response will depend on the individual personality. A rich person might decide to give a million pounds or so to make the prayed-for cause succeed. A writer might feel urged to publicise the cause. An unattached young person might give up employment and work for the cause as a volunteer. All those things would have happened because of the praying.'

'You seem to be talking about concerted prayer offered by a large number or people. That would hardly be our scene. We need secrecy. What do you think about individual efforts?'

'It might be the same thing on a smaller scale. Look, one of the people I met was this marvellous girl called Abigail Fordham. She is highly ambitious and will soon be ordained into The Church of England. She makes it quite obvious that she intends to become a bishop or archbishop. She prays for it. I know she does because she told me. Well, perhaps her prayers and her actions reinforce each other. It's the actions – what she says and how she behaves – that make people see her as bishop material. But her praying makes her remember what to say and how to behave.'

'That makes sense, Fred. Your ideas are worth thinking about. You have done well. Right now I want to put the subject on the back burner because there have been some dramatic developments while you were away and I need to bring you into the picture.'

She told him everything that had happened recently. Some of it Fred took very much in his stride because it agreed with what he already suspected. He was fully aware of the Thaqib project, and he picked up the fact that Nshila was doubtful about his status as an evil-doer, and confused about her own attitude towards the reward. There was credible evidence that the Prince was a danger to the country and ought to be eliminated. But it was not conclusive, some of it being a conversation overheard, and interpreted, by just one man.

And then Nshila told him the latest development, the intervention of Jilly Jordan. Fred got very excited.

'That solves all your problems. If the Prince is going to die anyway, then you don't have to feel guilty about removing him yourself. You don't need to assess his level of evil-doing. In fact, if Jilly gets to him first – and is never discovered – then you can claim the hit as your doing and pick up the reward.'

'That's unworthy, Fred. Getting paid for a service you have never provided! And it would make Jilly bitter. We don't want vendettas inside the profession.'

'Sorry. But suppose he did get there first. What would you really do?'

'Abort the project.'

'And lose the reward?'

'Yes.'

Fred asked for a coffee break and time-out for reflection. During it, he marshalled his arguments.

'Let's look at the reward. You have hardly mentioned a cash fee, and I have wondered why. Maybe you don't really need any more money or maybe you foresee dangers in concealing the transaction. But the client has mentioned non-financial rewards that would give you status and influence. You haven't dismissed them. They might even lift you into the ranks of people who are forever above suspicion. That could be an advantage business-wise.'

'In meteorology you mean?'

'No, of course not: as an assassin.'

'Just possible, Fred, if I continue in that line. But I'm not at all sure I shall do so.'

'Well, status and prestige are enjoyable, surely? You might be offered a whole new range of quite legitimate appointments. And I don't hear you grumbling about that MBE they forced on you. There could be bigger things available.'

'That was an accident. It happened because budget cuts had gone so deep that a government department couldn't pay me. A national honour was the best they could come up with. And it was really hard to get myself nominated without the nature of my service being recognised. We had to do a lot of fudging and manipulating.'

'But in this case, the client claims to have huge influence in such matters. How would you feel about a peerage and a seat in The House of Lords?'

'I don't need stupid jokes.'

'No. No. No. Please. Just give me a chance.'

'Carry on then. I never realised that having an apprentice was meant to be a penance.'

'Look, I've told you about this astonishing girl Abigail Fordham. She's absolute dynamite and she reckons she is going to climb right up the hierarchy of the church, and become a bishop and end up in the House of Lords. I laughed at her, and argued against her, but I also learnt a lot about seats in the Lords and how they are going to be won. She was quite sure about it. Whatever reforms are trumpeted to the public, the same old people are going to have influence and the same old people will be sitting on the benches. The reasons given for their presence will be different, but the people will be largely unchanged. And our would-be client in the Thaqib case did say (I remember you telling me) that he could swing almost anything except marrying into the Royal family. Isn't that true?'

'Yes, but we don't know how serious he was. And even if it was true, there's still the problem of breaking the link between myself as an assassin and myself as the recipient of an honour. It will have to be awarded in my real name, and the client will immediately know who made the hit.'

Fred thought hard about how to answer. And simultaneously part of his mind marvelled at the odd situation. Here was he, the apprentice, seeking to guide the master at a time when she was in doubt. What a responsibility! Out of the air a story line hit him.

'There is one way in which the connection could easily be broken. Just suppose that the reward was money. If the person earning the reward doesn't want to be known, then he or she can request that it be given to a charity. The charity gets an anonymous donation – which is happening all the time. The giver knows that the money is payment for a hit job, but has no idea who made the hit. It's easy.'

'Except, Fred, that the reward here is not money. The nature of the reward is such that it identifies an individual. How does your story cope with that?'

Fred was not to be stopped.

'How does this line grab you? It's off the top of my head and I'm sure we can improve on it. But try it. Our negotiator explains that his principal is descended from a colonial administrator in the old British Empire, who seriously wronged an African chief by deliberately altering a boundary. He did this in order to end a long-running dispute and thereby please the colonial Governor.

'In the culture of those days, playing dirty tricks on ignorant natives was no big deal – they were seen as having no importance. In later years, when attitudes had changed dramatically, he came to feel ashamed and guilty and regretful about what he had done. He realised that he had done serious harm to a whole tribe by denying them grazing land that had been theirs for as long as anybody could remember. There was no way he could put it right. His family had seen the thing affecting his mental health. "My principal" (this is your negotiator speaking) "has become aware that some descendants of the wronged chief are working in this country." Your negotiator explains that his principal would feel his debt to be partly repaid if he could benefit some tribal notable in a dramatic way.'

'You are into fantasy-land, Fred.'

'Are you sure? There are all sorts of long-forgotten issues being dragged up today because powerful nations have developed guilty feelings about their past actions and the victims are able to boost their national egos by demanding an apology. This country recently made a formal apology for the Slave Trade. Americans are feeling bad about what they did to the Indians and Australians about the Aborigines. And what about the Elgin Marbles? I'll bet the British Museum ships them back to Greece eventually. My idea is a bit more extreme, that's all.'

'Ingenious, Fred. We should have to improve the story to make it credible, but the underlying concept is good. Well done! I need time to think about it. Go back to your embassy and make yourself useful. I will send for you in a few days.'

Chapter Twenty-One

Whose Problem?

She was not a heavy drinker. A glass of wine, half-refilled was the norm. The evening after that long talk with Fred the bottle was half-empty before she noticed. I am trying to make the problem go away, she thought: just looking for oblivion so that I don't have to worry any more.

But she stayed awake and the problem stayed too. Her apprentice was dead keen that she should take the contract and carry it out. She, herself, saw too many difficulties and an uncertain reward. Yet what sort of teacher was it who acted chicken in front of her pupil? Her pride was offended.

Then two new visions impacted on her confused mind. One speaking against the project, and one more helpful.

Much of the talk with Fred had been about breaking the link between the doer of the deed and the receiver of the reward. Fred had offered – just – a credible solution. But they had talked little about Jilly Jordan. How did he affect things? Without him, her motives – if she accepted the contract – would be the removal of an evil-doer, the challenge to her skill, and her interest in the reward. Jilly's inclusion added a competitive thrill. Would that change her behaviour? Was she likely to take stupid risks in order to get to the Prince first?

The risk-taker who lived inside her skull – and was continually at war with her more cautious self – had something to say.

'Stop worrying about yourself. Think about others for a change. You are not the only one with a problem? How about the client? He or she, whoever he or she is, seems desperate to place the contract and is risking exposure with every day of delay. If you don't sign up, he (or she) is back to square one. Look, girl, do you remember those lectures about disputes and negotiations that you attended in the Open University course? The big idea at the time was that if each party knew more about what the other really valued, then there might be scope for an agreement that transcended whatever piddling matter had triggered the dispute. You bought into that idea at the time. How about applying it now?'

It took Nshila three days to reach a decision. During that time she annoyed Gillian and Peter by being abstracted and forgetful. Important things went undone – she only fed Rasputin regularly because of his importunity. She was likely to accept a risk to her security that she had never accepted before. But she was attracted by the ingenuity of Fred's proposal, and the skill that it would require. Finally she called Fred in.

'Fred, when I was doing my MBA, and studying industrial relations, we were told that negotiations often ended in failure because each side thought only of its own narrow objectives. It was argued that if the two sides knew more about each other's problems, they might find ways of helping each other that would outweigh their immediate differences. We are going to break with convention. We are going to have a conference with the client and get a wider understanding of his position. It may give us new ideas about how to do the job. And before any meeting, we are going to refine that plan of yours and give it some credibility.'

Chapter Twenty-Two
Strange Meetings

Because secrecy was vital to both sides, the identities were concealed and nobody was quite sure who he or she was meeting. Both assumed that it was not 'the principal' but a close associate, with delegated authority. Both also expected some level of disguise. They didn't expect that they might one day meet their opposite number in another environment and recognise him or her.

Several meeting places were proposed by one side and rejected by the other. Camber Sands, on the Kent coast, offered excellent security but was deemed too uncomfortable for lengthy discussions. It was also very windy and the tide came in fast: running before the sea would be a distraction. A Thames cruise, surrounded by tourists, would offer the participants anonymity, but was rejected because of the 'imprisonment' factor: once on the vessel one could not get off it at will. There was a case for less romantic places, like roadhouse-type restaurants offering 'Three course Sunday lunch for £11.99p' and all used by big families. The noise would make eavesdropping impossible, but might also mean that the parties could barely hear each other. And there was the danger of poorly-supervised children putting jammy fingers on their clothes. The final solution was the show house on a site offering 'Exquisite Executive Residences' at 'negotiable' prices. The show house was warm, comfortably furnished and had a fully-stocked bar.

Fred felt immensely proud of his role as negotiator. Nshila had wanted to do it herself, but had reluctantly given way to logical argument.

'We must look at the objective,' Fred had said. 'We want them to procure a peerage for our nominee, and that nominee will turn out to be female and black. Don't you think it's dangerous if our main negotiator is also female and black? It only needs one person to say 'curious coincidence' and we shall be in trouble.'

'Here's another point. If we succeed, you will be a public figure, making speeches in the House of Lords and appearing on television. However well you disguise yourself now, you can't avoid personal mannerisms and habits of speech. The people who engineer that peerage may well follow your career. They may see behaviour that is suspiciously like the behaviour of our negotiator.'

'Well done, Fred. Good thinking. But will things be that much better if you go instead? I mean, you are known to them from the Virginia Water visit and they surely have photographs of you. And you are black, too.'

'But my skin is not as dark as yours, and I would have to be disguised anyway. Look, I'm not much darker than Gillian's husband. And who else have we got?'

The make-up artist welcomed the challenge. She had made several images for Nshila and Fred offered a different challenge. She asked, 'How about a keen young head teacher? I can make him look about thirty, and he can be the trouble-shooter sent into a failing South London school to sort the place out. He can have some worry-lines, and thicker eyebrows to make him look menacing. I'll give him some pills to make his face look a little jaundiced: they won't cause more than a mild feeling of sickness.'

Fred was unhappy about the drug-induced pallor, but he was the one who had volunteered for the job and it had to be done. Together, the two worked carefully through what should be said at the meeting and what should be concealed. It was all based on Fred's earlier idea of separating the doer of the deed from the recipient of the reward. Nshila spelt out his duties.

'Keep the story general, Fred. We came to this idea because of our shared national background. But remember that other societies have debts of honour and family obligations. They have conflicts of interest that cause one person to do wrong to another, and later regret it. Don't talk Africa to them. Talk Mafia. Talk Russian Revolution. Talk looted art works from World War II. They won't be expecting literal truth from us, so you can be a bit dramatic. Make them see that this is a solution to their problem and then they won't dig too deep. After all, they have handed out peerages to some pretty awful types in the past. You have heard of Lloyd George, have you? No? Undisguised trading of honours for cash? It's true – believe me. When they finally identify me as a candidate they will be relieved at my suitability.'

When the meeting took place, it was the client side that opened the dialogue. 'I hope you accept that we are totally serious in this matter. We have talked it through many, many times and we can see no better solution than eliminating the Prince. Can we take it that, if we agree terms, your principal will do the job?'

'I wouldn't be here,' said Fred, 'if we were totally negative. And there's one thing I can say immediately that may help you. We don't want money. However much you are offering, we don't want it. My principal has heard nasty rumours about new methods of tracing transactions, and off-shore banks giving in under pressure. We are playing safe.'

'Then there must be something else you want. Otherwise, like you just said, you wouldn't be here.'

'Yes. It's a long story, but quite by chance – without knowing it – you have suggested a way in which my principal might be able to right an old wrong and discharge a debt of honour.'

Later that day, Nshila pressed Fred for every detail that he could remember. To her great relief he seemed to have done well. He had painted an exotic but marginally credible world peopled by usurped princes, forged title deeds, men in iron masks, competitors sold into slavery, unacknowledged heirs and looted grave-goods. He remembered the exact words he had finished with.

'My principal feels he will have discharged his obligation if he can bestow honour and power upon some representative of the wronged family. He knows that two members of that family received an expensive education at an international school in Africa, called St Albans. He knows that they now live in this country. But he has been unable to trace them. Can you, with your resources, identify one or both of these people?'

The reply was guarded. 'We can probably manage that, but there may be a difficulty about national recognition. It's not possible to achieve an honour for somebody who has made no major contribution to our society, or who doesn't belong to it. And the more significant the honour, the more notable the person has to be. We can get an OBE for any lollipop lady in the land if she is nominated by enough school-children. If we are talking about a peerage, we need a high-profile contributor. The popular belief is that you just give a huge donation to a political party and then order the ermine robes. That's seldom true. There may be a few cases when the nominee is a personal crony of the Prime Minister, but normally there has to be something else. Yes, we can identify the people you talk about, but if none of them measure up – or can be given the chance to do so – then there's no hope.'

'Explain that a bit more.'

'It's a matter of public reaction. We want ordinary people to say, "Oh! He's the man who did XYZ – that's why he's got a peerage". The XYZ has to be a matter of some substance. Our PR people can build it up considerably, but they can't fabricate it out of thin air. We can find projects that, if successful, would justify the honour, but they naturally demand a high degree of skill and competence. So there has to be a match between the person and the project. If we have a name, we must look for projects that the named person might cope with.'

That was the end of the first meeting. It had been fairly cordial.

The second meeting took place at a hotel on the Thames. The hotel had bought one of the old Oxford barges (originally owned by the colleges and used for watching boat races) as a 'feature' to attract customers. The client's representative was the same person as before, and Fred again stood in for Nshila. Since there was now some familiarity, the conversation moved faster. 'What have you been able to find out?'

'The first bit was easy. We traced the family. Two members of it attended a school called St Albans and now live in this country. One is a teacher at a school in Margate. I have to tell you that he is negative as a candidate for a peerage. He teaches science at a fee-paying school for the sons of rich, over-privileged parents. If he taught counselling-skills at one of the new City academies, we might have a chance. As things are, it is hopeless.'

'Is that the end of the story?'

'No. The other family member is his half-sister, a woman named Nshila Ileloka. She came to England to study at LSE and has done well for herself. She has a First Class degree, and an MBA from the Open University. She owns a consultancy firm that specialises in meteorology and has become a respected expert in her field. She already has an MBE for services to inter-cultural understanding. If she had a higher overall profile, she could be suitable.'

Fred had difficulty restraining his anger at that point. In his view Nshila was way ahead of some recently ennobled characters. But he managed to keep his cool.

'Surely it is possible to fix that? The major PR agencies can create or destroy an image at the drop of a hat.'

'Within limits, that's true. But have you thought of all the steps necessary?'

'Surely you explained them at the last meeting. What's new?'

'We are happy about the acceptability issue, but we have further work to do on competence and agreement. This woman obviously has skills. But are they the right skills for any available project, and can she succeed? For instance, if the only credible project we could find was about undersea exploration then she wouldn't do, would she? Another worry is that she might not accept our invitation. We can't tell her the real reason why she has been chosen. She might not want the job, and with good reason. So we have to build a good case for choosing her, and we have to persuade her to accept it.'

Fred kept silent and waited for his opposite number to continue. He broke some bread from the sandwiches provided by the hotel and threw it to the ducks. The client spoke again, sounding a little aggrieved.

'And you people seem to be saying "No peerage, no corpse!"' The representative felt that Fred lacked understanding of his problems. 'We still have work to do in order to be confident of keeping our side of any deal. If we handle it badly, there will be major political embarrassment and we will still have a clever, dedicated untouchable terrorist plotting actively against the country. Our part in this deal is hard to handle.'

Fred was too inexperienced to cope with powerful arguments like that. He promised to ask the principal about possible concessions. In return, the client representative promised to search out suitable projects and estimate to what extent they matched Ms. Ileloka's capability.

When Fred reported back, Nshila reminded him about Jilly Jordan and spelt out her attitude.

'You are doing alright, Fred, but remember that time is going by and Jilly may get to the Prince at any moment. It won't worry me if you and the client are still trading words with each other. I won't feel that I am on the job. But if we reach a deal, then beating Jilly to the hit becomes a matter of pride. I have to beat him, or find some way to take him off the board.'

'He has made no further attempt yet, has he? Perhaps he has decided that the task is too hard, and gone back to Brazil.'

'Perhaps he has. And perhaps not. And if he had made another attempt, and failed, would we know about it? We only know of the first attempt because somebody noticed the dart sticking out of the trousers. If it had fallen out unseen we would know nothing.'

The third meeting took place only three weeks later. Simon Trent had found a project that looked exactly right but that needed immediate action.

'The Republic of Anacanda', his representative told Fred. 'It lies just north of an old British colony – the one where Ms. Ileloka was born – and has friendly relations with it. We need the help of Anacanda in influencing another of it's neighbours. Anacanda is seeking overseas aid for a major agricultural development and has asked two countries for proposals – one from our government and one from a private consortium based in Belgium. There will be no big capital return on the project, but the goodwill value will be enormous. Our team is due there in about six weeks and at present there is no political front-person. It was thought that competent civil servants would be enough. I shall have no difficulty reversing that decision. I can get high level blessing for a black woman who is expert in everything to do with the weather. For that's one of their problems – rainfall in parts of Anacanda is variable and success will depend partly on the location and extent of the area chosen for the project. Some people will see it as a mistake to send a woman into a male-dominated culture. In this case it can be justified, because the President is known to be powerfully influenced by his wife. It's a bit of a national joke. Ms. Ileloka will be culturally and professionally acceptable.'

'But that still leaves the problem of approaching her and persuading her and briefing her.'

Behind his negotiator's face, Fred was euphoric. Would this woman the client had found accept the job? She certainly would. Could she be ready in time? Fred would pull out all the stops. He was so overjoyed that he took a step beyond his brief.

'If you were able to give me details about this Ileloka woman, my principal might be able to assist your approaches by using intermediaries in the expatriate network. Would that help?'

'It would. But another thing we really must have is a time commitment.'

'What do you mean?'

'We need to have a time frame for making the hit. This mission will take time to complete, and arranging to have Ms. Ileloka appointed as Head of Mission will also take time – even if you can help. There is risk involved, and heavy expense. We don't want to go through all that before we see action from your side. You should at least promise that the Prince will be dead before the mission returns.'

That stumped Fred. It was impossible to explain that Nshila couldn't make the hit while she was away in Anacanda. Fred had to guard the fiction that she was the unwitting beneficiary of the death, and entirely ignorant of the whole matter. Could he promise that the hit would be made before the mission left? No. That was beyond his remit, and he didn't even know if it could be done. He took a firm line.

'That won't do. It's not good business policy to deliver the goods before payment is assured, and you can't make payment till the mission is over. You have to trust us. But the principal is a man of honour. You deliver, and we'll give you a body.'

Reluctantly, the client side agreed.

The government approaches to Nshila, and the negotiations that followed, were easy to handle. Knowing beforehand exactly what they wanted, Nshila furnished naturally and spontaneously all the right answers. She was mildly worried by undertaking such extensive activity before she had worked out how to kill the Prince – but only mildly. The excitement and novelty and humour of the challenge had got to her.

Chapter Twenty-Three

Call Me Madam

This story is about me, Nshila. Mostly it's other people telling of me and my doings. This part, I must describe in my own words. There's no other way to put over the excitement and pleasure.

I did some day-dreaming, of course. I imagined myself standing in a magnificent debating chamber. I was wearing a splendid robe, somebody said, 'I call the Honourable Baroness, Nshila Ileloka' and I stood up to speak. Fantasising is fun.

'It's going to happen,' I told myself. 'The delegation, I mean. I am as suitable as any other candidate.' Some testimonials were required, and for that I applied discreet pressure to senior staff in my country's embassy. The dirt that Fred Mbwele dug up was quite sufficient. They fabricated records about my diplomatic skills and leadership skills and political connections.

There was no work on hand that I couldn't leave to Gillian and Peter. I had to buy clothes, of course. I had to meet an African Head of State and must appear in African dress. I just love the bright colours and the floating garments and the colossal visual impact they give you – not least the headdress that makes you so much taller. I had not worn African dress since that expedition to set up the weather stations (I still remembered the knock-out effect on Fred and Abel when they met me in the hotel that first evening). I gifted myself a week in Paris, which offers more choice than London. I spent half my time in museums and half in fashion boutiques.

Was I so excited about this project that I forgot about Jilly Jordan? No. But the plan I designed to neutralise him was so simple and obvious that I am ashamed to mention it. The early strategies I thought of required making contact with him in the UK environment. That would be extremely difficult. Ideas like buying him off or diverting him to another target, or framing him for some crime, or even killing him, all came up against that obstacle: I had no idea about his present alias or location or what today he looked like. The answer came in a conversation I had with Jessop. We were discussing Jilly's motivation, and Jessop said that he believed it was mainly pride. 'Once he is committed to a project, there is almost nothing he cares about more than success.'

'Say that again, Jessop. Did you mean "almost"? Did you mean that there really is something more important to him?'

'I think so. Everything I have heard about him tells of a passionate dedication to the rainforest where he grew up. I don't see how that can help you, but I think it's true.'

There was no point in pursuing my idea with Jessop, but if the information was true then surely there must be a communicative link between Jilly, wherever he was, and his remote home. If the right people over there became convinced of a major new threat to his homeland, they would tell Jilly about it and send some message like, 'Come home. We need you urgently.'

It cost money, of course: rather a large amount of money. But a fictitious multi-national organisation took threatening actions towards the rainforest, and a high level of local panic followed. I never got confirmation that Jilly had rushed home, but I felt confident. Sometimes you have to rely on probabilities.

Civil Service protocol demands that officials treat their political boss – even if he or she is appointed from outside and has less expertise than they – with formal respect. That meant that I got 'Madam' or 'Ma'am' or 'Marm' or even 'Mem' whenever they addressed me. I liked it.

At first, the respect I received may have been an artificial veneer, covering doubts about the competence of an outsider. It changed. I was well qualified for the assignment and felt justified in taking the initiative. The first thing I did was insist that every member of the party gain limited familiarity with the language of Anacanda. It borders on my own country, so our embassy had one or two speakers of the language. I got them along to give lessons. By the time my programme finished, all my team were able to use the normal polite phrases that indicate respect for your hosts, and all had some understanding of their culture.

More than that, I insisted that at least one member of 'my personal staff' should be included in the delegation. I made out that I was a fitness freak (partially true) and needed support if I was to be stuck in a foreign country for perhaps as much as a month. So Zach Kawero joined up as my personal trainer. Nobody realised that his real expertise was as a computer hacker and surveillance expert. Had we been challenged, we would have passed him off as a theoretical expert rather than an athlete. Zach brought sophisticated equipment with him.

I took every opportunity to talk personally with members of the delegation, officially and socially. They picked up an awareness of what I had done with my life and what qualifications I had achieved. A few of them were graduates of LSE and respected my First Class degree.

It was great being addressed as 'Madam'. It was also great to work in the environment provided for senior civil servants and their political masters. I mean, if I really wanted to have a genuine Constable on the wall of The Rain Consultancy I might just be able to find or borrow the necessary money but I would never, ever do so. A top civil servant, I found, could say 'Take away that Constable and get me a Stubbs instead'. All done on the taxpayers' money – like the carpet and the desk and the armchairs. People have an 'entitlement' that goes with the rank, and they feel bound to use it. It's good for the ego. And failure to use it is frowned on by whatever union or association the officer belongs to; it might cause somebody to say, 'If that privilege is not being used, could it not be discontinued and a bit of money saved?' For the first few days I went to the ministry and back by tube. Then somebody explained that the chauffeur-driven car at the ministry door – that I had walked past – was actually there for me, personally!

The journey to Anacanda kept up the standard. I enjoyed the VIP lounge and the complimentary drinks, and the comfort of first class travel. At other times I have emerged from the aircraft in a bedraggled state – made worse by a long wait for baggage, intrusive questions from immigration officers and searches of my belongings by customs staff. Nothing like that for my delegation.

We swept through the airport like royalty and I was looking close to my best when I shook hands with the Minister for Economic Development.

We rode into the capital along a broad, straight road flanked by jacaranda trees sporting their blue flowers. Outside the line of trees was the dry red earth that you see in so many parts of Africa, and the air was warm, slightly scented. I had that glorious feeling that warmth was guaranteed – no matter where I went I should never feel cold but always safe and free in loose, comfortable clothes.

I don't know how the delegation would have behaved under another leader. Perhaps they would have grabbed their opposite numbers and insisted on immediate, earnest discussions. I was having none of that. It's not the way to do business in the middle of Africa. We accepted all the entertainment that was offered, and returned the hospitality in the guest house (a minor palace) that had been allocated to us. I performed a balancing act that was difficult but enjoyable. At times I showed myself to be a knowledgeable woman of the world. At times I was mildly flirtatious. At times I played the modest woman and required my best civil servant to act the role of male escort and supporter. I paid special attention to the 'wives' of my hosts. I use the word 'wives' carefully, for in a developing African country you can make no assumptions. A cabinet minister may have a 'real' wife who is still pounding mealies in a remote village. He can't expect her to cope with diplomatic functions, so in the big city he finds himself a substitute. He needs, and usually gets, an educated, sophisticated, English-speaking girl who has probably travelled abroad. In terms of relationship she may be second wife (or third, etc.) or mistress or a one-night hire. You can never be sure. But you have to get them on your side so that they will speak of you as 'a normal woman'. This reduces any assault on the ego that their men may otherwise suffer through having to deal with you. They can say, 'She is certainly exceptional, but deep down she is just a woman.'

Regarding our purpose, the priority I set for my delegation was to find out as much as possible about the Belgian delegation that had preceded us. We knew that they had been asked, just as we were being asked, to recommend an agricultural development scheme for a backwards area in the North East of the country. The parameters were well defined. There were only a certain number of crops that could grow in the climate, and many of those would never find a market in today's competitive world. There were perhaps six credible alternatives. More flexible were the extent and location of the land to be planted and the degree of support to be offered. Anacanda expected that the successful bidder would provide seed, train staff, and guarantee a certain level of purchasing of the product for a number of years. They would also provide marketing expertise. Then there were the unspoken pay-offs for the people who would vote on the two proposals.

We had considerable success, often due to the civil servants. The data they collected was unspectacular, but very useful when collated. They were good listeners, and good at steering the conversation. They picked up a wide range of unrelated facts, which they faithfully reported and which I was able to integrate. Zach Kawero was able to install a spy camera in the office of the Minister of Economic Development. It picked up strong indications about the general direction of the Belgian proposal, together with a few lurid passages involving the Minister and his secretary.

For my part, I watched in the fire. The guest house was on the edge of town and, at night, there were numerous village fires close by. I found a sheltered hollow where I could light my own fire without arousing suspicion. As the embers glowed, I concentrated my mind on the people I had dealt with that day and tried to conjure up images of what they were now doing. That part was hard work. The better you know your target, the easier it is to evoke the picture: it can even be done without physical materials such as body parts or possessions. In this case I had only limited knowledge and needed things like handkerchiefs and headscarves and pictures and letters that the subject had written. Such items helped me visualise the man and trace an outline in the glow. It works best when the flames have died and there is a red glow at the heart of the fire. Throw your eyes slightly out of focus and think – think – think.

The picture that emerged of the Belgian proposal was worthy

but boring. They had produced a scheme that was sensible and workable, but unimaginative. You might have called it Teutonic. It accepted the parameters indicated by the host government, making no attempt to test them or improve them. It dismissed four of the possible alternative crops, examined only two in detail, and suggested that development should cover the area first designated, and nothing more. The support promised was generous: purchase of half the crop was promised at a fair market price for three years, and the Belgian government would facilitate marketing in the European Union. Finally, I saw an image in the fire of the Minister of Finance. He was looking at a letter received from a bank in Switzerland. I could see a number of zeros.

What bugged us was the motivation of the Belgian syndicate. That country had never been a huge player in the colonisation of Africa and no longer had any interests that it needed to protect. Why should it want its scheme to be accepted, when that could only mean spending a great deal of money for little reward? It made no sense. Why had they got involved in the first place?

We had a conference about it. Some people argued that the reasons for the Belgian involvement were irrelevant. They had no impact on our own objective. This was to create a political climate in which Anacanda could be persuaded to modify its policy of non-intervention in the affairs of its eastern neighbour. That was ruled by a mentally unbalanced dictator who was destroying the economy and reducing his people to poverty. The country had previously had a substantial trade with Europe, advantageous to both parties. There was also a significant British population. It was thought that Anacanda could exert a beneficial influence if old-fashioned anti-colonial prejudices could be overcome. We were to create goodwill towards Britain by solving their agricultural problem.

A different view about the Belgian involvement was that they must know something that we didn't know – and that whatever was being concealed in this way might be valuable, or might be dangerous if we remained ignorant. The man arguing this case most aggressively was Miles Strang.

Miles was the senior civil servant in the party, and in one sense my minder. He was supposed to show me the implications of anything I suggested: to spell out the pros and cons as they appeared to a person deeply involved in the machinery of government. He was supposed to examine the possible consequences of an action and look for pitfalls. He was supposed to say, 'If we do so-and-so, Ma'am, then such-and-such is likely to happen.' I liked him, and admired him because he was intelligent, considerate and courteous. I was sorry for him, because the Civil Service had killed whatever capability he might have had for fantasising, and replaced it with caution. Such a summary, of course, says as much about me as about him. He was certainly very useful. He kept worrying about the motivation of the Belgians.

'The sort of thing that might lie behind it – to give an example – is mining. A Belgian surveyor might have located deposits of a valuable mineral. His government might be trying to build up goodwill in the hope of winning the concession to extract it.'

He also saw weaknesses in the work the Belgians had done. 'You know, they quite failed to show our hosts how competitive world markets are today. They have told our hosts nothing about the activities of other third world growers. We have already done our hosts a service by opening their eyes.'

'That's a nice thought, Miles,' I answered. 'It's good to think that we are a bit sharper than our rivals. As to their motives, we must put that on the back burner for the moment, but keep our eyes and ears open.'

The time came when the welcoming formalities were over and we started northwards into the bush. Saloon cars and smart clothing were out: safari suits and Landover's were in. The only concession I allowed myself was a hat with a larger brim than usual and a neat little cockade in striking blue and red and yellow. It brought an outburst of humour from Miles. 'That shall be our Oriflamme,' he said, laughing. 'What's an Oriflamme?' (I had never heard the word before.)

'The Oriflamme, Madam, was the battle standard of the French Kings in Mediaeval times. I know it from a warlike poem I learnt at school. It's Henry of Navarre exhorting his troops before battle;

'Press where ye see my white plume shine, amid the ranks of war, - and be your Oriflamme today the helmet of Navarre.'

'That's bit cryptic, Miles. Tell me more.'

'Well, Ma'am, Henry didn't have the Oriflamme himself. He was trying to make himself King but he hadn't yet got there. He was telling his men, "Just you watch my helmet. That's going to be as good a talisman as the Oriflamme itself".'

Several others were around when we were talking, and the thing gained a special significance. If I ever forgot my cockade, somebody would ask, 'Where's the Oriflamme, Madam? How will we know where to follow if we can't see it?' It was very good-natured.

Getting to the area was an adventure for my staff. Some of them had been on package holidays to Morocco and seen tourist Africa. None had seen the reality of the interior. Our route took us across the rift valley – down one side and up the other. They were amazed to look down onto clouds and descend through them to the valley floor. They marvelled at the skill of our drivers as they negotiated unprotected bends with their wheels a few inches from a precipice. They enjoyed having to push huge fallen rocks over the edge so that we could pass. It was novel and exciting. Two of our drivers were armed with rifles, since animals were a possible, if unlikely threat, and because of poachers. These might mistake us for game rangers and open fire. We had a keen marksman in our group who delighted in the absence of safety rules and displayed his skill by selecting targets almost a mile away and hitting them regularly.

The more adventurous ones persuaded the drivers to let them have a turn at the wheel. One of them was handling the lead vehicle and caused the convoy to stop abruptly when he rounded a kopje and found a full-grown male giraffe straddling the road. He had never seen a creature of such size and immediately started reversing. There was insistent horn-blowing from the vehicle behind and much angry shouting. Then the proper driver took over and detoured carefully around the giraffe, which continued feeding from a treetop as if nothing had happened. Another of our party managed to drive into a ford rather too fast and stall the engine. His passengers had to stand up to their waists in water and push the vehicle slowly for twenty yards. Emerging, they found leeches hanging onto the fleshy parts of their legs and were unreasonably distressed. I laughed.

Inevitably, we sometimes came up behind heavy vehicles, creating huge clouds of dust at they rumbled along poorly-maintained dirt roads. Miles Strang, driving for the first time, made an attempt to pass and quickly abandoned it.

'It's worse than the MI on a winter morning in driving rain. There, you are driving into total darkness but at least you know there's nothing coming the other way.'

One of our local team spoke to me in his own language.

'What's he saying?' Miles asked.

I laughed. 'He's telling me that if there are people on the roof – on top of the baggage load – they will signal to you when it's safe to go. Then you put your foot down and pray.'

One adventure caused us to lose a day. A dust cloud behind us turned out to be caused by a large private car – one of the old Chevrolet vehicles with a bonnet as long as the flight deck of an aircraft carrier. The occupants were clearly in a hurry and overtook our convoy at dangerous speed. Passing our lead vehicle, the driver turned too quickly to regain the right side of the road. Instead of the steady, gradual turn appropriate to dirt roads, he wrenched the vehicle sideways and skidded. We watched as it slithered uncontrollably from one side of the road to another, hit a large rock on the right hand side, turned over and threw two passengers into the bush. We were lucky to find everybody alive – two inside the car and two in the bush. We had to drive them to the nearest hospital, which was fifty miles away.

Miles was one of those who had never experienced the true Africa, and he became increasingly interested in my origins – in a pleasant courteous way. Once we passed very close to a village and he asked, 'Is that the sort of place where you grew up, Ma'am?'

'Yes. It's pretty much the same.'

'Could you have been one of those women over there?'

'You mean the ones carrying water pots from the river and the others pounding mealies? Yes. I could have been one of them.'

I could see him turning it over in his mind – comparing my life story with his own. 'It's not like my Mum's street in suburban Swansea, is it? Could you ever go back there, and live like that?'

'In one way, Yes. I could manage quite well without all the sophistication of western life. I could do all the things one has to do to survive. In another way it would be quite impossible.'

'How's that?'

'I'm so westernised now in my attitudes and patterns of thought. And how you think influences how you speak. I would very soon be saying things that offended the tribal culture – which is totally male-dominated. They would never find me acceptable. I would say things I was never supposed to know or talk about.'

'Have you noticed,' I went on, 'how I always ask one of you to make contact with village people if we need something – like information about any dangers along our route?'

'Yes.'

'I do it because the people you will speak to are the senior male members of the village and they will be comfortable talking to you. More so than if I went myself.'

'Interesting, that. I'm learning a lot on this trip.'

One of the fascinating things about ex-colonial Africa is the mixture of place names. You find local heroes remembered alongside romantic names introduced by eccentric European adventurers. I met an example of this when the local staff reported that Harpers Ferry was out of order and a decision would have to be made about crossing the swollen Zuweli River.

On hearing the name I had visions of some American expatriate getting sentimental about the civil war. It seemed I was wrong. Percy Harper had been an Englishman who had farmed land on both sides of the river and got rich by doing so. He had got tired of native canoes, and ordered a genuine river ferry from England. Being an eccentric (some people thought him mad) he had rejected normal designs and gone for the type that hauls itself across the river - pulling on an underwater chain. Only a few survive, but this boat still existed, long after Percy had died and the local people had reclaimed the land. But it was poorly maintained, and worked on average seven days out ten. Often, it sat unattended at one bank or the other. The latest news to reach us spoke of 'a short delay' which in that part of the world means a minimum of two weeks.

I took no part in the conversation about our travel options but I remember many of the place names.

'If Harpers Ferry is out, then we don't have to go down Stanley Steps, which is a difficult route in spite of the new vehicle track. We can leave the heights by Nalolo Ravine and then turn west to West Lunga and Yeta's Drift. After that there's a good road up the escarpment and we can hit the main highway at Roger Young's Kraal.'

'With the river this high, Yeta's Drift may be impassable.'

'True. If it is, then the only option is to go north to Jubilee Bridge, which means struggling through Chavuma Swamp – with all those bugs eating us.'

'We could avoid that by keeping straight ahead at East Lunga and using the longer road to Jubilee Bridge, past the Lobola Hotel.'

'Good idea. A night of luxury would suit me fine.'

'Unlikely. They won't have room for us. They are usually full of rich Americans on bespoke safaris.'

The decision eventually reached was to try Yeta's Drift. It proved passable, though with some difficulty. I never got to see the Lobola Hotel, or Jubilee Bridge or Old Namushakende that stood on its west bank. Roger Young's Kraal was nothing to sing about. I would have preferred the long curve of Mwanawina's trail – the route he had taken a hundred years ago, so I was told, to launch a surprise attack on his enemy.

We reached the proposed development area. We greeted the Chief and his advisers, went through the polite formalities, and got started. A major oddity soon appeared. Our brief suggested that we use as one boundary of our study the present limit of cultivation. It was easy to identify that line - we could see where crops had grown and been harvested or were still growing, but it was not logical. The facts and the theory differed, for no very obvious cause. There were geographical features, mainly a ridge of high ground and a thick belt of trees, that suggested a division between heavily watered land and land that received far less. This line should have coincided with the cultivated area. It didn't. There were large areas of land that should have been watered and productive but appeared dry.

We spent three days establishing good relations with the local tribe. On the third day Zach Kawero, who was best with the language, raised the subject with the chief. He got a strange answer.

'We can't cultivate those fields you talk about because it doesn't rain there. Your science may say that it ought to rain there, but your science is wrong. It never happens – at least not enough to do any good. Don't ask me why. I don't know. Mbangwe might know, but I don't.'

Chapter Twenty-Four

Mbangwe

Who was Mbangwe? We soon learnt that he was their witchdoctor and a highly respected person. My team members responded to the knowledge in different ways. At one end of the scale were the men who thought him a total irrelevance. He had nothing to do with the climate and should be ignored. Other people said that, whatever he could or could not do, he surely knew all about the fields that were uncultivated. And to ignore him would be an insult to our hosts. At The other end of the scale were Zach Kawero and I, both believers. Publicly, I joined myself to the middle group to justify talking with and about Mbangwe.

It was Zach who got the information we needed, talking with the tribal elders.

'Mbangwe is old, highly skilled and a past-master at rain-making. It falls, they tell me, where he calls for it and nowhere else. And his idea of the right place ends where the cultivation ends. No rain falls on the uncultivated area because he never demands it.'

'Why on earth does he do that?'

'We can't be sure of that, because the elders were reluctant to say anything critical about him. But one old man said that when he was a boy the tribe had been in conflict with very aggressive neighbours who encroached on their lands. This fellow believed that Mbangwe had caused rain to fall on the land that was held by his tribe but not on the disputed patch. So the enemy decided that poor land was not worth fighting over and gave up. Mbangwe was a big a hero. But he has used the same call ever since, and the line of cultivation exactly matches the furthest advance of the old enemy.'

'But that enemy is long gone. Why did he not change his call and make that land productive again? If he is as skilled as they claim, it must have been within his competence.'

'Nobody seems to have an answer to that. There are several ideas one can dream up, but none are convincing. Maybe the tribe had too few men to work the land. Or the enemy were still feared. Maybe he thought they would come back if things were better, and decided never to give them the chance. Maybe he tried, and his spell failed to produce any rain at all, so he went back to what he knew worked. Maybe, as he got older, he forgot what he had done, or was too lazy to change his habits. But all this is primitive stuff and we can't really take it seriously.'

Our sceptics thought all this was ridiculous; I knew it was not. The present pattern of rainfall had been engineered by man, and could be altered again.

The area suitable for cultivation could theoretically be enlarged. By how much? Could it only be restored as far as the largest limits the tribe had ever enjoyed? Or could it be extended far beyond that? An answer was badly needed because all previous plans had assumed a growing area of a certain size and that size was too small for viable production of some crops. There were two that had been excluded from consideration by comparatively small margins. Both these would be viable given a 25% increase in available land.

It was clear to me that I must concentrate on Mbangwe. But to do this risked losing the confidence of the many unbelievers on my team. I had to justify my personal actions, and provide others with useful, interesting, credible tasks while I got on with the job.

The task I devised for them was to review the research work that had identified suitable crops and their possible market. Was it thorough? Was anything missed? I also initiated them into a weather-modelling program that I had brought with me. Getting the best results from this needed considerable skill. Gillian was an expert, and I was semi-competent, but it would be hard work for a novice. However, these were intelligent people and they might be able to make some deductions about local rainfall as it ought naturally to be. For instance, they could make comparisons with other similar areas. It was interesting that the person who emerged as best user of the program was a tall thin man who I had previously seen as a nonentity. His name was Emrys White-Walker.

I explained my focus on Mbangwe by my belief – attributed to my tribal background – that we had not been told everything. I had to embark on a careful, confidence-winning strategy and find the underlying truth. I used Zach to defuse any chauvinist objection to my enquiries, asked a lot of discreet questions and thought hard.

Mbangwe was maintaining a situation that we disliked, but was it necessary to treat him as an enemy? Were we looking at a win-lose situation or could it be turned into win-win? If not, then the obvious solution was to kill Mbangwe. But would that help? I would be left trying to manipulate the rainfall myself, and despite my success at Gillian's wedding I doubted my skill. And the stakes were much higher. A wet wedding is a minor disaster compared to the well-being of a tribe. And I was totally against killing Mbangwe, who had done nothing wrong.

There just had to be a way of creating a win-win situation. I needed to know much more about Mbangwe himself. I needed personal contact, but could hardly go myself. It would offend all the local rules.

I sent Zach. He didn't go willingly. He has always been a bit scared of me, and when he realised that I was a bit scared of Mbangwe he felt worse still. I made a big song and dance about the details of his role. He was to be the expatriate African, unimpressed by western habits and believing that true wisdom was only to be found here in the heart of our continent. He could say whatever seemed acceptable about me and my mission, provided only that he listened and looked and reported accurately to me. After long negotiation with the tribal elders, he obtained an interview with Mbangwe.

The outcome was unexpected. Zach was knocked off balance by Mbangwe's welcome. 'Have you brought a cameraman with you? Will my picture be in the paper?' Mbangwe held up a month-old copy of *The Times* with a picture of a minor Royal on the front page. Zach floundered for a moment, and then replied that preliminary interviews were not usually filmed, but if there were to be a follow-up (which was probable) then a full team, including cameramen, was mandatory.

Zach had a hard time, for Mbangwe was full of himself and inclined to illustrate his power by long-winded examples of what he had done, frequently straying from the point. Zach's evaluation came down in the end to this:

> He has been a powerful operator and will retain influence in his tribe for some years. But he is past his prime and sometimes gets things muddled up. He is inclined to ignore the tasks that demand the most concentration and focus upon those that he can perform quickly and without effort. One of these is rain-making. He can do it with his eyes shut. He sometimes uses it just as a way of showing off his power.
>
> I did notice that he relies on 'props' to aid his concentration much more than you do. Quite small objects associated with your target apparently allow you to get results. I have even seen you working with no aids at all – just closing your eyes and doing it all by mental effort. Mbangwe is surrounded by bits and pieces, and seems dependent on them. I saw that on his wall he has a crude picture-map of his tribal area. Goodness knows where it came from, but it seems intrinsic to much of his work.
>
> I also realised that his eyesight is poor. He wears glasses, but I think they are more for prestige than any practical use. With or without them, he often makes mistakes.

That report was very useful. It seemed likely that in his rain-making Mbangwe associated his spells with this tribal map on the wall. If that was true, maybe we could somehow doctor the map and use Mbangwe's own skill to further our ends. So the next thing I did was ask Zach to bug Mbangwe's hut with a few cameras.

'No. No. Absolutely not.' I had never seen Zach so obdurate. I asked if he was scared. 'You bet I'm scared! I've taken a few risks for you in the past, but this is way off limits.'

Where could I look for help? The answer came in the unlikely, gangling form of Emrys White-Walker, who had demonstrated aptitude in the use of my weather-prediction program. He must have heard me talking with Zach, and he volunteered.

'I can do that.'

Needing to know more, I asked Miles what Emrys was like.

'We recruit people like Emrys quite often. The Civil Service tries very hard to recruit the best brains in the country, and a few of them are so extraordinarily bright that they have trouble fitting in.'

'I'm surprised. Surely the environment is just what they are looking for?'

'Perhaps they are, but they are so accustomed to trusting their own intellect that they are apt to exceed their brief. For instance, a supervisor might give a recruit like Emrys a difficult task, feeling confident that it would be done well. The Emrys-type then goes beyond his instructions because the further steps seem to him quite obvious; it never strikes him that another course might be preferable. The supervisor doesn't expect this, he wants the Emrys-type to stick to his brief and report back so that the further steps can be debated. The Emrys-type has gone too far, and caused embarrassment.'

'How do you cope with them, then? How will you cope with Emrys?'

'Oh! I won't have to. They rattle around from job to job causing general mayhem until they find a slot that perfectly suits their talents. It's a bit like the party game called "Pass the parcel". In fact, Emrys doesn't belong to my department. He's been assigned to this trip by his proper boss, a man called Simon Trent. I'll bet you that Emrys has five or six jobs in different parts of the service and finally becomes our recognised expert on a remote but vital subject. He'll be happy, and he'll progress through the salary scales but he'll never get a KCMG. He's here now because Simon doesn't know what to do with him.'

'He's a Welshman. He graduated with outstanding honours from the University College of Wales at Aberystwyth, and came top in the entry examinations for the civil service. He's got a strong Welsh accent and infuriates people by being too frequently right. He looks odd, too, doesn't he? The word "gangling" might have been invented for him. He's tall, with long arms and legs that seem to be attached only loosely to his body. He looks like one of those wooden puppet figures worked by string that can still be found in antique shops.'

The great thing for me about Emrys was that he had no fear of a dirty old man in a mud hut. He felt he was quite smart enough to do the job without being discovered. And he was. A few days later his concealed camera gave us footage of Mbangwe working a rain-spell, and he did indeed use the map. He ran the palm of his hand slowly around it anti-clockwise while murmuring the words of power. It was not clear whether he could see the map well, because his eyes were shut the whole time. We got a good view of the map, which looked like the work of some long-dead missionary. It showed the boundaries of the tribal area accurately, and populated it with small drawings of local features and people. Conceptually, it was the sort of thing a child draws, but the execution was much better. It was very faded – so much so that some of the outlines had disappeared.

The plan was obvious: create a map that looked much the same and substitute it for the existing one. Mbangwe, having poor eyesight and suspecting nothing, would call for rain to cover the area designated on the map. He would never know that the area had been altered. Rain would fall on the area where we wanted it.

It was a hard task to make a credible substitute out there in the bush. We had none of the facilities a draughtsman requires. But four days later our small team – Zach, Emrys and I – had a product that we considered good enough to offer a chance of success. We made it to the exact dimensions of Mbangwe's map so that it could be overlaid on the original within the same frame. That frame, we knew, was an old rectangular frame in heavy dark wood that might once have been host to a landscape or a portrait. You find the most amazing things in remote corners of Africa: possessions prized by expatriate Europeans, abandoned when they left or died, and acquired by local people. Often they are thought to confer prestige in some obscure manner. I remember that in my father's hut when I was a girl there was a picture of a European gentleman with long side-whiskers in formal dress, with a top hat. The part of the title that had not been obliterated said W.E.GLAD. There are numerous relics of that sort. Some of the most interesting ones are of German origin and come from the days of German rule in East Africa when Von Lettow-Vorbeck fought the British and they had a gunboat on Lake Victoria.

I had a big shock one night when the embers of my fire sprang up and died down again. Suddenly I was in London, not Africa. I was seeing a room with large windows, and through one of them I could see Tower Bridge. The man in the room was my apprentice, Fred, and he was doing something with a round flat dish. What was it? I could imagine him experimenting with herbs and chemicals, but the substance in the dish looked like nothing more exotic than a fruit pie! He seemed to be poking tiny things into it. They might have been fragments of glass. I was furious. That impossible ill-disciplined apprentice was attempting food-poisoning. I was more furious than otherwise because I could do nothing about it. I slept badly that night, but decided in the morning that I must put it on the back burner and concentrate on the present job.

How would we substitute our own map for the one on Mbangwe's wall? When there is a physical object involved there is only one option. We identified a time when Mbangwe was likely to be absent from his hut, watched him go, and sent Emrys. Zach kept watch from a safe distance in order to signal if Mbangwe was seen returning. It proved necessary, and the signal was given, but Emrys was slow to respond. When Mbangwe returned, he found Emrys sitting on a stone suspiciously close to his hut. He stalked up to Emrys aggressively.

They say that academically clever people can be short on common sense and cunning. Emrys is not. He stood up smartly and gave Mbangwe a long harangue in Welsh. Mbangwe had some knowledge of English, but this sing-song torrent of multi-syllable words defeated him totally. He may also have been afraid of the gangling. Was this puppet-like thing perhaps being activated by an unseen power above him? Mbangwe broke contact and disappeared into his hut. Emrys told us later that he had recited one of the most lurid passages from a tale in The Mabinogion.

Did it work? Yes. During the next ten days there were three storms, and rain fell just where we wanted it. A multitude of small flowers sprang up to carpet the ground. They must have been lying dormant for years. There was no noticeable decrease in the rainfall over the normal area. Well done, our side! Well done, Mbangwe!

That left us with the problem of convincing officials back in the city. Quite reasonably, they argued that rain in an unusual place one year was no guarantee of a repeat performance. We anticipated their doubts, and prepared a case. The core feature was climate change triggered by global warming. I had a long e-mail correspondence with Gillian in London, getting the latest theories and shaping them to support my arguments. We also found some men from that area who were prepared to say that the limits of rainfall had been gradually extending westwards. And we suggested physical changes that would increase the probability of rain – the planting of a certain type of tree and the erection of what we called 'weather towers' to attract lightning. We designed and commissioned a series of irrigation ditches.

And we paid out money. We bribed more people than the Belgians had done, and we bribed them better. Possibly the most effective item was the deal I did with the President's wife. Whenever she was in London, she said, she was extremely bored with the entertainments offered – both by the British government and her own embassy. When she was next in London, would I personally show her something 'a bit more raw and raunchy and exciting?' I felt I had enough contacts to manage that.

But final deliberations on matters like that are long drawn-out. All the parties affected must have their say, and those who are forced to make sacrifices must be pacified. They must be given sweeteners. We left for London with good reason to feel we should win, but aware we were still vulnerable.

As the green fields of England appeared below us, I remembered seeing Fred Mbwele in the embers of the fire. I was sure to be greeted by some trouble or other, sparked off by his impatience.

Chapter Twenty-Five

Experiences Of The Apprentice

Fred Mbwele felt badly about being left behind. It was worse because Zach Kawero had gone. Fred was aggrieved. He thought, 'I know what it's all about. I have been in on the negotiations. I know who the target is and I know about the peerage. Zach knows nothing. He's aware of her dark side, but he keeps away from it and he's outside the loop on this thing.'

He talked to Gillian and Peter. Gillian was slightly worried by Nshila being absent – she always felt more comfortable when there was somebody to fall back on if necessary – but Peter saw it only as an opportunity. He had prepared the ground by talking to Nshila.

'Do you mind if I make a few field visits while you're away? I'm sure we can get more business from that tour operator who specialises in the Isle of Man. That place has a micro-climate all its own. It would make an illuminating study.'

Fred could see the boss was doubtful. Perhaps she imagined Peter in hard-drinking sessions with bent local worthies, and doing deals beyond his remit. I suppose, Fred thought, that if you employ an ex-criminal, then doubts will persist. He could almost see her mind working. But it was only a brief moment before she agreed. Having placed her trust in him, she was going to keep it.

Maybe I can be like Peter! The thought was reinforced, rather than negated, by the instructions Fred received himself. He got a heavy-handed warning about not experimenting, a long reading list and an entry card for the British Library. He could come to the office freely, but if he needed anything from her flat he must ask Gillian to let him in. It was so unexciting that he protested vigorously and often. Eventually he won a concession. She would teach him one bit of practical witchcraft, on condition that he followed her other instructions religiously.

She showed him how to use The Companion. He – The

Companion – was a rather nasty spirit that could be attached to an enemy. From the moment the spell was cast, the target experienced a malignant presence just behind him. If he turned round, there was nothing to see. When he faced forward again the presence was again felt. It was accompanied by the faintest unpleasant smell. The presence projected a threat of horrible but unknown things about to happen. Targets were likely to act irrationally in the attempt to evade it. Some had jumped into water. Some had taken drugs to dull their sensibilities. A few had killed themselves.

It was a very nasty spell. Nshila showed him how to operate it, but only gave him the words appropriate to the lowest level. It worked (in the version she showed him), by making some representation (drawing, photograph or model) of the target, burning one of her special powders, speaking words of power and marking the representation with vertical strokes to show how many hours the persecution should run for. Nshila set up a demonstration against a VAT inspector who came to the consultancy about some trifling inaccuracy in her returns and was thoroughly unpleasant. She set the clock for just ten minutes. The man nearly fell down the stairs as he tried to look behind him. He turned around before he entered the lift, as if inviting somebody to enter before him. There was nobody there. In the foyer, he stared into the mirror and opened and closed his eyes repeatedly. He made a call on his mobile, and dropped the instrument when turning rapidly on his heel as if somebody had spoken in his other ear. Then the time expired. He sighed with relief and walked out into the street. Fred was told not – repeat not – to try the trick for himself, and she locked away her stock of powder.

Nshila had been gone for six days. Fred was pleased with himself for not giving in to temptation – so far. On every one of those six days he asked himself, 'What does she expect? She has a keen young apprentice and she leaves him alone to read a lot of dreary books and denies him any opportunity to experiment. It's not realistic.' It was made worse when he found that some of the books – which he tried seriously to read – were so inconsistent. There were great chunks of unbelievable rubbish and then tiny gems that had the smell of truth. Of the latter, some were only hints about what might be achieved, without any practical instruction. He learnt much about what people believed, and what they claimed to have done, but little that he could test.

He was scared of disobeying Nshila, but as time passed he managed to convince himself that minor crimes would have no serious consequences. 'She needs an apprentice,' he told himself. 'She's very competent, but she's in her thirties now and she needs somebody young and vigorous to help her. She won't want to lose me, so she won't hand out any very terrible punishments. And she likes me! Anyway, if I keep my mouth shut she may never know that I have made a few trials. I might even do something to help the present project along. When she comes back, she still has the problem of killing Prince Thaqib. The Anacanda business is about making sure the client can reward her. If she came back and found him dead, she could walk into the House of Lords with no more effort. She would be grateful to me!' So by day ten, Fred was looking for practice opportunities. After the manner of young men, he conveniently forgot the moments of blind terror when he had looked into her 'emotional intensifier'.

The great idea came to him in a bar: the bar on the concourse at Charing Cross station. His embassy sent him from time to time on visits to significant nationals working in England. He had been to a meeting at Herne Hill and returned to London too late to report to his boss. He wasn't in any hurry to reach his lodgings, so he stopped for a few drinks. He liked the anonymity of places like that – all sorts of people drifting in and out, talking in languages and accents from all over the world. He liked listening to snatches of conversation on unrelated subjects. He liked the fact that nobody accosted him or took any interest in him. It was like being a fly on the wall.

There was a television screen in the corner, and it showed, briefly, a flash of some religious dignitary pontificating on this, that or the other. He reminded Fred of the Reverend Tom Clutton who had been his least favourite contact at Hedgewood Theological College. He was a lecturer in Biblical Sources and was the rudest, most conceited, most arrogant man Fred had ever met. Nobody had a chance to make a case against his theses because he never listened long enough to grasp what they were saying. He had a range of 'trigger words' that set him going, and as soon as he heard one – or thought that he had – he launched into a derogatory tirade intended to make the other party look an idiot. Fred hated him. Sitting in that bar at Charing Cross Fred realised that here was the ideal person on whom to try The Companion. Up to then he had identified no likely target, mainly because target reactions were known to be unpredictable. A target with low mental stability was more likely to lose control and injure himself. After all, Fred reflected, the VAT Inspector might easily have fallen down the staircase and broken his neck. But the Reverend Clutton was ideal. He was far too confident to lose control and he fully deserved some low-level harassment.

But did Fred have the knowledge and resources needed? In particular, did he have the powder that she had burnt? Just possibly he did. He remembered that when Nshila had demonstrated The Companion, she had spilt a small amount of it over the edge of the saucer. There was a chance it had not been noticed, or had been swept onto the floor. At least he could look for it. Another problem came to his mind: in the demonstration, the target had been close by. Was proximity necessary? 'It's irrelevant,' he thought. 'I want to be there anyway to observe what happens.' He decided that he could take the first step without much effort by looking for the powder. If there was none to be found then he was stymied anyway.

Gillian let him into the flat readily. He had only to explain that Nshila had promised to lend him a book, and then forgotten. He would search her shelves for it and maybe read for a while to see whether he needed to take it away. The story gave him a reasonable time in the flat without arousing suspicion.

As he closed the door behind him he had an instant of panic. He had entered Nshila's home by means of a lie and with an intent she would condemn. Would she know? Did she know already? Was there some spiritual or electronic link by which her belongings were protected? He stood still for thirty seconds wondering whether some terrifying apparition might form out of the air or some agonising pain grasp his stomach. Nothing happened. He started his search.

There was no powder on the table, and none on the floor. He was about to give up when he realised that the table was not set directly against the wall. There was a radiator between them. On the top of the radiator was a small quantity of the magic powder. It might just be enough. Suddenly there was a faint hissing sound and Fred's stooping form shot erect as his fears revived. From the edge of the breakfast bar, the green eyes of Rasputin were watching. His studies of mediaeval witchcraft had told Fred about witches' familiars, of whom cats were the most common. Might Rasputin at this moment be communicating telepathically with his mistress? Unlikely, Fred thought, as he relaxed. Mediaeval familiars would have had no experience of inter-continental contact. But they did talk to their mistress when she was present. Rasputin would be asked about his life in her absence and he would surely tell. For a moment Fred considered abandoning the project – after all, he had not yet touched the powder. He could confess to the intention but claim Brownie points for restraint. His macho self spoke up. It said just one word – 'Coward' – and Fred was committed. He told himself 'Cats don't remember things for long. By the time she comes back he will have forgotten all about it'.

Carefully he swept the powder into an envelope and put it into his pocket.

He looked round the flat again. It was the first time he had been alone within it. One thing in particular caught his eye. On the table close to him was a glass ashtray that contained a pile of clear transparent discs, rather like CD discs except that they were slightly smaller. Idly, he picked one up and put his finger through the hole. He twiddled it round while continuing his survey. His glance lighted on the ashtray that held the other discs and he noticed that underneath it was a beer mat advertising his favourite brand of lager. He knew that Nshila also drank it, and he realised that he was thirsty. He imagined himself opening one of the cans that must be waiting in the fridge and pouring the golden liquor down his throat. Nshila would never begrudge him a drink. He was opening the fridge door and as he did so the disc fell from his finger onto the floor. He stared at it. It was no longer transparent. It was opaque, and it was coloured a deep, ruby red. And then it dissolved. It gradually disappeared, exactly as a lump of lard turns liquid in a frying pan. Fred was scared. This was clearly some sort of magic. Was it going to trigger something else? Fred grabbed a book at random and went out into the office. He managed to put the disc and its behaviour out of his mind.

In order to look normal, he spent a few moments chatting with Gillian and Peter. Then he left. Going down in the lift he looked for the first time at the title of the book he had taken. Poetical Works of Alexander Pope! He shuddered. If Gillian or Peter had noticed the title, they would wonder why on earth he wanted it and become suspicious.

Sometimes these projects have their own momentum. If Fred had not had the powder, he would never have investigated the cost of a journey north. He had little money, and rail fares had just increased. He was shocked at the quoted cost of a return fare to Leeds. On protesting, he learnt that various concessions – available to young persons and senior citizens and those travelling at certain hours – reduced the cost dramatically. So a week after his 'vision' at Charing Cross Fred purchased a mid-week off-peak return and experienced another journey north by the east coast main line. He found the scenery on that line to be boring. Flat, featureless and uninspiring. The only memorable event was a spirited and quite tuneful rendering of The Lincolnshire Poacher, by a party of four young men going home to Grantham. Other passengers were annoyed and complained. The singing calmed down, but Fred moved to a seat close by and listened to every word. The first line had grabbed his attention,

'When I was bound apprentice in famous Lincolnshire,
Full well I served my master for more than seven years,
Till I took up to poaching, as you shall quickly hear.
Oh, 'tis my delight on a shiny night in the season of the year.'

Seven years! Would his apprenticeship last seven years? No. She had only specified five. And surely he would have some big adventures before that. Maybe he was starting on one now! The choir then started improvising new words, crude and sexually explicit as is the way of young men. Fred loved it. After they had left the train, Fred amused himself by composing his own verses.

In the afternoon he was booking into a small and rather sordid bed-and-breakfast place half a mile from Hedgewood College. Sitting on the bed, he found that it had the usual four legs, but one of them was half an inch shorter than the others. The bed rocked whenever he moved.

The best plans are simple. He knew that from the door of the old potting shed in the college grounds it was possible to see the lecture room where Reverend Clutton performed. He established that the gardeners were at work in a remote area and set up his gear in the depths of the shed. As a witchdoctor's den it was unconventional, but adequately dingy, dirty and smelly. Cobwebs brushed his hair and mouse-droppings littered the shelves. Bright sunlight slanted through the door and fell on scraps of food, shards of old flower pots, assorted loose bolts, and twigs from worn-out besom brooms. The rest of the place was darker by comparison. But a ray of sun sparkled on a piece of metal sticking out from behind an old notice board propped against a wall. Investigating, Fred found a riding crop with a silver handle and a dog collar and a short length of chain – all new. Somebody else had been making use of this location. Who? For what? Perhaps it didn't matter. He got down to business.

Candles provided enough heat for the tiny quantity of powder and created a small but definite cloud of smoke. Fred uttered the words of power slowly and carefully, and marked Clutton's photograph to give him twenty minutes of misery.

He had timed his actions to coincide with the end of Clutton's lecture. It was spot-on, and the results were immediate. The usual end-of-lecture pattern was for students to exit first and the teacher later. That day, the door flew open and Clutton emerged first, brushing at something at the back of his neck and shaking his head. He started down one of the many paths that led through the grounds, and suddenly side-stepped as if to allow somebody behind him to overtake him. Nobody was anywhere near. Twenty yards further on he looked wildly all round him, shouted 'Go away', lost his balance and fell into a small, prickly bush. At the bottom of the college grounds there is small lake, with benches beside it and a statue. The statue is large and fat, and stands on a large, fat plinth. Nobody knows who it represents and it stood there before the college was founded. It is commonly referred to as St Always. Clutton sat on a bench for a time, pulled a book from his briefcase and seemed to make a great attempt to concentrate on it. He never kept it up for more than seconds. Then he would sniff the air with an expression of disgust, twist his head rapidly left and right, and shake himself as if something unclean might be sticking to him. Finally, he focused on St Always and must have thought that perhaps his persecutor was hiding behind it. It was like the way children behave when one is trying to catch the other and the fugitive puts a tree between him and his pursuer. As the pursuer moves right, the fugitive does the same so that the tree trunk is always between them. Clutton did exactly the same, except that there was no fugitive. Then he gave up and sat down on the bench again with his head in his hands, until the time ran out and The Companion went off duty.

At the last moment, Fred himself had a strange experience. For a fraction of a second, he thought he saw The Companion. The light was falling on Clutton through the leaves of a tree and possibly what he saw was only a shadow. But on his left shoulder and falling halfway down his back there appeared to be a grey sack-like thing that grew bigger and smaller rhythmically as if it was breathing. It was slimy, and appeared to be attached to Clutton by suction as if it was some kind of slug. Most of its weight seemed to be at the bottom of the sack, as if its being had concentrated there to gather strength for a new attack. Had Fred seen The Companion, or was it his imagination? He thought, 'I must ask Nshila', and then remembered that she was never going to know about it. Another regret was that he had no way of telling Clutton why this horror had visited him.

The event took place in the morning, and by mid-afternoon Fred was back at Leeds station checking the times for London trains. On the platform he met the now-Reverend Alice Abigail Fordcombe – returning to pick up possessions from the college and transfer them to her London flat. She was full of enthusiasm about her curacy, and her new boss and his fashionable City church.

'Almost as soon as I get there, Fred, I'm going to be involved in a high-profile wedding – men in tail coats and top hats – women in fancy fashionable gear. It's great.'

'Surely you won't have much part in it will you? You'll be right at the bottom of the totem pole.'

'Yes,' said Abigail. 'Maybe I shall just be carrying a candlestick or something. But I'll see how it's all done and work out how to do it better when my time comes. I'll make some useful contacts, too. Just watch my progress, Fred.'

Fred could have scored a few points off her by saying that he had just taken a big step forward in his own profession. Wisely, he kept silent and just exchanged addresses and phone numbers.

Back to the books. That was his intention after the Hedgewood experience. He had to make up time if he was to satisfy Nshila that he had kept his promise. Several days were spent in the British Library studying archaic texts. In the evenings he read more popular texts about English witches in medieval days: all the claims made by them and the accusations made against them. He also struggled through most of The Golden Bough by Sir James Frazer: the edited version rather than the original thirteen volumes. Fred learnt a great deal about the times Frazer lived in, and what was then accepted as science. Scientific, by modern standards, Fred decided, it was not! The man had correspondents in obscure corners of the world, and they wrote to him about what they thought the locals were doing, and why they thought the locals did it. Frazer printed the lot!

But some of the beliefs and practices were so frequently reported, from widely different parts of the world, that they gained credibility. Some of them almost demanded an immediate trial. That was a temptation Fred resisted till Abigail called him about her society wedding.

'Fred, you have to do me a favour.'

'Try me.'

'The caterers for this wedding have been let down by their staff and are desperate for people to serve at the reception. They have asked me whether any of our regular helpers at the church could stand in. (Double the standard rate, of course). I've only found one. Will you help me? I'll never forget it if you do.'

'I might. Will I get to see all the celebrities dolled up in their fancy gear?'

'That you certainly will. We even have a genuine prince on the guest list. You can't get much better than that.'

'What prince? Prince Who of Where?'

'Prince Thaqib. You must have heard of him.'

Fred was incoherent with excitement and Abigail had to ask three times, 'Are you still there, Fred?' This was Nshila's current target, and he, Fred, Apprentice Witchdoctor, was going to be a waiter at a meal where that target would be present. And he had just read about a neat form of assassination that would fit the scenario perfectly. He had difficulty putting the right degree of reluctance into his reply; difficulty in making it sound as if he was doing Abigail a big favour at a heavy cost to himself, and deserving of a big pay-back later.

The way the spell worked, according to Sir James Frazer, was that the practitioner got hold of an uneaten portion of the food that had been served to the victim. That portion had to be made poisonous, and since things that have once been connected remain connected, the food already consumed would become poisonous inside the victim.

Fred had no difficulty in acquiring a small quantity of poison. He mixed some into one of those tiny pots of jam that are found on the breakfast tables of hotels. At the required time he reported to the caterers on site for a two-hour session of intensive training. He turned up without having a precise plan of action and mentally prepared to be disappointed. But in his heart he felt that this was a marvellous opportunity and he took notice of any detail that might help him.

Events proved favourable. The man in charge had experience of using unskilled labour; his policy was to give them thorough training for the simpler tasks, and juggle the tasks of his regular waiters so that no newcomer could achieve a major foul-up. So Fred was not required to serve different vegetables with different spoons or rush to the kitchen for obscure spices and sauces. He had to serve the first course, which was pre-plated and set on the tables before the guests arrived. During the main course his duty was to re-supply the proper waiters, and then he had to serve the dessert, which was described on the menu as Deep Brandy-bottom Fruit Pie.

'Marvellous!' he thought as he looked at the preparations. There were about twenty pies – separate but identical – and each of them was already cut into twelve pieces. The tables were round ones, each seating twelve people. Nothing could be easier! All that the waiter had to do was lean over the guest, put his cake slice underneath a section of pie, and deliver it to the plate.

'Why bother with witchcraft at all?' For a moment Fred toyed with the idea of doctoring just one segment of pie and making sure that he delivered that one, and no other, to the Prince. The thought was gone as soon as it arrived. The death would be physically caused – it could be investigated by ordinary physical means and seen as a crime.

What did he have to do? Fred thought fast. He must retain a piece of the pie eaten by the Prince – that individual pie and no other. He must poison it within an hour or so, while its partner was still inside the Prince. He must also ensure that no other guests ate any of the ten pieces remaining, for those would be subject to his magic just the same as the one eaten by the Prince. He wondered if the magic might extend to all the pies, for they were made of the same ingredients. Unlikely, he decided, for at the moment he acted each pie would have its own clear identity.

It worked. He took one pie and removed one segment and threw it away. He then started serving, going first to the lady on the Prince's right hand and moving anti-clockwise round the table. This left him one piece short as he approached the Prince again. He took a second pie, served the first segment to the Prince, secreted the second in a pocket of his waiter's jacket, and concealed the rest of the pie on a shelf in a corner, intending to pick it up later and destroy it.

He found a secure location, took the slice of pie from his pocket, lifted the pastry crust and smeared a thick layer of his poisonous paste on top of the contents. Task completed! Death for Prince Thaqib and big rewards for Fred from his delighted mistress! Those were his thoughts. How quick would the death be? He hoped to be able to observe events, but the caterer discovered the need for an extra crate of champagne and Fred was one of two people sent to fetch it. Nothing dramatic had happened by the time he returned, and the caterer no longer needed him. He was sent home with a brief word of praise but no wiser about the success or failure of his endeavours.

The London evening papers operate at amazing speed. The wedding had started at 11.00 in the morning and he had served the pie about 2.15pm. The late editions of the evening papers – hitting the streets at about 5.00pm – had it all on the front page. 'Food poisoning at society event. Celebrities rushed to hospital'. It told of five guests being rushed to hospital from a society wedding with painful symptoms typical of food poisoning. Terrorist activity had not been ruled out. Amazingly, the report said, there had been no deaths and the victims were in a stable condition. Their names were given. The list included Prince Thaqib.

What could possibly have gone wrong? The truth hit Fred like a hammer blow. He had forgotten to retrieve the ten segments of pie! He grabbed the paper again and compared the list of sick guests with what he could remember of the names on the place cards. Yes! Those stricken had been on the same table as the Prince. Second helpings! That had been the cause. It was an excellent pie, and some Oliver Twist-like spark had asked for more. One of the other waiters – or an enterprising guest – had noticed the pie left on the shelf and served some of the remaining portions.

Failure! The Prince was still alive and unintended people had suffered. Fred was furious that he had so misjudged the type and quantity of the poison. And then it struck him how awful it would have been if he had got it right and those other four guests had died in agony. He had been saved from committing a dreadful crime. And he gained some satisfaction from knowing that the witchcraft part of the plan had worked perfectly. It was the physical element that had let him down. Being honest with himself, he had to confess that he had been careless. As soon as that slice of pie had been eaten and activated, his concentration had lapsed.

This story was one that Nshila must never hear.

Chapter Twenty-Six
Found Out

'You stupid, ignorant irresponsible young man.'

It was about twenty-four hours since the plane had touched down at Heathrow, and about twenty since Nshila had escaped from an airport beset by baggage-handler strikes, eco-demonstrators and anti-terrorist precautions. She had reached her flat in the late evening, been enthusiastically greeted by Rasputin and fallen exhausted into bed. The next day had been satisfactory, all the events of her absence having been dealt with correctly, and sometimes brilliantly, by Gillian and Peter. It was not the same when Fred Mbwele responded to her summons and knocked on the door at 6.30pm.

It took only fifteen minutes to get Fred started on the true story. She had the advantage of having seen him in the fire. It only needed the word 'pie' to tell Fred that she knew something, which meant that she might know more. How much more? When must he tell the truth, and when was it safe to lie?

He was no match for her, often making mention of people and things that invited new questions. He spoke of Abigail Fordcombe, and was asked why she had felt able to contact him. Why were they on such terms that she could ask him to act as a waiter? Fred had to admit that he had met her on Leeds station. What was he doing there? Nshila also remembered showing him how to use The Companion, and felt that Fred had probably been unable to resist a trial. She asked him about it, and Fred was scared of telling an outright lie. She was also aware that very few people – even honest ones – remember every detail of a story when asked to relate it. She felt quite safe in saying, 'You have not told me everything yet – have you? What about the bits you left out?'

Rasputin made it worse. He sat all the time on the radiator where the powder had been split, and glared at Fred without blinking.

So Nshila got the whole story, and gave judgement in the words

'You stupid, ignorant, irresponsible young man.'

She stared at him for a moment, making a big effort to control her temper. Then she said, 'I need a little time to think about this – what you've done and how to deal with you. Go out now and get me an Indian take-away from that place in Aldgate High Street, and two bottles of red wine. Get something for yourself, too – birdseed, maybe, and get a birdcage from that pet shop on the corner. You may be facing four weeks as a parrot, with Rasputin to watch you. Here's some money.'

Walking up Fenchurch Street, Fred's youthful optimism began to return. 'She can't be all that angry with me,' he reasoned, 'if she plans for us to eat and drink together. She's cooling down already. I'm sure she would hate the idea of a gutless unimaginative apprentice who sticks to the rules all the time. That's not how she operates herself. All that stuff about bird seed has got to be a joke. She's not going to turn me into a parrot.' Passing Aldgate Pump, he thought, 'I don't even think she has the skill to turn me into a parrot. I've never heard her talk about transformation. I don't think it's her scene at all.' He returned to Eastcheap with Nshila's Indian take-away, and the two bottles of wine, but no bird seed and no bird cage. Instead he had a monstrous spicy pizza for himself and a six-pack of their favourite lager and very little change.

The reception was not what he expected. Nshila had used the time to alter her image and create an intimidating environment. She was dressed all over in black and sat in a high-backed carver chair that looked almost like a throne. She had fixed the lighting so that she was largely in shadow, while bright light shone on a low cushion a few feet in front of her.

'Put the food in the oven and sit there.'

Without quite knowing why, Fred did so. Later, he tried to comfort himself by rationalising his behaviour. 'I stood no chance in direct confrontation,' he told himself. 'And it was true that I had fouled up. She had a right to tear strips off me.' He found it more difficult to admit that her appearance and attitude and demeanor made him afraid. He knew she was unpredictable, and there was a chance that he had gone too far in ignoring her instructions. She might – just might – be intending some serious harm. He had never seen her like this before and he felt psychologically overpowered.

When he sat on the cushion it was worse. He could see her only dimly against the unlit background. Her ebony skin colour and black clothing made it hard to pick out her form. But he could see the whites of her eyes and the flash of scarlet fingernails when she moved her hands. Sometimes she seemed to be unnaturally tall. He could tell when she moved, but what those movements were, and what she was doing, were impossible to pick out. He himself was isolated in a circle of bright light.

'Look into my eyes.'

'Keep looking.'

'Sit still.'

Fred could feel some force tampering with his mind. Was he being hypnotised? Was this how a rabbit felt when it was paralysed by the sight of a stoat? She spoke six words in a language unknown to Fred and then seemed to be crooning softly in a slow, sinister manner. Fred felt his limbs freezing up till he was unable to move. In both legs and feet he experienced vicious muscle cramp of the type that sometimes afflicts humans in the night. It was very painful. The usual human response is to move the afflicted limbs as much as possible, even getting out of bed to stand on the floor and hope that changes of position and temperature will cause the spasm to pass. Fred couldn't stir. Would it pass? When it happens naturally, there is a time limit – the muscles gradually relax and the pain passes. The mind knows what will happen and finds reassurance. This was not natural. It was happening because she willed it. The muscles would only relax when her will relaxed. Fred had a moment of panic.

Rasputin jumped off a chair and stalked between them to examine an empty food bowl. Nshila's concentration wavered and Fred felt a lessening of the pain. Good. The muscles were unfreezing. No – she had recovered. The pain returned. Worse than before, as if she was trying to make up for the momentary lapse.

It seemed to go on for ages, but the clock had moved on just five minutes. And then the pain was gone – not gradually as happens with muscle cramp, but suddenly as if somebody had thrown a switch. Fred was sweating all over. His shirt was damp and he was trembling and shivering. His legs felt weak. He thrust them out in front of him and allowed his body to fall back over the cushion so that he was arched over it. Then he sat up again. Nshila turned the lights on. The other-worldly atmosphere was gone. She was still a smart impressive woman, but she was smiling at him and there was no threat in the air. He could see a small tear in her skirt – presumably due to a fit of anger from Rasputin.

'Feed the cat, Fred, and then come back and make yourself comfortable. Don't worry. Nothing more is going to happen. Just don't forget the experience.'

Nothing was said. Nshila left the events to point the lesson. Instead, she took Fred through his activities while she had been away and helped him to recognise his mistakes.

'Don't ever attempt witchcraft for personal pleasure, Fred. There is always danger, and there are always side-effects. You set The Companion on Reverend Clutton for no better reason than revenge. You were lucky nothing went wrong. I must check some of the obvious points.

'Does anybody know what you did? Does Abigail know, for instance, or Peter or Gillian?'

'No. They know I came to the flat, but I'm sure they believed what I said about borrowing a book.'

'Did anybody see you entering or leaving the potting shed, or did you leave anything behind?'

'No.'

'Did Clutton catch even a glimpse of you? Since you could see him, he must have been able to see you.'

'No. I'm sure he never did. He was far too concerned with his own troubles to notice anything at all distant. If I had been beside him, he would have known, but I was at least a hundred yards away.'

'That's good news. Now for your attempt on the Prince. I can understand that you wanted to be helpful, and I can understand that the opportunity seemed to be heaven-sent. I don't condemn you, for intelligent rule-breaking. After all, I have broken rules happily enough myself. But your effort was truly extreme. I never told you to have a go at the Prince. I am not yet even bound to the contract, and I could still refuse it. Do you understand?'

'Yes. I've got that.'

'Now, there are times when we want it known that witchcraft has been or will be practised – usually in order to create fear. There are other times when we want it to leave no trace, so that observers treat what has happened as an accident. Your efforts left five people in hospital. There must have been some sort of investigation, and if that turned up the fact that a casual substitute waiter had left early, then people would be looking for him. They would get your name from Abigail. Do you know what happened?'

'Yes, I do. Abigail told me when she rang up to thank me for my help. The caterers were successful in hushing it up and avoiding an official enquiry. They cooked up a story about the jug of cream on that table being filled from a batch that was past its sell-by date. They worked very hard to pacify the sufferers and made some un-refusable offers of compensation – like catering free for a private dinner party in the home. They got away with it.'

'You have a lot to be grateful for, Fred. Last point, can you tell me where you made your biggest mistake?'

'Leaving the pie behind to be found. That must be it. I should have made sure nobody except the Prince could eat it. I could hardly have walked out with it, but I could have accidentally dropped it on the floor and put my foot in it. I can't understand why I forgot to go back for it.'

'Good. That's enough, now.'

Fred opened the door and was almost through it before he remembered the magical discs. He hesitated and tuned back. He had come clean about his more dangerous adventures. It was a good moment to clear the slate completely.

'Nshila, while I was in here looking for the powder something very weird happened to me.'

'I think I've heard enough craziness. Have I got to put up with more?'

'This was not something of my doing. It was quite innocent.'
'Go on.'
'You had left a pile of clear round discs in an ashtray. I wondered what they were and I picked one up. It was in my hand while I went into your kitchen to get a beer out of your fridge. As I opened the door, it fell out of my hand onto the floor, and it had changed. It was not transparent any more. It was opaque, and dark red in colour. And it melted. It was amazing. I was standing there with the bottle of beer in my hand, staring at this disc, and then it dissolved in front of my eyes. There was a pool of water for an instant and then it evaporated. Nothing else happened, as far as I could see. Do you know what it was?'
'Sit down and wait.'
Nshila took a large file from a bookshelf, sat back in her chair and leafed through it. Fred sat quietly, but felt the pressure building up as five minutes extended to ten, and then fifteen. At intervals he made impatient noises; every time she responded with 'keep quiet' gestures. Finally, she spoke. Fred sensed that she had been disturbed by what she had read.
'Those discs were sent to me by a god – I didn't know at the time what they were or what I would have to do with them. They didn't seem to connect with anything I knew. I thought I had better do nothing till some message came – which explains why I left them out so carelessly.'
'What are they, then? Tell me, please.'
'In this file I have copied and pasted passages from the oldest known texts on witchcraft and magic. When you told me how your disc behaved, it rang a bell for me. I have read about these things, and been told more, but I have never actually seen one or handled one. In my mind I had formed an image about what they might look like, but that image turns out to be quite wrong. That's why I have never recognized them till now. They are not African in origin, though they are known and used there. They come from Northern Germany and the Baltic States and Scandinavia. I imagined them as being made out of wood – like a section through a branch of a tree. When I was given these I just thought, "Computer discs" and

my mind ran along that track. Fred, what was uppermost in your mind when this happened?'

'That's easy. I was thinking of a cold lager as a reward for a job well done. I was visualising the toggle coming off the can and imagining the feel of the liquid as I swallowed half the can in one go.'

'Yes, that fits. These are finding discs. Their oldest known use was to seek out a victim in his hiding place. Witchcraft was often independent of physical contact and once the rituals had been performed the victim died anyway. But there were some cases when the predator wanted to be present at the end and the victim hoped to escape by hiding. A finding disc like this allowed the practitioner to follow a trail and uncover the victim. It never failed. If his enemy had one of these the victim was helpless.'

'That's a very different situation from uncovering a beer in your fridge.'

'It is. But the tools of our trade are flexible, and maybe the principles operating here were similar. You wanted a beer and the image of the can was clear in your mind. The disc picked up that image and led you to the thing you sought. It probably changed colour gradually as you moved to the kitchen. You didn't notice, because you knew where the beer was and you didn't need to be led to it.'

'That's pretty useful. No more looking for things like insurance certificates and railway tickets and business cards that you can't find.'

'Useful, Fred, Yes. But don't let thoughts of trivial uses drive the nastiness from your mind. Just imagine a victim shivering in his dark, damp hiding place, and knowing that the disc was bringing his killer nearer and nearer.'

She turned back to the file and read more.

'There's worse yet. It seems that if the user had sufficient mental power, the victim could not only be found by the disk, but killed by it. The moment his last defense was stripped away, the disc dissolved and the life force in the victim dissolved too. No blood – no wounds – no screaming. Just the instant shutting down of all physical activity. This is nasty stuff.'

'Yes. But none of that makes the things evil in themselves, does it? The world is full of things that can be used for good or bad purposes. And you're not going to make evil use of these discs, are you?'

'No, I'm not. I know now why I was given these discs, and why I didn't recognise them. My purpose, I promise you, is wholly beneficial. You and I are going to take these discs and have a little treasure hunt out in the country, Fred. This last chapter of your adventures has been useful.'

Chapter Twenty-Seven

Rowan Hall Again

As the light faded, Nshila walked Fred around Rowan Hall. Unoccupied for years, it contained only items that had been forgotten or rejected by the last owners, or were too heavy to move, or were built-in or were broken. There was a huge, rough oak table in the dining room, and three cheap, unmatched chairs in the main bedroom, and an assortment of brooms, mops and garden tools. There was dust everywhere, and old newspapers lay in corners. Some windows were broken.

She explained what they were there to do. It took a long time, because she had never told Fred about her interest in the place. The story of Edwina Awford and her search seemed irrelevant to him.

'Why are we doing it at all? Why does it matter to us whether Edwina finds whatever it is? I'm sorry for the woman, of course, but she's not our responsibility. Surely we ought to be concentrating on Prince Thaqib? You don't seem to have made any plan for eliminating him, and time is running out.'

'I want to buy this house, Fred. I think it's the most beautiful building I've seen in this country. I want to buy it and live here. Being a witchdoctor doesn't stop me being a woman, and giving way to fancies now and again.'

'What? Are you going to commute into London every day from Reading?'

'No. It will take ages to renovate the place, and even when it's done I will still live most of the time in Eastcheap. But I'll spend some weekends here, and one day I'll retire and live here in peace and luxury.'

'What was that?' Fred was shocked by a sound from the back of the house. A door had slammed, and was followed by bumps and scraping noises.

'She's just come in from the garden,' said Nshila. 'Those noises came from the garden tools as she put them in place behind the door of the porch. She doesn't always put them in the same place relative to each other. Sometimes you'll find the spade to the right of the rake, and sometimes the other way round.'

'I get it, now. You don't want to share the house with her. You want to help her find whatever it is so that she'll leave, and go wherever her husband has gone.'

'That's right.'

'But you're into witchcraft and magic yourself. Don't you want to make friends with her? Don't you think you might learn from each other? Surely it would be fun to co-habit?'

'Idiot! Every woman wants to be mistress in her own house. You can't feel in charge if somebody else is making free with the place.'

'So you want to dispossess her?'

'I suppose so. But she wants to go. I feel great sympathy for her – forever searching for something she can't find, and unable to leave without it. She desperately wants to move on. I can feel it.'

Nshila had brought two canvas chairs with her, and a folding table. She got Fred to set them up in the kitchen, and placed a small camping stove on top of the old cast iron cooking range that was still built into the wall. She fetched water from a butt outside the window and made tea. Then they sat opposite each other and she went into the details.

'I got the idea as soon as you told me of your adventure with the discs. Maybe, just maybe, they can help us locate what Edwina is after. We have to picture a range of items that might be the right one, and walk about with a disc in our hand, watching for a change of colour.'

'Surely it's very hit-and-miss? How can we guess what it is? And the disc dissolves and disappears. How many of them have we got?'

'Eleven. There used to be twelve, but you used one up looking for a beer. But they don't dissolve and disappear unless they have "found". So if we picture an object, and there is nothing like it anywhere in the house, then the disc won't "find" and we shall still have it. The house is empty and there can't be that many things hidden in odd corners.'

'That still leaves us thinking of a wide range of items.'

'Quite true. But we have a few clues. It has to be the sort of thing that would remind a woman powerfully of her dead husband. We're going to make a list of possible items and try them out one by one.'

'Are you going to be any use at that? I mean, you've never had a husband and never been widowed. And it could be anything. Suppose it was something they bought on a special occasion and it reminded them both of how much they loved each other? We could be looking for anything from a casino pass to a china dog.'

'Don't make so many difficulties. Between us we can imagine a range of things that might have the necessary sentimental value. And big items like a china dog are out – they would have been found long ago. It has to be small and easy to lose.'

'Or get thrown away by accident.'

'Stop it. You're not being helpful. We must each make a list of possible items, and compare them.'

They were interrupted by a loud gurgling noise that seemed to come from directly overhead. 'Bath water,' said Nshila as she recovered herself.

'I don't understand,' Fred said. 'There's no water connected to the house. How can Edwina take a bath? How can she make physical noises out of nothing and at the same time move physical objects like those garden tools. Surely she has to be a spirit or a physical entity? One or the other? How can she be both? And if she's living here, why don't we hear every movement she makes? What we actually hear is intermittent. And could she appear to us if she wanted?'

Nshila was getting annoyed. She wanted to get on with the project, not answer endless questions.

'I don't know. This sort of thing is outside my field. But there's nothing in the history to suggest malignancy. I very much doubt if she's going to play tricks on us, or start throwing things. Let's get on with the list.' In a few minutes they had fourteen 'possibles';

Cufflinks
Document or letter
Tie pin
Postage stamp
Credit card
Photograph
Coin
Letter opener
Nail file
Key
Regimental cap badge
Identity disc
Banknote
Medal

There were interruptions while they compiled it Doors were shut. Steps were heard on the stairs. Curtains were drawn back upstairs as if somebody liked to sleep with moon and stars for company. Gradually the noises ceased.

They separated the list into 'likely' and 'unlikely', judging that mundane things like 'Tie Pin' and 'Cufflinks', though easy to lose, were not likely to have the necessary romantic element. The 'likely' list was headed by 'Document' and 'Photograph'. They argued over

Banknote
Coin
Medal
Identity disc
Regimental badge
Key

Nshila was keen to cut things out. Fred was different. He imagined all sorts of strange associations, offering imaginative examples.

'Suppose they were in a foreign country and saw some wonderful object that they both wanted. They added up the local currency in their pockets and found that there would be just one tiny foreign banknote left. They reached their hotel starving, but they still had that single banknote. It became a talisman for them. And how about a key? They might talk about each having the key to the other's heart.'

She agreed that people did fix on the strangest things as tokens and reminders, but she was convinced that they must go for the normal and the probable first. 'We must go for the obvious before checking out the bizarre.'

The house was almost empty and there was no point in thinking that items might be 'behind' something or 'underneath' something or 'inside' something – the 'somethings' were not there. They had also assumed that Edwina would have searched the few fittings that remained, however unlikely they might be. She would have checked that no document had been used to patch one of the light-shades that still hung forlornly on leads in one or two rooms. She would have pulled out the drawers of the old oak table to make sure that nothing had been pushed over the back of a drawer and become trapped behind it. She would have taken out the old newspapers used to line clothes drawers to see that there was nothing underneath them. She would have poked inside the sockets beside the fireplace in the reception rooms – the sockets that had once held rods and wires that rang bells in the kitchen.

They were looking for things that might have slipped into a gap, or fallen down a small hole, or dropped from a person's clothing during a DIY job and been walled up behind a skirting board or floorboard. Such items were certain to be invisible. Only the search-discs gave them an advantage. Fred made another objection.

'If we find something, how will we know whether it is the thing Edwina values? We might find half-a-dozen items – and one of them the special one – and never know it.'

'I don't have all the answers, Fred. It could turn out as you suggest. But I'm hoping that Edwina will react. Anyway, we're not stopping now.'

'If she does react, will we feel her beside us, or see something?'

'I don't know – don't know – don't know. How many times have I got to tell you? Maybe you will feel her emotions and I won't. Or maybe the other way round.'

It was one of those experiences that defy planning. Actions that seem simple have unexpected complications. For instance, the discs discovered three locations, revealing five coins of different denominations and different currencies, but none of them could be thought of as a person's treasured possession or fetish. 'If we found a Spanish Doubloon then it might qualify,' said Fred, 'but this mix of Dollars and Francs and Roubles is useless!'

'And three of our precious discs have dissolved. Eight left. We have to be more selective. Any ideas, Fred?'

'Yes. Let's eliminate some of the items less likely to be lost. If we guess right, and they don't exist, then the disc won't dissolve and the items left to check will have been reduced. Think about a medal that Ned might have won in battle. Edwina might well be fixated upon it, but because it's a precious thing it's likely to be kept in a secure place and not lost.'

They tried Medal. They found a silver medal labeled 'Mixed Doubles, Eastbourne 1999' lodged under the wainscot in the dining room. The date put it long after Edwina's death and therefore useless. Seven discs left. Fred made another suggestion.

'We are getting down to Document and Photograph. Both of them are common items and we might get more than one. If, say, we go for Document and find one that's useless, and lose one of our seven discs, are we going to try Document again or not?'

'Maybe we can use the discs better,' said Nshila. 'Till now, we have followed the direction that made it grow redder, going all the way till it dissolved. Suppose that we note the direction but then move on to another part of the house to see if there are other leads? Then the disc won't "find" and we can still work with it.'

It worked, but it brought new problems. They tried with Document. They got four 'indications' but lost a disc. It seemed that the disc didn't always wait till a human hand was on the object. It was apt to dissolve prematurely. That happened with a document that had been used to cover up an airbrick low down in the wall of the kitchen. Obviously there had been a draught from it and somebody had glued a piece of parchment over it, and painted it. Their 'Document' was a page torn from a garden centre catalogue. They ought to have rejected that lead because the parchment had clearly been used deliberately. But Fred went too close, and the disc in his hand dissolved. Six left.

They tried the second 'Document' lead and encountered the dreaded problem of an item that had slipped too far. Between floorboards, a corner of white paper was visible. The eyebrow tweezers from Nshila's handbag gripped a corner but only tore it off. Nshila was angry at her carelessness. Fred suddenly stood upright and froze.

'She's here!'

'What do you mean?'

'Edwina. For a second or two some other person's thought was mixed with mine. It was extraordinary.'

'Were they friendly thoughts or angry thoughts?'

'Friendly, I think. They were supportive of our efforts and willing us to succeed. Rather like somebody who has given up hope and suddenly gets a new suggestion from a friend.'

'Let's go on then. You had better get this floorboard up.

They managed it, but found only a 'flyer' to advertise a Mediterranean cruise. It was most frustrating. Five left.

Nshila made a decision, 'We still have two leads on 'Document'. We're going to leave them for the moment and try with 'Photograph', taking great care not to let a disc get too red. Then we'll review all the leads, trying to pin-point the locations and assess their probability.'

They did it. But they lost another disc when Fred was startled by the noise of the lavatory cistern flushing. 'Blast you, Edwina!' he exclaimed, dropping a disc onto the top of the oak table where it turned red and dissolved. Looking under the table, they found a pornographic photograph stuck to the underside with blue-tack. Somebody had been trying to conceal his interests. Four discs left.

But they had two leads on Photograph to add to the two on 'Document'. One of each was in the main bedroom. The second

'Document' lead was in what seemed to have been a Games Room and the second 'Photograph' one was in the Drawing Room. Cracks between the floorboards in the bedroom yielded a bill from a long-dead local dressmaker and – a most exciting find – a love-letter beginning 'Darling Edwina'. 'This has to be what we want,' exclaimed Fred.

But as they read it, hope faded. The letter contained endearments from time to time, but mostly dealt with building work on an outhouse that Ned wanted Edwina to commission from a contractor. It was hardly a letter that a woman would keep close to her heart.

They passed to the two leads to 'Photographs'. One, the disc had suggested, was in the downstairs toilet, where hiding places were limited. Poking around behind the cistern dislodged a picture of a wire-haired terrier. Not what they were seeking. The other lead suggested the dining room, but neither Nshila nor Fred could see any place where they had not already searched. They risked another disc. Nshila held it, both of them focused their minds intensely on the concept of 'Photograph' and both moved together, holding hands, round the room. To an observer they would have appeared ridiculous. But to the left of the window the disc began to glow red.

Yet there was nothing to be seen. The wallpaper was flat, without joins or any suspicious bulge. What had gone wrong?

Suddenly Fred spotted a faint vertical line beside the windows. He pointed it out. 'Shutters,' gasped Nshila.

'What do you mean?'

'At one time it was common to cover windows overnight with wooden shutters. These were inside the glass, and when not in use they folded back into a recess so that they lay flat against the wall. That's what we have got here. They have been painted over several times and covered with wallpaper as well so that they are almost invisible. Get a knife from somewhere and open them out.'

'She's here again. I can feel her. She's urging us on. We are winning.'

It took them fifteen minutes to break through the layers of paint and wrench open the shutters. A photograph fell out. Fred grabbed it and held it up.

It showed a young man in military uniform standing proudly in front of an older man – a man in a more ornate uniform with masses of gold on his chest and shoulders and cap. This older man was pinning a medal on the younger man's chest. This time they must surely have found it. This was what Edwina had searched for all these years. On the back was written 'My darling Ned and the Lord Lieutenant.'

They had little time to look at it. Fred had certainly had no experience like the one that followed. Even to Nshila it had a novel quality. A haze seemed to develop around them, as if a cloud was forming with themselves at its centre. The photograph grew misty and they saw it for a moment as if through tinted glass: grey glass, or light blue. They were holding the photograph between them, each with one hand on it. Yet it moved. They felt it taken from their fingers and moved slightly away from them as if it was being examined by somebody with longer sight. Their hands were frozen in the position they had used to hold the photograph, but the thing itself was six inches beyond their hands – and quite steady.

Two more things happened. The photograph dissolved. It happened slowly and steadily, beginning at the edges. Little by little it disappeared until there was nothing left. They heard a faint sigh, and an intense feeling of relief, exaltation and joy engulfed them both. It was so strong that it had a physical effect, bringing them close to tears and unable to speak for fear of emotional breakdown. It reminded Fred of the moment when he read the notification of his degree. It reminded Nshila of the feelings she experienced when sinking into a hot bath full of scented foam. Both of them were briefly but intensely happy.

And the house was silent in a way it had never been before. It felt friendly and restful. They sat on the floor in the dining room, their backs propped against the wall, and slept till morning.

That same morning, Nshila put in an offer for Rowan Hall. Before the day was over, it had been accepted.

Chapter Twenty-Eight
A Sideline

Nshila was seriously pleased with herself about the perceived success of the Anacanda mission. All her friends heard about it, though the version differed depending on how much they were aware of her occult practices. Reactions also varied. Gillian was absolutely delighted by knowing that it would bring economic benefit to an under-privileged people. Her Pakistani husband took a more cynical view and asked who was going to make money out of it. Fred Mbwele saw it only as a means to further the Thaqib contract.

'Now the peerage business is settled, and Edwina has gone wherever Ned went to, we can get on with killing the Prince. How are we going to do it? I've got a few ideas.'

'Calm down, Fred. For a start, the peerage business is not finally settled. The client needs some indication from Anacanda that our proposal has been accepted, and that they will speak appropriately to their megalomaniac neighbour. And I won't be bounced into hasty action by somebody who has the patience of a butterfly.'

Put in his place, Fred felt a need for sympathetic company and decided that Reverend Abigail was his best bet. They had always found it easy to talk, discovering that their wildly different views never provoked conflict. It was as if the strategies each adopted were utterly irrelevant to the other and could be examined academically. It was a Friday morning when Fred found Abigail closing off her counselling session in Fig Tree House, the curiously-named building in which much parish business was conducted.

'Good to see you, Fred. Will you just run an errand for me, while I freshen up? Then we'll have an alcoholic lunch together and you can give me some ideas for my sermon on Sunday.'

'Yes. What must I do?'

Abigail gave him a large bunch of keys, picking out the longest one. She pointed through a window towards the church itself, and a small door set at ground level.

'That's the door to the crypt. I'm responsible for looking after it and nobody else ever goes there. At the moment the door is unlocked. Go down the steps and you'll find yourself in a tiny hall with three doors. There is a label hooked onto one of them. It says WC, and this key fits the door.'

'WC? Really?'

'It's a tiny joke started by my boss, Canon Orberry. The WC just means Wine Cellar. He moves in some pretty exalted circles and when he entertains he offers the very best. But he likes to conceal his stocks, to avoid being seen as rich and privileged. The WC notice is to discourage investigation – in that location people are going to expect the other thing - and vile and dirty as well. They won't even try the door. He told me to bring up five bottles of Chateau Vassar '85 and I have forgotten. You can do it for me.'

Twenty minutes later, they were sitting in the restaurant section of the Admiral Benbow and the five bottles were in a supermarket carrier bag under the table. Abigail – off duty till Sunday morning – was fresh and cheerful in plain clothes, but annoyed that Fred had gone quiet and thoughtful.

'What's bugging you, Fred?'

'That crypt. It was dark, and I dropped your bunch of keys so that I was unsure which one I needed. And the WC notice had fallen down. I didn't know which key to try or which door to try it in. Anyway, I opened the wrong door first.'

'Which one?'

'The middle one.'

'There's no light in there. I don't suppose you could see anything at all, could you? Black as night, I expect. So you tried another door, right? And you blanked out whatever you had seen, right? You wiped it from your memory?'

Abigail felt she had hinted clearly enough that Fred should forget whatever he had seen. But Fred was not firing on all cylinders: he failed to pick up the hint.

'My eyes had become accustomed to the gloom, and I saw some

pretty weird things. There were some chains hanging from the walls, and a slab of wood that looked like the top part of a pillory, and a schoolmaster's cane. In the corner was a wooden frame that looked like the rack they used to torture Guy Fawkes.'

Abigail stared hard at Fred. She had no innocent explanation ready. She had taken just enough alcohol to be careless, and she felt just enough trust in Fred to tell the truth. It might be better, anyway, than fabricating an unlikely story.

'We are both a bit unscrupulous, Fred. Right? We have different objectives and different methods but we don't let conventions stand in our way. I'm quite sure you are into the black arts – magic and spells and the supernatural: it was obvious enough from the questions you were asking up at Hedgewood. What do you think are my main weapons?'

'Sex, of course. That's no mystery. A girl with your face and figure and come-hither attitude can have any man she wants. While she has them they do her bidding because they want to please her. When she's tired of them they do it out of fear. And because they are afraid of being blackmailed. I've nothing against that, Abby, and I feel sure you can get your bishopric.'

'There's another way, Fred. The people I want on my side are powerful men, and powerful men sometimes find release and relaxation in the opposite experience: the experience of submission.'

Fred gaped – and caught up fast. In his explorations of the internet he had stumbled on sites that linked what he had seen in the crypt with what Abigail was saying. He grabbed some tissues from Abigail's handbag and mopped up the beer he had spilt in his agitation.

'You do things to them! Restrain them! Hurt them! Punish them! And they like it! Pay money for it! You're one of those people who advertise themselves on websites wearing thigh-high boots and fishnet stockings and wielding a whip!'

'Not quite, Fred. Nobody pays me. I don't advertise. But there are men in high places who have a deep psychological need for that sort of thing. It's the only way they can escape from the constant burden of being the one in charge.'

'Surely you can't get that many such people?'

'I don't need many.'

Fred worked on the idea, pondering the angles.

'I suppose it's better than sex as a threat to hold over people.'

'Certainly. In these liberal times even clergymen are likely to own up to past sexual misdemeanours. The brave ones will say "Publicise it all! See if I care! It just makes me look human." The other thing is better. No Dean of a cathedral would want seriously humiliating pictures appearing in the tabloids.'

'Surely they don't pose for you!'

'No, Fred, but I have good technology. I have one or two concealed cameras that feed digital images straight into my computer. Then it's all on the hard disc. Everybody in the business does it, but actual use of the material is extremely rare. I have a couple of Archdeacons in the records, but I don't suppose I shall ever look at the pics again. You'll be there now, of course, but only as a figure peering in through the doorway. Opening the door triggers the recording.'

A memory of his own adventure at Hedgewood came back to Fred.

'I found some gear hidden away in the old potting shed. A dog collar – dog, not clerical – and a length of chain, and a riding crop. Were they yours? Were you into that scene already?'

'Beginning. Early on, I was focused on sex, as you suggested. But one of the strange visitors the principal imported was a young RC priest who was struggling with the idea of celibacy. He had a book that described methods of "mortifying the flesh" and I borrowed it from him. It was pretty extreme. One day I surprised him having a go at flagellation. I hate to see things done badly, and I said "I could do that a lot better for you than you can do it yourself." He handed over the birch twigs and I took a few swipes.'

'What happened?'

'He yelled a bit and danced about. Afterwards he said that he had never felt cleansed of sin to quite the same degree. He asked me to do it again, and I rather enjoyed it. The experience got me thinking. Don't imagine I have given up sex – it's too much fun – but this works even better.'

'Are you going to get serious about that sort of thing?'

'No more than I am now. It can get expensive and it can become hard to conceal. I'm never going to be more than a GP.'

'General Practitioner? What on earth do you mean?'

'Look, Fred, men who want that sort of thing have varied, specialised, kinky tastes. For every such taste there is a specialist somewhere. I refer men to the appropriate specialist. It needs care and good judgement. I'm still learning.'

'How is that? Surely a specialist is glad to have clients pointed his way – or her way – since I suppose these specialists are all women. It must mean good money. I mean, if a medical GP refers a patient to a hospital the hospital doesn't turn down the case.'

'It might do, Fred, if the case demanded some special, sophisticated and expensive piece of equipment that they didn't possess. Remember that these people I am talking about are individuals with a limited budget and equipment shortage can be a serious problem. They don't want clients referred to them for a service they can't provide. And there are issues of security and confidentiality, too. I need to get known as a person who makes reliable judgements and is always discrete. It takes time.

Abigail could see from Fred's expression that he was shocked. A counter-attack was in order.

'This won't come between us, will it? Anyway, what were you doing in that potting shed? Why were you interested in the equipment I left there?'

'First question – No. I am just amazed at your range of interests. Second question – Pass. I would like to tell you, but my boss would be against it.'

'This boss you speak about. She must be quite impressive. I would like to meet her.'

Chapter Twenty-Nine
Celebratory Dinner

News came from Anacanda. Good news. The British proposal had been accepted, and in their next meeting with their neighbouring state they would advance the British cause. A small dinner party was arranged at The Savoy to celebrate success. Conversations were at times confused, because different people had different levels of knowledge. There was a cast of seven.

Sir Gilbert Griffick, KCMG, knew almost nothing. He was Her Majesty's Secretary of State for Third World Relations and was present to show that the success of the mission had been noticed at the highest level. His presence made sure that the food and drink were of the highest quality.

Maurice Heckmanfield was the Permanent Secretary to the Ministry. He was the one who had conceived the project – deeming the objective a good one, and achievable. He had chosen Miles Strang as the leader of the mission but had given in to persuasion when Simon Trent recommended Nshila Ileloka as a political appointee. Maurice suspected that Simon had a personal motive and would gain from Nshila's appointment. But he had met Nshila before the mission departed, so he knew her personally and knew of her legitimate achievements. He had decided that she was very suitable for the job and that Trent's motives hardly mattered.

Miles Strang. The most senior civil servant on the mission team. He had worked closely with Nshila on all aspects of the mission that did not involve the supernatural. He had come to like and respect her, but was still unable to work out how she had succeeded. The strategies he had discussed with her did not seem powerful enough to have got those results. Some other force, he believed, must have been at work.

Simon Trent, junior minister in another department. Well known and often feared as a political fixer. Simon was the only person present who knew that Nshila was to benefit by a seat in The House of Lords, and that this benefit was to come to her (he hoped) as an unexpected and anonymous gift from an assassin. Simon was also the only worried person present. He was worried because the assassination had still to be completed, and because a problem had arisen in regard to the peerage. He had a need to communicate with the assassin and was faced with the usual sequence of delays and cut-outs. He was quite unaware that the assassin was sitting at the table with him.

Solomon Kubaka – Anacadian Ambassador to Great Britain. He was the one who had delivered the good news. He was a jovial, expansive character who liked people around him to be happy. He knew almost nothing about the project, but his government had seen it as a good deal; and that was enough for Solomon.

Araminta Kubaka. She was Solomon's wife and had recently arrived in the country. Maurice Heckmanfield had been keen to include her because he felt Nshila might be embarrassed if she were the only woman in the party. Araminta was descended from Portuguese traders and was several shades lighter in colour than her husband. She was a large woman, dressed in very bright colours and loaded with expensive jewellery. Her prime objective, it appeared, was to collect invitations to hospitality suites at major English sporting events. There was immediate rapport between Araminta and Nshila, the latter finding her directness and ebullience attractive.

Nshila Ileloka – the unofficial guest of honour. She was the only one fully aware of how success had been achieved. She was almost certain that Simon Trent was her client and was grateful that her previous meeting with him had been undertaken in the safety of her aunt-like disguise. She sensed a level of concern in Simon and knew that problems with the contract might be a cause – but clearly she could take no action immediately. She loved Araminta and resolved to mobilise Mike Fanshawe on her behalf. Mike would be able to get her some invitations.

Understandably, the conversation was guarded and dwelt on issues of general public interest. But the food and the wine were excellent and they all enjoyed themselves.

Chapter Thirty

Simon's Problem

The day after the celebratory dinner Simon Trent slept late. It was partly due to drinking more than usual, which he had done to divert his thoughts. Crawling out of bed, he opened the window and was disappointed to find a dull, overcast day with the wind in the wrong direction. He could hear nothing from the zoo.

Simon sought to compensate for his modest physique by a fit and healthy image. He had a cycling machine in his flat, and a rowing machine and a treadmill and a set of weights. Frequently, two cups of tea and an exercise session and a cold shower would drive away depression. It worked, but worked less well than usual. He lit a cigarette – in defiance of the Minister of Health (whom he hated) – and reviewed his options.

The crisis had two elements – time and restricted numbers. Unfortunate revelations about a man recently elevated to the peerage had drawn public attention to the subject and one of those already on the next list also had a very dubious past. An edict had been issued that the current honours list must be decided quickly, and must not be too long. The message was, "Let's get this over with the minimum of public attention". Simon had to tell the assassin that he must deliver on the contract earlier than expected. Further, his ability to manipulate appointments was reduced and the place he had mentally designated for Nshila Ileloka was being contested. The supporters of Graham Schwarz were pressing his claim hard.

Who was Graham Schwarz? Simon asked himself the question angrily. Schwarz had made an awful lot of money from a fishing fleet; a fleet that used environmentally disastrous methods to gather huge catches. They also had little respect for the fishing limits of other countries and had been prosecuted many times. When that happened, Schwarz made it clear that the fault lay with the captain of the vessel concerned and was a contravention of his company policy. The company paid any fines imposed with a flourish of righteousness and the captain lost his job and his pension. Most of this was unknown to the public due to the Schwarz public relations machine. The public went on eating Schwarz Superb Seafood in happy ignorance. It wasn't very good, and the labelling on the tins held a few clues. But the labelling was in the smallest print and there was a great deal of it. Most people gave up trying to read it.

Business friends of Schwarz believed that morality was an unsatisfactory quality, militating against commercial success. They admired the fact that his public relations machine worked so well. It had successfully concealed the fact that his two divorced wives had received niggardly settlements. Any misdemeanours they had committed in response to his treatment were exaggerated, while immoral and illegal activities by Schwarz himself were concealed. He was charming to his friends, but if one of them should fall from favour he found a vicious enemy.

Schwarz was also an art lover, believing art to be a good investment and a source of prestige. He had a valuable collection of old masters and contemporary celebrities. Like all seekers after honours, he had made huge gifts to the political party of his choice. He had also given a valuable painting to the National Gallery and topped up – by a huge amount – the appeal launched to stop The Bridge Into Eden going to America. He had friends in high places.

The people pressing for Schwarz were arguing that the activity for which Nshila Ileloka was to be rewarded had taken place only recently. They did not attempt to deny her worthiness, but they said that more research was needed. In most cases, they argued, extensive enquiries would be made about the background and antecedents of a nominee. Had there been time for such enquiries? She could be included in the next honours list, they pointed out. And the activities for which their candidate was nominated had taken place earlier. He was already a public figure. And he looked right, physically, having a dignified image that made people see him as upright and responsible.

Simon reluctantly accepted that he would have to make contact once more with the assassin. The procedure had been slightly simplified since the affair began, but there was a fixed time-window within which he had to ring a certain mobile number. The window was from 3.15pm to 4.30pm. He remembered that he was expecting a lunch-time visit from Rodney Bezzle, who was the most powerful of the Schwarz supporters. It would be better, he thought, to avoid that meeting. Rodney was off on a lengthy fact-finding mission to Las Vegas, which meant that a new meeting could not be scheduled quickly. He would have more time to muster anti-Schwarz arguments. And his plotting would not be confused by extra pressure.

Simon phoned in sick, reflecting on the many times he had made his mother do it in order to avoid some lesson for which he was ill-prepared or some pointless and probably painful activity on the sports field. He fell asleep for several hours over a thriller and woke at 4.20pm. He grabbed for the phone.

Chapter Thirty-One

Fred Tries Again

Simon Trent's call was relayed to Nshila by Jessop on the dedicated secure line – the one with voice modification. She learnt that the Prince must be dealt with fairly quickly. She pointed out that death could happen after the announcement of the peerage just as well as before, but the response was negative. Simon insisted that she deliver on the contract first. She was not really surprised. She also learnt that Simon was having problems with the peerage nomination.

Nshila was not greatly worried. All along she had sensed hesitancy in the client and had restrained herself from total commitment. If the client was unable to meet his obligation then she was under none to make the hit, nor take the risks involved. The deal would collapse, but the client would still be in debt to her for her success in Anacanda. She decided that she would tell Fred about both the new time schedule and about her doubts. He would be disappointed.

But when they next met, another matter took precedence. It was a grey, overcast Saturday afternoon and her favourite rugby team had just lost their match. She was surprised when the office bell sounded – the cow bell. Normally she got no unexpected callers at the weekend because nobody expected the office to be open, and there was no bell-push linked to her flat. Sometimes people called by phone to set up a visit, but unexpected calls were few. She only heard the cow bell because the caller was vigorous and insistent. Her mind said, 'Young, eager, enthusiastic, inconsiderate. It has to be Fred.' Resigned, she let him in.

'I've had a dream!'

'Amazing! And I suppose it's so important that you have to rush round here and tell me!'

'Yes. You'll agree, I know. It's about the tin you recovered from the hut, that night at the village. You never told me what you found in it, but I know you use it now for household objects like pens and keys and hanks of string and library tickets and expired credit cards and data sticks – things you seldom want but won't throw away. I have seen you searching in it, even tipping it out to find the item you want.'

'This is accurate but boring.'

'The next bit won't bore you. In my dream I saw that the bottom of the tin was actually a piece of paper. It was a dirty white, and stained brown in places, and cut exactly to the size of the tin. It could easily be mistaken for the tin itself, or make you think it was just a lining to stop the bottom of the tin from rusting. In my dream, I knew – I was absolutely certain – that there was something vital on the other side of that paper.'

'And was there?'

'I don't know. I was just reaching in to get my finger underneath a corner, and I woke up.'

'So you've come round here on a Saturday evening because you think I'm so careless that I failed to explore that tin thoroughly? Honestly, Fred, I didn't get where I am now by making mistakes like that!'

'Sorry – sorry – sorry. But people do overlook things. The contents of the tin must have been pretty exciting. Surely it's just possible you failed to notice the paper on the bottom?'

She thought the idea was stupid. But she humoured him. Sure enough, the bottom of the tin was indeed covered by a tired piece of paper and it did fit the tin exactly, and it was easy to mistake it for the metal of the bottom. She had done so. In fact she had to put her glasses on now to see it. 'After all,' she thought, 'I'm in my thirties.'

With great care she lifted the paper out and turned it over. Crash! Fred knocked over a chair as he recoiled from the table where they were working. Nshila herself was shocked, and stepped backwards under the impact. Faded, the image was, but unmistakeably it showed a terrifying airborne devil that seemed to be rushing towards them with malignant intent. Neither of them could quite define what was so frightening about it – what artistic trick had been used to make it so lively and so mobile and so evil – but there was no doubt of the effect.

'I know what this is, Fred. And your dream was right. I wonder why it was sent to you. This is the second time you have brought me a gift.'

'What is it?'

'It's Kwaname's own original of The Culler.'

'Who is The Culler and what do you mean by "original"?'

She told him the legend, just as she had heard it long ago in the hut under the baobab tree. How, in the early history of humanity, The Culler had formed a liking for a particular witchdoctor: a man of unique skill. He gave that practitioner a picture of himself and explained that correct copies could be used to persecute any victim provided two conditions were met. First, the victim must have taken the image into his possession, knowingly or unknowingly. Second, The Culler had to be activated at a particular moment. This was done by a symbol, drawn on the back of the paper. Nshila illustrated the idea.

'Suppose I had a good version of The Culler, drew a small picture of an ambulance on the back, and managed to get this into the possession of the victim. Then, the next time the victim saw an ambulance, The Culler would materialise in the air behind him, inspire the most unbearable fear, and drive the victim to disaster. Most witchdoctors planted The Culler on their victim by concealing the image within a gift.'

'Give me another illustration.'

'Well in English villages where the street frontage is all built up, it sometimes happens that new houses are built behind them. The access to those houses is often through a narrow alleyway. In parts of Kent such a thing is called a twitten. If my drawing was obviously a twitten, then the next time the victim entered one, or a narrow overhung passage like that, The Culler would materialise.'

'That's not very reliable is it? You don't know when the trigger event is going to happen, or even if it will happen at all. And how can you be sure your drawing is going to be good enough?'

'You can't, but if you know the habits of the victim, you can choose a situation that he is likely to experience. And as to the accuracy of the drawing, its power depends partly on the imagination and concentration of the witchdoctor as he creates the image.'

'Suppose the victim looks at the picture of The Culler and throws it away. Is he safe?'

'No. To be safe, he has to pass it on to another unknowing recipient. And if he has no knowledge of witchcraft, he won't think of doing so. He is far more likely to hang on to the thing and try to figure out what it is. Remember, too, that the victim may be unaware that he has received The Culler at all. A good way of delivering it is within the pages of a book. The receiver knows nothing about it till he turns the relevant page. Or it might be wrapped round a wine bottle, and then gift-wrapped over the top. The thing might not be unwrapped for days, but the victim would be at risk straight away - from the moment he received it.'

Fred thought it over. Then he asked, 'What does "a correct copy" mean? Do some work and some not?'

'Yes. That's one of the mysteries. Nobody knows which details are essential and which are not. Copying was tough. It must have all been done by hand, as medieval monks used to copy religious manuscripts in remote cloisters.'

'How was it passed on? How did a witchdoctor get one? How did Kwaname get one?'

'The most common thing, so he told me, was a gift from an old man to a younger one – either before death or through a promise given. Sometimes it happened through theft from a dead man's estate. Normally those versions worked, though sometimes nasty-minded old men passed on a dud copy, after destroying a good one out of spite. The other method was allowing a fellow professional to make a copy, or making copies for sale.'

'Dud copies must have died out, then. People would have found that they didn't work, and destroyed them. The survivors must be good. This one must be good. I mean, if this is a good one and you made a copy to give to me, and that copy never worked, then I would know it. I would destroy it and ask you for another.'

Nshila sat quiet for a moment with her fingers to her temples, trying to remember things said to her long ago. In her mind she saw the sun baked ground outside the hut, and heard distant sounds from the village – a dog barking and an aggrieved wife screaming, the buzzing of flies in the roof of the hut and Kwaname mumbling to himself. In the present, rain pattered on the skylight and Fred waited patiently.

'There's more to it than that. You know how the experts restore paintings, don't you, and the way they reconstruct texts that have been partially burnt or buried in the sand for centuries?'

'Yes. What of it?'

'Kwaname told me – I remember it now – that sometimes a good copy could be made from a dud one. Nobody knew why. The dud one must have differed from the good one in a single feature, and when copying from it, the witchdoctor sensed something wrong and altered it. That's not so strange as it sounds. I've heard of old texts that seemed to make no sense until somebody queried a single word. They said, maybe, "this word is currently translated to mean PLACE but it could also mean PLANT". When the change was made, it all became clear.'

'And sometimes scholars have two copies of a text, and the text of one can fill in the gaps in another. It's possible that a witchdoctor had two non-working copies but was able to make a third that worked. There are many unknowns where The Culler is concerned.'

'I can follow that. But it's all academic. Kwaname left you this copy and you trust Kwaname. It's got to be a good one.'

'I think you're right. I saw him use it once. The job was not wholly successful, but The Culler did appear as planned. This was his copy. In fact that faded charcoal mark in the bottom corner was my doing.'

'Hey, get off it!' Rasputin had walked across the table and left two dirty paw marks on the picture.

'I expect it will still work if we can get those off.'

'Do you think he may have spoiled it?'

'Possibly. I've told you, nobody knows for certain.'

'Let's try it. Let's try it just as it is. Let's have a go at the Prince!'

'Why not get the paw marks out first?'

'Well, we have got one change to the picture that may damage its efficiency but may equally well be harmless. If we start scrubbing out the paw marks we shall probably leave traces – discolorations - around the spot, and they will be wider than what we rub out. We will have made a second change. If we try now, and it works, then we leave the paw marks alone. If it fails, then we have nothing to lose by trying to get them out. Let's try.'

Nshila was reluctant to experiment with The Culler. She explained why.

'He has limitations. Don't ask me why spirits have things they can and can't do. But it's a fact. Just like some humans can run fast but can't add up, so spirits have different capabilities. The Culler is excellent at chasing fast in straight lines, but he is not very manoeuvrable. So if the victim is constantly turning corners, he can't respond fast enough, and overshoots. Imagine an oil tanker chasing a London taxi and you can see what happens.'

'The other problem comes when the victim escapes the planned death. The spirit seems to get his kicks from the victim running away from him as fast as possible. If the victim provides a good chase and The Culler then catches him, the result is a squashed corpse - not totally flat, but sufficiently flat to destroy vital organs. In current British society that would get an awful lot of forensic attention. If the victim twists and turns too much, then the demon may be baulked of his prey. He hates that. He takes out his anger on the witchdoctor who summoned him.'

'What happens then?'

'If the witchdoctor doesn't know the words of power, or fails to speak them quickly and clearly, he or she gets the full treatment.'

'What's that?'

'Look, I only know what Kwaname told me, and he was vague, offering more than one version and sounding as if it was largely hearsay. It seems to start with the appearance of that thing we both saw as a drawing. It's bad enough like that, but imagine it live, and moving towards you. Imagine it not at eye level, not a remote thing in the sky, but threatening you from a position about fifteen feet above the ground and twenty yards away.'

'Sounds scary. What next?'

'The immediate effect is that the victim becomes paralysed with fear. While he is immobilised The Culler throws some sort of trap around him. Kwaname spoke of a ring of light that hovered all round the victim, about four foot off the ground. Then he recovered the power of movement and tried to run. Every time he ran into the ring he was thrown backwards and the ring shone a tiny bit brighter. He bounced around inside it, running panic-stricken in all directions. Every time, he seemed to run slower, as if the life force was being sucked from him'

'If it was just a ring, why did the victim not duck underneath it?'

'Because he was in such a panic that he was unable to think straight. Then he became exhausted, and fell to the ground and something like a dirty blanket seemed to form on top of him. It gradually changed colour and began to look more like lead. The victim was suffocated and died. There were never any marks, Kwaname told me.'

'Do you know the words of power that will stop all this?'

'Yes, I remember them. Kwaname was very careful to make me fix them forever in my mind. He was not keen on using The Culler and didn't want either of us to get swatted. He worked out a mnemonic for us – one of those rubbish jingles that you never forget and which has a relationship to the words you need. Like the first letter of each word in the jingle being the same as the first word in the spell. Or like Cockney rhyming slang with "plates of meat" for "feet" and so on. I remember it. What I don't know is how soon the words have to be spoken to prevent any lasting damage to a possible user. Maybe he will be saved if the words are spoken before the ring of light appears, or maybe not. Maybe he suffers some degree of damage the first time he hits the ring, and it gets worse with every encounter. I am not too keen to try.'

'Wait a moment. If the spirit itself is so poor at ducking and diving, how would it get here to hit us if it had started at, say, The

Savoy Hotel?'

'Don't ask me. I just know that it can. Maybe the restrictions only apply when it's hunting. Maybe at other times it can enter hyperspace like the starships do in science-fiction stories.'

'But you know the words, anyway. We're safe, if you speak them quickly enough. Let's try it. I know Prince Thaqib is a target at the moment, and I know he is attending a dinner at The Savoy this evening. He'll leave by the main entrance, which is a short road – no turnings off it at all – leading into The Strand, which has thick traffic all day. We can do it now, and he'll be in the mortuary before midnight.'

'Very clever, Fred. And just how are you going to fix that he accepts the copy in time for this event?'

'Look, it's a formal dinner. They'll have a seating plan and name cards. Beside each place setting there will be a fine white napkin. All I have to do is slip the picture between the folds of the napkin. As soon as he unfolds it he will have taken possession. It's a doddle, mistress.'

'And what is the signal going to be? What will the drawing show?'

'The names of the wines will already be printed on the menu. We just sketch a tilted bottle – as if it was being poured out – and write the name of the wine beside it. When the waiter starts pouring Prince Thaqib his glass of Chateau Whatever, The Culler will respond.'

Nshila was shaken by his enthusiasm. It took her too long to frame a refusal, and before she was ready her mad, over-eager apprentice had grabbed the picture and rushed to the office photocopier. He was going to make a copy as insurance, in case anything happened to their precious original. She was furious.

But inside her head, the adventurous, experimental part woke up. 'Chicken!' it said. 'Gutless – unadventurous – feeble! Here you have a fine chance to test a procedure, get rid of an enemy, and educate your apprentice. And there's no possible danger because your apprentice will be here with you, and you know the words of power. Do it! Do it! Do it!' When Fred came back, she raised a practical issue.

'We have to plan this sensibly. I can believe that you are able to get into The Savoy and slip The Culler into his table napkin. But until you get there, you won't know the names of the wines. You won't be able to complete the drawing. Anyway, do you have the concentration needed to visualise the sequence of events as your pen or pencil moves? Mental power is an essential element in our craft.'

'Well, maybe I do, or maybe not. You are always telling me I have the concentration powers of a butterfly. Could you do it here, before I go? You're powerful enough to put a strong message into the bottle picture, and I can write the name beside it when I find out.'

It was done, and Fred was off to The Savoy. He was back shortly before the scheduled time for the dinner. 'Mission accomplished.'

Nshila reminded him again of the trouble in store if the Culler turned back upon his users. But can one maintain the highest level of vigilance for ever? Even the keenest sentries sometimes fall asleep at their posts. Nshila was in the bathroom, experimenting with a wig that would extend her range of disguises. Fred must have been dozing, and he missed the sight of Rasputin rocketing into the bedroom to hide under the bed, his hair sticking up in fright. Animals are more sensitive than humans to paranormal phenomena.

Nshila sensed nothing until she heard Fred cry out in panic. She rushed from the bathroom, looking ridiculous with a towel thrown over her shoulders and the wig still on her head, to find the room already full of a ghastly red glow. It was apparently centred on a ball of fire hanging just below the ceiling above the door. The ball had only the beginnings of a face, but there were lines upon it that managed to suggest intense evil and seemed to be growing stronger each moment. Fred was paralysed, standing rigid with his face twisted in terror. But there was no ring of light yet visible. Crisis! What were those words she needed?

They came to her, and she spoke. As she did so, there was a deep growl, like an angry, dangerous dog. The Culler started to fade.

She revived Fred with a comforting hand and a heavy slug of whisky. He was really, really scared. Nshila was scared, too, but made a big effort to conceal it. Fred had been in deadly danger and was very lucky to escape. Her own efforts to frighten him into obedience had enjoyed only limited success. The Culler had done rather better. She noticed, thereafter, that Fred addressed her less often by her given name and was more inclined to say 'Mistress'.

'You know what this means, don't you?'

'Yes. The spirit failed to get the Prince. I wonder what happened.'

Next day the first edition of the evening paper screamed;

MIRACULOUS ESCAPE OF PROMINENT DIPLOMAT.

The text told how Prince Thaqib, leaving The Savoy Hotel late the previous evening, had been seen to run fast into The Strand, where traffic was heavy. Amazingly he was not run over and entered one of the roads that lead up to Covent Garden. He had been found in a few minutes by a member of his entourage sitting on the kerb in a bemused state.The Prince was not available for comment, but it was thought that he might have heard or seen an activity that was preparatory to an assassination attempt. A spokesman said, 'Sadly, these things happen at times in our country. Eminent men like the Prince are aware of it. The short road leading from The Strand to The Savoy is a restricted space, and the Prince would naturally have sought an open area instead. I am pleased to say that he has no serious injuries.' The report added a strange postscript.

'Several bystanders claim to have seen a bright, fastmoving globe of fire also emerging from The Savoy entrance. However, the descriptions are so varied that little credence can be given to them. More exciting were the statements made by passengers on the top deck of a Number 27 bus. They all agreed that the bus had been struck by a round, flat fiery object that sent an electric shock through the steel. This was felt powerfully by those who touched any part of the framework.'

Chapter Thirty-Two
Embassy Party

Nshila was not a dedicated party-goer. She thought that many parties relied too much on alcohol and too little on a good mix of guests. However, she felt unable to refuse Fred's invitation. His embassy was celebrating the fifteenth anniversary of independence. All the staff were allocated invitations to distribute, the number being dependent on rank. Fred got slightly more than he should have received due to his father's influence. He asked Nshila, Peter, Gillian and her husband. Nshila was allowed to bring Mike Fanshawe and Zach Kawero also got invited. Fred said that the party would include a 'special friend' of his own, but would say no more. Dress, it seemed, was to be 'smart but optional'. Fred said that senior figures would certainly wear the formal gear appropriate to their culture. So there would be Europeans in dinner jackets and Arabs in long white robes and Africans in national costume. He told Gillian that if she wanted to try Pakistani dress to please her husband, that would be OK. He told Peter that a suit printed in broad arrows would be a poor joke. Nshila had no trouble making up her mind – it was going to be the long figure-hugging dress in a shade just lighter than purple. Mike Fanshawe invited them all to meet at his flat and go on to the embassy together.

That was the event at which Nshila met the Reverend Alice Abigail Fordcombe. She was the 'special friend' Fred had refused to name. She was the last to arrive at the flat, and Peter saw Mike Fanshawe register the impact as he opened the door. Abigail was wearing the conventional black cassock and dog collar of the Church of England and had a small cross hanging from her neck. But the cassock had obviously been tailored to emphasise bust, waist and hips, and to end high enough from the floor to show expensive shoes with a medium heel, slim ankles and sheer tights. The outfit said 'Woman' in large letters and 'Priest' in much smaller ones.

The dress of the others was varied. The Rafiqs had decided to ditch the Pakistani image, and Javed, Gillian's husband, wore a dark blue blazer embroidered with the badge of his sailing club on the breast pocket. Shirt and trousers were cream. Gillian wore a bias-cut silk party dress with puff sleeves in a deep apricot colour. She looked marvellous. Mike and Peter and Zach had decided to play safe with dinner jackets, but Mike's was white and the other two were black. Nshila had known Zach for years and mentally labelled him as a tall black nerd – words he sometimes used to describe himself. Seeing him in a dinner jacket made her realise that he had matured and changed. He had fewer spots, more confidence, held himself more upright and looked like a young professional. Peter Grace in a dinner jacket managed to look more like a gorilla than ever. But he did not clash with anybody. Finally, the host of the little party, Fred, had decided on a white dinner jacket with an electric blue shirt and a yellow bow tie. He clashed with everybody.

It was a good event. The start was boring, because the Ambassador observed the old procedure of a receiving line, and everybody had to be announced, and shake hands with him and his wife before mixing with the throng. But after that it was fine. The guest list was so varied that one had no need to pretend knowledge of the people one met. It was quite OK to say 'Who are you and what brings you here?' The food and wine was excellent, and there was enough space to circulate without having to push people aside.

The friends split up. The Rafiqs were greeted by another mixed-race couple and went off to explore cultural differences from a culinary viewpoint – all tastes were catered for. Fred was snared by one of his bosses and sent off on party business: he escaped quickly, but the process was repeated several times. Peter and Zach operated together as a woman-seeking pair and had, it seemed, a good deal of success. They looked so odd together that they aroused curiosity.

That left Mike Fanshawe and the Reverend Abigail and Nshila. It was weird, because Nshila could see that Mike had judged Abigail and found her wanting. Mike, if he wanted something, would conceal his desire and work behind the scenes to achieve it. The Reverend Abigail was different. Her appearance and her manner proclaimed that she had a lot of offer and would use it openly. She was not going to be reticent about it. Mike, being there as Nshila's escort, wanted to distance himself from that attitude.

Her conversation with Nshila was certainly open and direct. 'I have heard a lot about you from Fred and I have been wondering whether we are to some extent in the same business.'

'What business would that be? I own a meteorological consultancy. I deal in charts and temperatures and isobars and so on. You are a religious professional. Can we really overlap?'

'We might. I mean, you sent Fred up to our theological college to learn a bit about Christianity, but it was quite clear that his interest was spirituality in the broadest sense. He was groping for supernatural power. If he works for you, he must have been following instructions you gave him.'

'He doesn't work for me, you know. He's a countryman of mine. We met on an assignment I carried out back home a few years ago, and he wanted to renew the friendship when he was posted to London.'

Mike intervened, taking drinks from a waiter, pressing them on the group, and trying to direct Abigail's attention away from Nshila.

'Abigail, is that one of your top brass over there? The tall thin ugly fellow dressed in purple. Do you know him?'

Abigail looked – and looked away. 'Not well, and yet too well for comfort. He's one of the puritanical old guard who looks down his nose at people like me. If I had lived in his diocese he would never have ordained me.'

'How did you get ordained, then?'

'By finding a bishop of the modern, free-thinking sort and forging a connection within his diocese.'

'It all makes your organisation look a bit fragmented. Don't you wonder sometimes whether outsiders might see the whole outfit as a sinking ship?'

'Right now, perhaps. But you wait a few years and the dinosaurs will all be dead and my lot will have revitalised the Church of England as a vibrant explorative think-tank that integrates the physical and the spiritual.'

A new voice. 'You sound very broad-minded for a priest of your religion.'

None of them had been aware of Prince Thaqib moving up behind them. Introductions were made. The Prince indicated that he had heard about Nshila from Fred, and wanted to meet her. His skill with women was so great that he conversed with both Nshila and Abigail in a way that made each feel the principal object of his interest. However, Nshila remained guarded in her responses while Abigail was more forthcoming. She said nothing about her activities in the crypt, but made no secret of her ambitions and her desire to meet powerful people.

'I might be able to help you in a small way. You say that you ride, and that you hunt whenever you get a chance. I ride out with The Snargate Vale quite frequently, and I would love to be your host at some of our meets.'

'Prince, that would be marvellous. But I'm usually dependent on others for a mount and I'm not sure I could get one for a ride over at Snargate.'

'No problem at all. My people will find something suitable for you. And bring your friends, if you like. It would make splendid day out. It will be fun to have a hunting parson, like in the story books.'

'Excuse me, please, but are you talking about Hunting the Fox?'

None of the group could understand, afterwards, how they had failed to notice the approach of Araminta Kubaka. How was it possible, in a small sailing dinghy, to miss the approach of a supertanker? But suddenly every one of them, including Prince Thaqib, felt six inches shorter. Her figure, impressive at any time, was exaggerated by a flowing African tent-dress and a six-inch hair-style.

Her interest in Hunting the Fox was so obvious that the Prince quickly extended his invitation to include her.

'And a horse for me? You will provide for me that?'

'Certainly, Madam.' But Mike Fanshawe, the only one who rode to hounds regularly, could see that the Prince was estimating her weight and wondering if anything in his stable could carry an inexperienced rider of that bulk. He must have thought of a suitable animal, for he renewed the invitation, clearly including all the four people. He said to Abigail,

'Why don't you phone me sometime to arrange a day? The Vale have their first meet of the season on October 26th and that will give us about three weeks' notice. And if we miss the first one, well, we ride out quite frequently all through the winter.'

The Prince moved on, and Nshila looked around for Fred. Their eyes met across the room and a tiny head movement signalled her need.

'Fred, here's a job for you – highly important. Prince Thaqib is here, in full Arab dress including Kaffiyeh and Naga. If we ever attack him again, we shall probably need body parts. Finger nails and toenails will be very hard to get, but there may be hairs sticking to his Kaffiyeh. If you see him go to the men's room, follow soon after. It might just happen that he takes off his headdress and you have a chance to touch it – and maybe pick a few hairs off it. I'm not too hopeful, but it's a chance, and if you succeed it will save us a great deal of plotting.'

Later in the evening there was a short encounter between Abigail and Fred. Abigail was pleased with herself and couldn't resist sounding off.

'I've just pulled off a referral, Fred, and got that menace Graham Schwarz out of my hair. It's great!'

'Referral? What do you mean? Oh. I suppose you're talking about your GP role and those awful things you do in the crypt. And referrals are dodgy, you said. Why is this an achievement?'

'Because this specialist is right at the top of her profession and very, very choosy. I had to pull out all the stops. But it's worth the effort. Schwarz kept saying that he wanted 'extreme' and now he's going to get it. Mistress Meg – that's her professional name – is more of a sadist than most. Schwarz is going to get some surprises.'

'You don't seem to like Schwarz.'

'I don't. He's offensive and disgusting.'

'Tell me more. Who is this Mistress Meg and what's she going to do to him? She sounds friendly enough. Meg is a pet-name, surely?'

'Yes. I think she uses it to conceal her true personality. The name has pleasant associations – like Meg Merrilees in the poem and the novel. I know her speciality, and I guessed right about Schwarz being suitable. I don't know much about her personally. She's so careful of her true identity that few people know it. And if I did know it, professional etiquette would stop me telling you. As for what she's going to do to him, that's easy. She's going to subject him to a range of humiliating and degrading experiences – and take a lot of money off him.'

'How did you manage the referral, then, if she's so guarded?'

'I was dead lucky, and had her pointed out to me in St James's Park. She was in a good mood and allowed me to talk to her. She gave me no contact details, but she asked for Graham Schwarz's phone number and said she would contact him. She's just been through on my mobile to say she has accepted him, and to confirm my finder's fee.'

'Lucky you. Sometimes, Abby, I think you have more than your share of luck.'

Fred was called away for more hosting duties, and put the conversation out of his mind. Anyway, this was one part of Abby with which he was not quite comfortable.

Later on he made an opportunity to report to Nshila about his contact with the Prince and to hand over a white envelope that disappeared into her handbag.

'The spirits were with me, Mistress. I was in the washroom with the Prince, and because I was re-arranging the towels he assumed I was one of the junior staff of the embassy – which I am, of course. He took off his headdress and asked me to hold it for him. He spent almost five minutes brushing his hair and combing his moustache, so I had plenty of time. Better still, he must have been to the barber recently because there was plenty of loose hair.'

'Well done, Fred.'

Chapter Thirty-Three

Rural Interlude

'We are not going to act, Fred, unless the client solves his nomination problem. Whatever means we might use to terminate the Prince, there would be some risk of detection and we have no obligation to take that risk when the client is in doubt about the reward.' Nshila had learnt about the client's difficulty and passed the news to Fred. There was a need to overcome the nomination of some competitor and no way had yet been found of doing so.

They were talking in an unusual location. Not the flat in Eastcheap but a quiet pub on the border of Kent and Sussex. Fred had been sent by his embassy to call on a respected national now living at Northiam. He had moaned to Nshila about the difficulty of reaching the place by public transport, and she had been moved to help him. She decided on what she mentally labelled 'An English Day' – one on which she would forget her responsibilities and enjoy the rural areas of her adopted country.

Getting out of London had been terrible, of course, but there were a few good memories. Here, on a corner in the Old Kent Road, had stood The Kentish Drovers, with its evocative sign showing shepherds driving their sheep to market in London. It had still been there when she first arrived in England and she loved to picture those rustic peasants trudging slowly, day after day, up to the big city. It must have been more like life in Africa then, and wildly different from today's mad rush. Mixing fact, now, with fiction she recognised the point where James Bond had lost a skirmish with his enemies. Not the Bond of the special effects films, but the original Bond of the spy novels. Driving a huge lorry loaded with colossal rolls of industrial paper, the villains had cut the ropes and allowed their load 'like the lavatory paper of a giant', to squash Bond's following Bentley. A good story, she felt.

Then the Sidcup bypass, the Swanley bypass, and onto the M25 for a few miles. Fast, but almost a pity, she had felt, that the old route down tree-shaded Poll Hill was missed out. At the bottom, she resisted the instinct to bear left when wanting to leave the motorway. Was this the only motorway junction in the country where, to leave it, one had to go straight on? Once, just once, she had got it wrong and struggled through sixteen miles of heavy motorway traffic to reach the next exit.

Climbing the Sevenoaks bypass, she had anticipated and enjoyed cresting the rise and viewing what Kipling called;

'The wooded, dim, blue goodness of the Weald'.

The roads were slower and winding after Tonbridge Yet the small hills and valleys of Kent had their charm. Once, she found herself going down a steep slope and looking at cattle on the reverse slope ahead of her. It seemed as if she was viewing them from above. And some of the trees were turning yellow and brown for autumn. They were beautiful.

Even Fred was enthusiastic about the broad swooping curve of the Lamberhurst bypass – fast down to the crossing of the tiny River Teise and fast up again to the Scotney traffic island. 'It's like a bird swooping to take a fish,' he said.

Early afternoon had found them at Newenden, a few miles from Northiam, and Nshila had given Fred the car to make his visit. She herself had spent two happy hours watching a cricket match – perhaps the last of the season – on the field opposite the pub, grateful that her time in England had enlarged her understanding of the game. When she had started watching, the scoreboard had said 'VISITORS 104 – WICKETS 9 and alongside, NEWENDEN 18 – WICKETS 1'.

By the time she had seen the BMW approaching from the Sussex side of the small hump-backed bridge, the score had progressed to NEWENDEN 92 – WICKETS 7. Twenty minutes had been lost while the fielding side searched for the ball in the stream that bordered the ground and, presumably, separated Kent and Sussex. The conference took place after Fred had returned and consumed his first pint. He was, as always, keen on quick action.

'But waiting for the client may mean that we miss opportunities for the hit. There must be moments when it is safe and sure, and others when it is less so.'

'That's true, Fred, and we know of one event that gives a perfect opportunity. Fox hunting is always a risky business, and we have been invited to join one.'

'So you can fix it for the Prince to be thrown from his horse and break his neck. Great! When shall we do it?'

'We don't know yet. The Snargate Vale rides out frequently in the autumn but we don't know which days the Prince will ride or when he will invite our party.'

'I can fix that. The invitation was aimed at Abby in particular. I'll get her to prompt the Prince.'

'Another thing, Fred. We have to plan the practical details in advance, in case the client only gives us a small window.'

'What do you mean?'

'Well, suppose that the client makes contact on a Thursday and says that he has found a way to disqualify the other candidate and my nomination is certain. I shall be obliged to complete the task. If the hunt is scheduled for the next Sunday, and we are invited, then there are just three days to make all our preparations.'

They were interrupted. A cricket ball rolled in through the door and stopped against the bar. A white-clad man retrieved it and was immediately involved in an argument with another man who followed.

'Did it bounce on the road or on the grass before it?'

'I can't be sure.'

'If it bounced on the road it's a Six. If it bounced on the grass and rolled, then it's Four.'

Appealed to, Fred, was unable to answer. Nshila, who felt committed to the home team, said 'On the road. I heard it clearly. It's Six.'

'Mistress, it seems an awful pity that we can't help the client with the nomination problem. Could we intervene ourselves to discredit the other contender?'

'Why should we solve the client's problem for him? We would

have to take some sort of positive action, and that increases risk. I don't care overmuch if the contract falls apart. I had a great time in Anacanda, and the government has benefited. They'll owe me. Sooner or later there'll be a payback, and I won't have had to kill anybody at all. Also, if you remember, our last attempt was not very encouraging, was it?'

'But if we don't go ahead Prince Thaqib will still be alive, and still plotting, and still a threat to the country.'

'Yes. I suppose that all the other aspects had blinded me to the moral imperative. But is it my responsibility? I wasn't the one who learnt about the plot.'

'Doesn't matter. You know now. And you are, perhaps, the only person capable of removing him permanently and discreetly. I just wish we knew the name of this new contender for that last peerage.'

'Well, we don't.'

Fred hated her negative attitude. This was his first involvement in a really big activity and cancellation would be a psychological let-down. He was going to fight it. He needed alcoholic support. Having established that Nshila meant to drive home, he went to the bar for another beer. That in itself was a problem, for the pub was a free house and stocked about twelve brews, all with fancy names. He ended by asking the barmaid which was the strongest, and returning to the table with a pint of Poachers Potion.

'Mistress, surely it can do no harm to find out who this nominee is? He or she might be somebody who we could discredit very easily. Then the whole project would go ahead as planned.'

'Unlikely.'

'I agree. But we won't be any worse off. If the nominee turns out to be whiter than snow, we just drop the matter. It seems a bit feeble not to try. I don't mind doing the necessary work. I'll make sure I keep your name out of it. Can I have a go?'

'How would you go about it?'

'I've two ideas. You remember how you introduced me to "scrying"? How you made me concentrate on the Prince and form his image in my mind and try to see what he was doing?'

'I remember. But where did you get that word "scrying"? I've not heard it.'

'Oh, it was in one of those books I got from the library about Elizabethan witchcraft. It was a word used by her court magician, Dr Dee.'

'Interesting. It might work. Who would you try to overlook?'

'That man called Simon Trent. You seem to think that he, or his boss, is our client.'

'The evidence certainly points that way. What was your other idea?'

'A simple one. You've told me a lot about the Anacanda trip and it's obvious that Zach Kawero became friendly with that man called Emrys White-Walker. Emrys was on secondment from Simon Trent's department. Am I right about that?'

'Yes. Go on.'

'Let's get Zach to meet up with Emrys and pump him. Emrys is a Welshman, and they are all as garrulous as a cage of monkeys. If Zach gets enough beer inside Emrys, he will give us the name. And we will have done nothing illegal. Can I have a go?'

'You can try your second idea. But if you get the name you are not – repeat not – to do anything more. You are not to start searching for skeletons in his or her cupboard. You give me the name and I decide what, if anything, to do.'

Chapter Thirty-Four

An Unguarded Tongue

Zach Kawero was not easily persuaded to pump Emrys for information. He liked Emrys, and didn't see why Fred should be making the request rather than Nshila. He checked it out with her. He was told that she was trying to save her own time by giving Fred simple tasks. He was also assured that nothing Emrys said would be used against him. With the proviso that he could only devote limited time to the proposal, Zach agreed.

It turned out to be much easier than expected. He arranged to encounter Emrys, apparently by chance, as he left work one evening. They adjourned to The Bowler Hat in Maiden Lane and Zach set the scene by moaning over his own misfortunes.

'It's not the cost of the equipment, so much, Emrys. Generally, the added functionality of a new item will justify the price. But the frequency of change means that I have to pay out again and again. I've just about wiped one lot off my credit card bill and suddenly another big purchase becomes essential. And there's also an opportunity cost associated with the time needed to get on top of any technological advance. I spend so much time learning that I have fewer hours to exploit the learning.'

'Zach, if you're upset, just listen to my troubles. I'm going to be transferred again.'

'Why? Where to? I thought that after the Anacanda assignment you would stay put for a year or so.'

'I was meant to, but now they say that a vacancy is coming up in one of the social services departments that exactly suits my qualifications and interests. It's a perfect match, they say, and I'm to move at the end of next month.'

'Well, is it a perfect match? Will you like it?'

'Can't tell. But that garbage about suitability is what they always tell me when they want to get rid of me.'

'I find that hard to believe.'

'It's true. My trouble seems to be that I am constantly asking questions and they don't have the answers. They could find them easily enough, but being ignorant upsets them. They get annoyed at looking inadequate. I had a row with one of them just four days ago. He as good as told me to stop using my mind until I had a few years experience and concentrate on doing what I was told. Get me another beer, Zach. London Pride, please. I don't like that other slush.'

Zach was soon back with two mugs of London Pride. He had also got double whiskys as chasers. He remembered that Emrys had drunk chasers before.

'Will you be sorry to leave Trent's department?'

'I won't be sorry to leave him, but there's a fine old argument going on about the Honours List and I find that very interesting indeed. It's also ridiculous and Gilbertian and pathetic – a national disgrace. But interesting, for sure.'

'Gilbertian?'

'Yes. You know, that fellow who wrote comic operas a century or so ago. The Pirates of Penzance was one, and The Mikado and The Gondoliers'

'Oh, him. I remember. Statements of the obvious that mocked human behaviour. "When everybody's somebody then no one's anybody". Things like that.'

'Yes. You will be interested in this, because one of the characters in the plot is the boss of our Anacanda adventure – Ms. Ileloka. They want to give her a peerage.'

'Good idea. She deserves it. Does she know?'

'Definitely not. Nominees are never approached till it's all cut and dried. That's not happened yet.'

'Is there a problem? I would have thought that after what she did in Anacanda she would be a strong favourite.'

'She is. And I agree with you that she deserves it. But the number of these things is limited, and there's another candidate who has powerful backing. There's a big dispute about who gets the last place. I'd like to see what happens, and I hope that your friend gets it.'

'Don't you like the other candidate?'

'No. I don't like him and I don't like his supporters. They are a crowd of arrogant bullies who think that money will buy everything. And the man's record makes me feel that Wormwood Scrubs would suit him better than the House of Lords.'

'Has he got a name, this creature?'

'I ought not to tell you, but, confidentially, the man is called Graham Schwarz.'

'Never heard of him,' said Zach. But he told Fred, and Fred had heard a lot about him.

Fred burst into The Rain Consultancy, flushed with excitement.

'Mission completed! I've got the name and I know what to do.'

'Quiet, Fred! Gillian and Peter are struggling with a dicey contract. You had better come into the flat.'

Fred contained himself only as long as it took them to sit down at the table. 'It's Graham Schwarz,' he said, 'and I know just how to fix him.'

There, Fred stopped. He knew that Schwarz was going to involve himself in an activity that would, if publicised, get him utterly disgraced. But he knew it through Abigail, and her weird practices were not to be revealed. How should he handle it? Perhaps by being honest.

'Look, Mistress, I can't tell you why I know this because I have made a promise. But this fellow Schwarz is going to be involved in a most degrading activity. Nobody who knew about it would recommend him for anything.'

'You have to say more than that. Don't reveal your source, but describe the activity. I might know the source anyway.'

'Have you heard of sado-masochism?'

'Yes. Sometimes I check internet sites that relate to witchcraft, and I see links to that subject. I've never followed them, but I know what it is. I am interested in power, and sado-masochism is all about the exercise of power. Some of the key words are the same.

'It's aimed at a certain type of male who enjoys being subject to a strong, sexy woman.'

'Go on.'

'Some of the experiences these men will pay money to submit to, if the women are impressive enough, are humiliating, degrading and disgusting. The whole scene is utterly weird, but it exists, and the men most often drawn to it are men in positions of power. They seem to want relief from their normal situation.'

'And is Schwarz into that scene?'

'Yes. And I know for a fact that he has signed up for sessions with a woman called Mistress Meg who is the most extreme practitioner of any. If we can get some good pictures of Schwarz being humiliated in her "dungeon" – that's the word they use – then he's a dead duck.'

'Who is this Mistress Meg and where does she live?'

'I don't know.'

'So what you are telling, me Fred, is that we have to find the real name of this woman, discover where she works, put a hidden camera in her apartment, record a session that she might or might not have with Schwarz, and retrieve the recording. Is that all? Dead easy, isn't it?'

'Don't be sarcastic. I've found out a bit more about the SM scene. Most practitioners protect themselves by secretly recording some of their sessions. Partly they do it because they might one day need to prove that whatever happened took place between "consenting adults". Have I got the right term?'

'Yes. The laws in this country are very relaxed. Almost anything can happen between "consenting adults". If a practitioner recorded the client expressing agreement then she would be safe from prosecution. It would still ruin the reputation of the client.'

'And that's the second reason for recording. The nastiest practitioners sometimes use the recording to blackmail past clients. Anyway, the point is that if Schwarz visits Mistress Meg there will probably be a digital record of what went on, inside her computer. All we need to do is hack into it, and Zach can surely manage that.'

'But we don't know the real name of Mistress Meg, nor where she lives, nor her email address.'

'That's all true, but we can get Snakesmith and Co. to follow

Schwarz and report his movements. Any deviation from his normal practice will identify the house he goes to. That will be Mistress Meg's address. Once we have got that, Zach can surely find out her telephone number, and that will give us the line she uses for the internet. That will allow Zach to get into her computer, and in seconds we shall have all the images we want. Can I go ahead?'

Nshila didn't like it. She felt she was being manipulated; that things were passing beyond her control and she was being pushed into actions too early. It was more difficult because she knew that after a period of reflection she would probably take that route herself. But she would have considered all the angles thoroughly, and she doubted if Fred was careful enough. His track record was not impressive. But she felt even worse about killing his enthusiasm.

She remained silent for so long that Fred feared she was going to decide against him. Unwisely, he came up with another suggestion.

'Of course, we could save time and effort by killing him. He's vile enough to qualify on your list of acceptable victims.'

'You really are impossible. You must know by now that I don't do things like that for personal gain. And there's always danger — not just from the law but from the spirit world.'

'How is that? You seem very capable in that world.'

'There is so much that we don't know. Sometimes I think that what powers I have are dependent on the use to which I put them. If I was less scrupulous, those powers might be denied to me. Anyway, your idea of killing Schwarz is out.'

'Very well, but can I try the other plan?'

'Alright. Get Snakesmith onto it, but come back to me as soon as you get the address. I want this to be done step by careful step.'

Chapter Thirty-Five

Executive Officer

Fred attacked his job with enthusiasm. He had persuaded his boss not to ditch the project, and that was good for his ego. He felt that if he could get compromising information about Graham Schwarz then success would be close: a grave for the prince and a peerage for his boss. He thought of himself as an Executive Officer in the original meaning of the term, the one who gets things done – getting dirty if need be – when instructed by an administrator. The administrator is a person a grade higher up who decides what it is that needs to be done. Impetuously, he rushed off to visit Snakesmith and Co.

Their response was not ideal. They were short of operatives and unable to promise quick results. Fred was surprised. He could see little difficulty in mounting surveillance on a single person.

'We are not talking about an ordinary person, are we? If you wanted surveillance on a suburban office worker of fixed address and habits, then one watcher might be enough. But Graham Schwarz goes everywhere, and often with no notice. Suppose he suddenly decides to check up on a fishing vessel in Grimsby? He doesn't leave home in the morning and walk to the tube station. He sends for his limo and gets driven to London City Airport and flies off in his executive jet. Even if we succeeded in following him to the airport, we would have no means of picking him up in Hull, always assuming that he went there anyway and didn't divert to Whitehaven.'

'Don't you have stringers – or whatever you call them – in all the big cities? You could use one of them.'

Geoff Snakesmith took a deep breath, shifted in his executive chair and scratched his ear. This man was naïve, he thought. Yet he didn't want to lose the business. He could probably recall Ed Giddins who had just traced an absconding husband to Carcassonne and been encouraged to take a few days off in the local warmth and colour.

'Not stringers, quite. It's true that we have reciprocal arrangement with agencies in other cities, but they are not always in a position to respond at once. Take it from me that we really can't commit ourselves to a fixed date. But what I will do is juggle some lesser assignments and promise to start watching before the weekend. Will that help?'

'I was hoping for more, but I understand what you're saying. Thank you. I accept.'

The Snakesmith offices were in a street leading off Edgware Road. Fred walked down to Marble Arch, turned east along Oxford Street and found himself a fast food outlet. He reflected on what he had heard. He ought, it seemed, to have made a more coherent plan before rushing into action.

A time scale. That was what he needed. The image of Charles Bwali flashed into his mind. Charles had been a close friend at university and had read Business Studies. At one late night alcoholic meeting Charles had extolled the virtues of a technique called Critical Path Analysis. It was supposed to make clear what actions had to be completed in order to reach a goal, and in what way each depended on another, and how they could be scheduled to get the project finished in the least time. Charles illustrated the procedure by describing the actions needed to get the barmaid into his bed. How nice it would be to have Charles Bwali here beside him in Oxford Street. Still, he must do the best he could.

A sudden access of zeal overcame him. There were good public libraries all over London and Fred adopted the old-fashioned strategy of asking a policeman. It worked, and ten minutes later Fred was immersed in An A - Z of Management Techniques. Here it was – 'Critical Path Analysis' and an example based on a dinner party.

It took him about three hours to get the job done. Delay followed delay because he was slow to realise what activities were inter-dependent and what activities could be undertaken at any time. For instance, hacking into Mistress Meg's computer (one activity) demanded knowledge of her address, and finding that address was a separate activity. On the other hand, devising a strategy to kill Prince Thaqib could be started immediately. It didn't depend on anything else. If it was ready before Schwarz had been discredited, that mattered not at all. Another problem was estimating the time needed for an activity when the method to be used was uncertain. Take getting the evidence, once Schwarz was known to be scheduled for some disgraceful act. If an armed raid was to be made, then evidence would be immediately available. If sophisticated computer hacking was needed, then several days might be needed. If the house was to be broken into, then getting Mistress Meg away from home might take longer still.

Fred drew boxes (called 'nodes' in the text book) and connected them by lines and arrows ('activities'). Beside the arrows he wrote 'lapsed time' trying to avoid extreme optimism or extreme pessimism. Beside each node he wrote the earliest date by which it could be reached. After two hours, the floor around his chair was littered with crumpled paper.

But he made progress. Adding together his figures, he got 36 days from the time Snakesmith started work until the final event. The clock in the library showed both time and date. It was 23rd September. Fred took out his diary and counted 36 days. It got him to Wednesday 29th October. There was enough time. But Snakesmith could not get started for three days. So 26th September was the real start date, and 1st November the earliest day in which everything could be in place.

He knew that the Snargate Vale Hunt would ride out on Sunday 2nd November and Sunday 9th November and that the hunting field was far the best place for the hit. The first date made the time scale very tight. The second allowed a bit of slack time. To make certain of the dates he tried the internet and found that the hunt had a web site. It gave dates and meeting places and illustrated features of a hunt in gorgeous colours. The meet on November 9th was at Goats Ferry.

Chapter Thirty-Six

Fred's Diary

Fred wanted a diary. Not the pocket version he had been using, but a big page-to-a-day one. Often there would be little to record but sometimes a great deal. There was nothing in the shops that late in the year, but he tracked some down in his own embassy. They had been set aside as gifts, and there were a dozen left over. The entries Fred made were a mixture of reported acts and his own thoughts about the project.

1st October

Snakesmith started covering Schwarz. All day devoted to legitimate business affairs and an evening at the Theatre.

October 2nd

Similar to previous day, but dinner at The Dorchester with his local MP.

October 3rd

Left work at 2.30pm and went to a gymnasium in Brompton Road. Left at 5.00pm and went home.

October 4th – October 5th – October 6th

The same entry on every page: Went to his office 8.30am. Left at 6.30pm and went home. Nothing suspicious.

October 7th

Schwarz reported as leaving his office at 2.30pm and travelling by taxi to a house in Cranley Place, South Kensington, where the upper flat (two floors) were occupied by Sensibility Services Limited. He remained there for two hours and, on leaving, appeared to be in an upbeat mental state. The Snakesmith agent pressed the bell and was answered by a strong, aristocratic female voice demanding a password. Not knowing it, the operator represented himself as a council employee charged to inspect the fire precautions in multi-owner buildings. He was told 'Your people were here last week. Go away.' He lacked proper identification, so he went. But he kept watch till midnight and saw three more middle-aged, well-dressed men arrive and leave. Is this the place?

October 8th

Brilliant idea! If Sensibility Services operates from the top two floors of a building then access must be possible from above. A proper 'dungeon' is in a cellar, but these people can't have a wide choice or premises. Abby is dead lucky to have a crypt: Others must have to fit out an ordinary room. I can get a skilled housebreaker to plant a hidden camera in whichever room Mistress Meg uses. Then I won't have to bother with hacking into her computer. Problem — how do I find the right housebreaker?

Different idea. N. could use the Hand of Glory to break all the locks and freeze every movement in the house. We could enter unopposed and film the place in detail. But how would we know the best moment to choose? We might find a frozen tableau of a harmless conversation that was not compromising at all.

October 9th

Schwarz went by executive jet to Aberdeen. Contact lost till 11.30am when local stringer reported seeing Schwarz enter the offices of the Port Authority. He left at 3.30pm.

October 10th

Went to Companies House (myself) and drew records for Sensibilty Services Limited. Found the absolute minimum of information, but the turnover is huge and overheads barely exist. Typical of a one-person business offering a high-value service to well-heeled customers. It has to be MM. The VAT number is the one covering 'Miscellaneous Services'.

October 11th

I'm mad to see finding a housebreaker as difficult. It's obvious. Peter Grace will have leads to one. Pour a few beers down him, and I'll know where to start looking.

October 12th

Schwarz followed to an address in Amersham. Belongs to Mrs. Backlead. Highly regarded locally and a Justice of the Peace. An elderly Schwarz relative?

October 13th

Schwarz all day at his office. Nothing suspicious.

October 14th

Got a lead from Peter and sat three hours in a dreary pub to start passing the word about a lucrative job for the right man. Expected no immediate response, and got none.

October 15th

Snakesmith rang early. Had tried to get me last night but failed. Schwarz had been again to the MM house. A week since the last visit. Does he have a regular appointment? Will he go on October 21st and 28th and November 4th?

October 16th

Marvellous! Unexpected phone call, and meeting with Al Rocket (real name?) in a burger bar. Job can be done, but very expensive. Can an embassy hanger-on borrow big money easily? Must try. Can't risk asking N. She might say 'No' and kill the project. Al Rocket promises camera installed and radio transmission working by end of the week. Al demanded deposit, and am now broke. Can hardly eat. Must use embassy canteen. Al not very impressive. Small. Huge feet. Toothbrush moustache. Claims to have been chosen by his boss – which makes him some junior member of a gang. But I've nobody else.

October 17th

Rang Abigail. Away on a mission week in Glasgow and not back till October 20th.

October 18th

Snakesmith says found taxi driver who had carried Schwarz to Cranley Place on 7th and 14th. Address well known to drivers who have delivered and picked up a variety of well-dressed and impressive men. Good tippers. Most drivers say it's a high-class brothel or a centre of sado-masochism.

October 19th

No news.

October 20th

Not a word from Al Rocket. Schwarz spent most of the day getting to and returning from Chepstow races. He has a share in a racehorse.

21st October

Got through to Abby. Asked her to pull out all stops to get an invitation for November 9th. Late call from Snakesmith. Schwarz was there again.

October 22nd

No news.

October 24th

No news. Frustrated.

October 25th

At last. Al rang late to say camera installed and running. Probably nothing to see this late at night, so don't be disappointed by blackness. Tried anyway, but he was right.

October 26th

Switched on the video link about 11.00am. Blackness for half-an-hour and then Mistress Meg in an admin routine – upgrading her files. Excellent visibility. Words readable on papers when they are in view of the camera. Appears to cross-reference clients with treatment expected and equipment needed. Very well-organised. The name on one paper might be Schwarz, but only a brief glimpse.

She looks normal. Amazing! But slouching about the house on her own, what else? Quite a big woman but very feminine. Dressing gown not tightly belted and Grade A legs showing at times. Full breasts. Narrow hips. Not a frightening image. Could be somebody's elder sister. Late twenties? Early thirties?

Chapter Thirty-Seven
What Fred Saw

There were no more entries in the diary. After watching MM at her admin tasks, he switched off for a time, having learnt from the watchers that real work began in the early evening.

Anybody able to view Fred at 7.40pm that day would have thought they watched a zombie. He was glued to his video screen with his mouth hanging open and dribble falling down his chin. He was utterly still. A mug of coffee stood on the floor in front of him, unnoticed and getting cold. His mobile rang, but he seemed to hear nothing except the sounds from the screen – a mixture of harsh commands and stifled cries of pain.

Incredible, he thought. The things that man is allowing her to do to him! Total physical surrender! And he seems to love it! And her! Is it really the same woman I saw slouching around in her dressing gown? Taller, yes – high heeled boots. But her stature, the way she holds herself. Figure-hugging black lurex top and mid-length black leather skirt. A sort of feminine demon king.

Wow! What was that she did to him just then?

Part of Fred was disgusted. Another part of him was fascinated. How would he react to a woman like that? The more he watched, the more he realised that in some weird way he might enjoy being in that man's position. No! No! No! How could that thought ever cross his mind? But he went on watching. What would she do to her victim next? This show he had to watch till the end.

It came. MM released her victim and pointed to a door. It must be a washroom, because the man entered it near-naked and came out fifteen minutes later looking like a Chief Executive or a top flight Civil Servant. By then, MM was in a very conventional dark grey suit with neat hair and modest make-up.

He wrote her a cheque. Fred knew that he could fix Schwarz. The next time he called on MM, Fred would have the whole session on tape. He could select stills from it and give the client sight of them. The chances of Schwarz being elevated to the House of Lords would be zero.

But Fred made a mental note to talk to Abby about this sort of thing. It was not really pleasant. She ought to drop it.

Abby called back about the dates. 'I can ask the Prince, certainly. I would enjoy a day in the field myself. But why are you so keen?'

'It's Nshila who is most keen. I think it's part of her admiration of things that are peculiarly English. She's never seen a hunt.'

'It may take a few days to fix. One can't always reach the Prince. I think that he is briefly away in his home country – something about beefing up the punishments they hand out to thieves. I'll get back to you as soon as I can.'

By then it was October 29th. Fred had recorded a Schwarz visit to MM and was moderately pleased with the results. But some of the extreme things that MM had done with the other client he had observed were missing. Perhaps November 4th would be better.

The other big problem was getting Nshila to start work on the assassination. Speed was now vital. He got to The Rain Consultancy to find the three of them discussing a business opportunity and was told to get lost for an hour – either keeping quiet in a corner or disappearing to a coffee shop. He stayed in the room and tried to read a book. But their conversation was quite interesting.

It was all about a request for weather forecasts from a firm called Sub-Saharan Multiwheels (or SSM). They operated haulage routes in all Southern African countries – Ghana to Maputo and Nairobi to Cape Town. Somehow they had heard of the weather stations set up by The Rain Consultancy and felt that the firm could help with route planning. Gillian, Peter and Nshila were arguing fiercely about what could be promised and what money could be asked for. Finally it was over and Nshila was free.

'Mistress, I am making good progress and there is a chance of making the hit on 9th November.'

'Are you sure? Will you get pictures in time and get the client's assurance that they are adequate?'

'I can't tell how long he will take deliberating, but I promise you those pics will do the job. Some of them will be truly extreme – real killers for anybody seeking appointment to a dignified place like the House of Lords. And you don't need to wait till the client has uttered, do you? He can't come to any other conclusion, so it hardly matters if he reaches it before or after the death of the Prince. What we need now is for you to get whatever materials you need. And you haven't even told me yet how you will do it. I'm not even sure if you have bothered to think about it.'

'You are a persistent little devil, aren't you? If you get everything in place – and that's a pretty colossal if – then three days will be enough for me to get ready, and to brief you for your role. Have I bothered to think about it? Of course I have. Why do you think I asked you to get samples of his hair? But I promise you that I'll think a bit more about ways and means. Is that all?'

'It's all I planned to ask. But if it turns out that your plans for the death need a lot of gofering from me, can you let me know in advance? I'm not finding it too easy to cope with this juggling of people and dates.'

Abby rang Fred on the evening of 2nd November. The Prince had been delighted to have his invitation accepted, and made it clear that he expected the whole party on November 9th. This meant Abby, Nshila, Fred, Mike Fanshawe and Araminta Kubaka. He had asked how many would ride, and Abby had confirmed for herself and Araminta. The Prince promised to find suitable mounts for them. He himself would be riding his usual grey.

On November 4th, Fred recorded Schwarz's visit to MM and was felt he had really hit the jackpot. MM suggested some activities to Schwarz, who seemed a little doubtful. MM teased him with his lack of courage and he agreed to submit. The pics were devastating. Fred spent all night editing and sent his selection off to the client by secure courier.

Chapter Thirty-Eight

The Small Print

The stimulus that caused Nshila to upgrade the Thaqib project came from Mike Fanshawe. He had been describing his experience as host to Araminata Kubaka.

'I took her to a rugby match. A mistake, you think? Well, she wanted "English", rugby obviously qualifies, and the season was just starting. It was hilarious. She thought the ball was some sort of fetish that each team was trying to plant in the enemy territory so that it could work black magic against them. And she was appalled that a man who had been thrown to the ground was allowed to get up again. She kept shouting, "Finish him, you idiot!" The scrum was quite beyond her, and I failed miserably when I tried to explain it. I mean, it's easy to say *what* is supposed to happen, but *why* gets you into heavy stuff about historical development. It's as bad as trying to explain why people like hitting a tiny white ball into a faraway hole, with bent sticks.'

'Did your friends like her?'

'Yes. Very much. She was so friendly and enthusiastic and outgoing. Some of them offered tall stories about the purpose of the scrum just to see how much she would believe. Somebody told her that the intention was to reinforce the magical potency of the fetish by urinating on it. She swallowed that, and said, "I suppose that's why they are all drinking from water bottles whenever there is a break in the play." I had an invitation to a party with the teams that evening, and I took her along. She recognised our scrum half, who is quite a small man physically. She swooped down and embraced him. He disappeared for a moment inside her robes. She remembered seeing him up-ended by an opposing forward and was very indignant. "You should have kicked him in the crotch," she told him. One of my cruder friends was amazed that any woman could be that huge, and dug a finger into her thigh. She turned round and gave him a hug like an anaconda and told him he was a marvellous, marvellous man.'

'She's a notable character!'

'She is indeed. She was very indignant about the sin-bin concept. She thought that just sitting in a box for ten minutes was a pathetic level of punishment. She got quite worked up about it.'

"In this country you have the stocks and the pillockry, I think. This I have seen in the expedition at Tussauds. You should have this for your sin bin! All people could throw the garbage. I think this word is audience precipitation. I should enjoy this."

'There was more like that, too. But I learnt one particular thing about her that you would find interesting, Nshila.'

'What's that?'

'She hates Arabs.'

'I'm surprised. She was perfectly civil to Prince Thaqib when they were together.'

'She had to be. She's a diplomatic wife. But it was when we discussed that meeting that it all came out. She sees Arabs as outwardly polite and courteous, but deceitful and evil-minded behind it. "Play them at their own game" is her motto. "Smile and smile and be a villain. Get everything you can from them, and then put a knife in their back before they do the same to you."'

'How did she get that way?'

'The slave trade, she says. In England we think of the slave trade only in terms of our own history and the Atlantic coast of Africa. But the Arabs traded down the East coast for some centuries before that. They followed trade routes through the island city of Kilwa reaching down into Mozambique and the mouth of the Zambesi and the regions inland from it. The trade included ivory, gold, spices, textiles, jewelry, porcelain – and slaves. The Arabs were sometimes in competition with the Portuguese, and Araminta is partly of Portuguese descent. She is married to an African and there might be an ancestor on either side who was sold into slavery. Anyway, hatred of Arabs has been handed down in the family.'

'By the way, she's dead keen on taking part in this hunt on November 9th. She swears that she knows how to ride, but I don't know her standard. She may be just a "trotting in the park" rider or she may be a real demon. And I'm afraid I can't be with you on the day to hold her hand. There's a week of meetings in Dubai that's an absolute three-line whip in my outfit.'

Something in the story made an impact on Nshila. She focussed directly on the task and set Fred to work.

'This is going to be a belt-and-braces job. Witchcraft-wise, we are going to simulate a horse jumping over a hedge and throwing the rider. So you have to go shopping – somewhere that sells soft toys. We want a grey horse, and we want a human figure in hunting gear of appropriate size.'

'If horse and rider are all in one, is that OK?'

'Of course not. The rider has to be thrown off. You must know that by now. When instructing the spirits, we have to get the small print right. When we mimic the event, the horse has to land safely and only the rider has to die. If we get it wrong, the spirit might kill the horse, too, and I don't intend to harm an innocent grey mare. If you can get an obviously male rider, that would be great, but it's unlikely. Gender neutral is probably all that's possible. Just don't come back with a figure that has a huge bust and sits side-saddle.'

'What about the practical part?'

'I haven't decided yet on the exact drug, but you are probably going to find yourself in a pharmacy, or maybe in a nightclub asking around for a supplier. On the big day you are going to be one of the people handing round what they call the Stirrup Cup. That's a drink the riders take in the saddle before the hunt moves off. It's usually hot toddy, with quite a modest alcohol content. You will have several glasses on your tray, and you're going to make sure that the Prince takes the one with a drug in it. The drug won't be strong, certainly not strong enough to kill him, but it will impair his judgement and increase the chance of his making a mistake.'

Fred had a hard time at the toyshops. Most of the horses were black or brown, and the choice of greys was limited. The riding figures were mostly astride horses – firmly fixed to them – or unmounted, with their legs together and incapable of being placed on a horse. Possibly because the traditional form of hunting had been made illegal, few figures wore the right gear. Fred spent three hours searching. He was despondent – close to giving up – when he passed a shop devoted to field sports. An assistant was preparing a new window display, and Fred was just in time to see him remove a horse-and-rider combination of exactly the right type. Diving into the shop, Fred asked if the proprietor would sell.

'Gladly. It's getting a bit worn, as you can see, and I've had a few passers-by get angry with me for displaying a politically incorrect image. I doubt if old Dobbin will be going into the window again. But are you sure you want him? I can't classify him as "saleable goods".'

Fred checked the final detail. Yes. Horse and rider were made in two pieces and only held together by a few stitches. He thrust a twenty pound note at the proprietor and rushed out into the street – horse and rider, unwrapped, tucked under his arm. He returned to Eastcheap, very pleased.

'Well done, Fred. The figure looks a bit heavy in the chest and might possibly be taken for a woman. But we'll drag a bit of the stuffing out and it will do fine.'

'What next?'

'I think I'll handle the drug part myself. But we need a location for casting the spell, and it ought to be geographically quite close to Snargate. Get down there and search. The ideal place is old and small and dark and deserted. Something that reminds me a bit of the hut under the baobab tree. Very few windows, please, and walls that you put nails into for hanging masks and bones and charms. Take a digital camera and bring me back some images.'

Two days later, Fred was back with three possibilities. One was a portacabin on a building site where the builder had temporarily run out of money. It was lonely, but quite easy to reach because of the track left by the builder's vehicles. The second was a disused garage on the edge of a village. It was one of the many small local garages that had been driven out of business by the diminishing margin on petrol sales and the increasing complexity of cars. Owners took them, these days, to agents appointed by the manufacturers, and those manufacturers were not interested in training and appointing tiny independent garages. This one had a discoloured sign outside saying 'Godber's Motor and Cycle Repairs (1941) Ltd'. The interior was large and empty. It was also noisy – the wind caused the corrugated iron roof to rattle, and various hanging cables banged against the walls. The third location was an old plate-layers' hut beside a recently closed railway line.

Nshila rejected the portacabin as unromantic and the garage as too near a populated area - also too large to have the right atmosphere. She favoured the plate-layers' hut.

She told Fred to get all the gear together and be ready for a start at noon on 8th November. She also said that she would be away from the office for the next two days since another project needed her attention. Fred wondered what it was.

Chapter Thirty-Nine

The Builder And The Priest

Nshila was just getting out of her car when a van drew up beside her. It was cleaner than the usual builder's van, and bore the legend 'Thaxted and Thorn Specialist Builders'. The driver introduced himself. 'Oliver Thorn, Ms. Ileloka. I'm the public face of the partnership. Thaxted is a bit more earthy, so we don't send him out for client meetings.'

'But is he a good builder? Are you a good builder?'

'Pretty good at most types, both of us, but when it comes to restoring places like this, then I reckon we are up there with the best. Are you the owner now? Has it all gone through?'

'We're exchanging contracts on Saturday.'

Together, they walked round Rowan Hall. Nshila's requirements were easy to express. She wanted the original house restored as nearly as possible to the way the original builders left it. She wanted all the accretions of later dates destroyed. Thorn immediately objected.

'No, you don't. You don't want it the way they left it. They had very high ceilings that made the rooms impossible to heat, and they had no plumbing and no radiators. Be realistic.'

She gave in. She gave in about other matters, too, as Oliver Thorn listed the many modern conveniences that she took for granted in normal life but would be missing in any totally accurate restoration. He also referred to re-sale value, which Nshila had never considered. The tour ended with Thorn understanding fully what she wanted, but having a great deal of discretion about the details. And then they went out into the grounds.

'Just about here, I want you to create a mound of earth, and build a round hut on top of it with a thatched roof. I want just one door, facing south west so that I can glimpse the river through those trees. And I want you to get the most mature tree that can be safely transplanted and set it beside the hut.'

'For Heaven's sake! Are you trying to build a 17th Century folly, like those young men did after seeing classical buildings on their Grand Tour? It's money wasted.'

Nshila was adamant. It didn't matter how hard it would be to find a thatcher, or how expensive, or what the structure was for. That's what she wanted, and if Thaxted and Thorn were unwilling to build it, the whole deal was off. The hut must have an internal diameter of about fifteen feet. The walls must be made of upright poles, the gaps being filled in with cement. She would have preferred dried mud, but in the English climate she would settle for cement, dark brown in colour. In her mind, she saw the hut under the baobab tree in which she had learnt so much.

'I think you're mad, Ms. Ileloka, but if that's really what you want, and you're prepared to pay, then that's what we'll do.'

'Good. Do it, then. Who's this?'

Approaching across the grass was a middle-aged man with a substantial grey beard. He wore a sweater in startling shades of purple and yellow, black trousers, and stout black shoes. On his head was a flat cap.

'It's Jehovah – alias your local vicar. You're going to love this. I'm off.'

'Ms. Ileloka? Good Morning. I'm Peter Proctor – Reverend Peter Proctor.' Briefly, he swept the beard aside to reveal a dog collar. 'I'm vicar here at St Martin's. I was passing, and saw the activity. I believe you have bought the hall? Is that right?'

'If you know my name, you probably know the answer to that, as well.'

Peter laughed. 'Yes, I do. This is a rural community, and you've done quite enough already to arouse interest. I doubt if there's anybody close by who doesn't know. I mean, getting rid of ghosts is quite an achievement.'

'Is that said about me?'

'It is. And a few ghost-hunters have been disappointed. Great boasts made by local young men and then an utterly boring, peaceful night.'

'People have stayed here overnight, then?'

'They say so. But nothing criminal. Just youthful adventures.'

'Well, I hope I shall be allowed to live in Rowan Hall without becoming a constant focus of attention.'

'The curiosity will die out in time. Will you be coming to the church at all? Are you that way inclined? Do you sing? We need a few new voices.'

'I might come. I'm a great admirer of English traditions, and your church is a part of that scene. I can't say I have a strong Christian background. Where I grew up they had a rather different view of spiritual activity.'

'I suppose so. But once people get talking constructively, it's amazing what one group can learn from another. I did anthropology at university, and I think that all religions have a common purpose. Maybe you can teach me something, and I, you.'

'Maybe, vicar. But no promises yet.'

On that note they parted.

Chapter Forty

The Spell

The disused railway line passed a mile from Snargate. Halfway down a long, long straight stretch stood the platelayers' hut. It was made of wood. It was large enough to have allowed six railwaymen to sit down inside it, if they huddled close together. It had an iron stove in one corner and a round, badly bent chimney leading through a hole in the roof. On the top of the chimney was one of those tiny round hats that were intended to disperse the smoke. The hut had one small window, black with dirt and partly obscured on the outside by a wooden shutter that hung drunkenly by one hinge. All around were green fields, with small trees blown one way by the wind and heavily populated by sheep. The car was in an old engine shed almost a mile away, left there after they had booked in at the hotel and checked that Araminta was also expected. Nshila and Fred had struggled along the track with all their materials.

The walls were adorned with devil masks, groups of bones, swatches of hair and scrolls of black paper carrying symbols and words. A small fire burned in the stove. It created a surprising amount of heat and flared up at irregular intervals, throwing strange shadows. Nshila cast incense upon it frequently. The atmosphere was hot, sweet, sickly and oppressive. It was also, to Fred, frightening. Nshila herself was frightening. She was dressed in a full, flowing black robe, and had a long black cloak over it. On her head was a hat apparently made of reeds. It was not conical, like the witches' hats shown in fairy stories. It was more like a squashed trilby. It came down over her forehead and almost covered her eyes. She seemed to have grown taller and assumed an aura of power.

On an old, scarred workbench against the wall was the model they had created to mimic the fall. The key to it was an old curtain rail holding a wheel between two flanges. The wheel could travel freely along the rail but could not escape from it. From the centre of the wheel a rod stood out, and onto this the horse was fixed, with the rider seated loosely upon it. The rail was curved – upwards towards an apex and then down again. The horse could be pulled in a horizontal direction by a string attached to its chest. By a controlled pull – Fred had been made to practise this again and again – the horse could simulate a jump and land on its feet. By a sharp extra tug as it reached the apex, the rider could be made to fall off. The identity of the rider was proclaimed by the hairs from Prince Thaqib's head, worked neatly into the white arab clothing.

Dirge-like music came from a tape recorder. Nshila threw more powder on the fire, wrapped her cloak closely around her and began the incantation. Slowly at first, and quietly. Then a bit more aggressively, with longer words and exaggerated hand movements. A silence. Then a quick crescendo of words, a final shriek and a nod towards Fred.

Fred jerked the string, and got it wrong. The horse rose quickly towards the apex and then slowed. The rider fell forward onto the neck of the horse but was not thrown off.

Nshila was shaking from her efforts, sweating heavily under her robes and headdress, and totally furious. Fred had never seen her so angry. She raised both arms as if to curse him – then lowered them and swore instead.

Silence for a few moments. Then she said, in an almost normal voice. 'There have to be more hedges than one in this hunting field. We must try again.' She made no further criticism of Fred, judging that it would make him more nervous.

The second time Fred got it exactly right. A short, sharp jerk as the horse approached the apex, and Prince Thaqib was thrown from his mount. The horse landed safely. In an unrehearsed movement, Nshila grabbed an old, discarded hammer from the floor, and struck three smart blows on the neck of the fallen rider. Belt and braces, she thought as she did it.

The walk back to the car was a nightmare for Fred. He had to carry all the materials – and offer support to Nshila who was exhausted. Several times she staggered and leant against him. Once she put her foot into a rabbit hole and fell. He dropped some of the gear and held out both hands to help her up.

'Thank you, Fred.'

The incident had a strange effect on Fred. He was surprised to find that he felt protective towards her. Next he felt admiration, almost awe, for her spiritual strength. What would it be like when he was a true witchdoctor? As a man, he would have more physical strength, but would he ever be able to match her in spirit? Overall, he felt good. He was learning, he had much still to learn, but it was a road worth travelling. Finally they reached the car. Nshila fell asleep and Fred drove to the hotel. He saw Nshila to her room, where she collapsed on the bed and slept. Fred went to the reception desk to check that Araminta had arrived. The night porter raised his eyes from a girlie magazine and gave him the story.

'Arrived? You mean erupted, don't you? I'm told Queen Elizabeth once passed this way back in 1554. I'll bet she caused less disturbance. Look at that!'

The porter showed Fred the registration book.

ARAMINTA KUBAKA
EMBASSY OF ANACANDA

Fred was also invited to look in the car park. There he found a stretch limousine painted in the garish national colours of Anacanda. Araminta had arrived!

Chapter Forty-One

The Meet

'Full English for me.' Nshila showed no sign of the weariness that had hit her the night before. 'We have plenty of time before the meet and only six miles to drive.'

She took a small pot of pills from her handbag and gave it to Fred.

'This is the drug. I will fix it for you to be one of the people who hand round the Stirrup Cup. Put one of these pills in the glass that the Prince is to take. It dissolves immediately. It doesn't affect the colour or the taste.'

'Ah! The pills is it? Young people like you should not be the drugs employing in the morning.' Araminta Kubaka kissed them both and settled her bulk on the designer chair chosen by the hotel for the breakfast room. It creaked alarmingly.

'I am the full English also, please. But I must have the tomato sauce on the fried egg, I think.'

Nshila and Fred had no further chance to speak privately, for it seemed that the chauffeur had been promised time off and Araminta was relying on her friends for transport to the meet. Nshila was relegated to the back seat while Fred drove – forcing his left hand hard against Artaminta's immense, jodphur-covered thighs whenever he needed to change gear.

The meet was held at The Oak and Ivy, a rather modern roadhouse-like structure whose red brick walls showed no trace of either tree or plant. The Prince, who met them as soon as they arrived, explained that it had replaced a more traditional building when Oxney Ales had sold out to a big brewer. The original Oak and Ivy had been deemed too small to generate the income the purchaser required. But with the new building, more land had been purchased and there was now plenty of space for the meet.

'Where is the Reverend Abigail?' The Prince was concerned

that she was not with her friends.

It was Fred who replied. 'She will be here soon, Prince. She had to take a dawn service at her church.'

'Good. I have a horse for her, and a horse also for you, Ms. Kubaka. I think I will wait for Abigail and see you both mounted at the same time. Right now, perhaps you would care to meet the Master and some of our senior members.'

Introductions were made. The Master carefully pointed out some of the more 'conservative' riders with whom Araminta might join up. His estimate of her was obvious. 'Noisy, ignorant, incompetent and stupidly brave'. He could see no fault in the major items of her turnout – the embassy Head of Protocol had done a good job – but he averted his eyes from her hard hat which, like the stretch limousine, reflected the national colours. He was much more approving of Nshila, who was dressed in a quiet tweed suit and wanted directions to some vantage point from which she could watch the hunt. Their conversation was just ending when a battered white mini-bus labelled 'St Aubyns Church and Hospice' drove fast into the car park and skidded to a stop amidst the Range Rovers and people carriers and Porsches and Mercedes. The Reverend Abigail got out, still in clerical gear.

'My battery was flat. I tried to start the car just before service and it never even tried. I cut my sermon in half and grabbed this heap from the pool instead. It isn't even licensed. Reverend Orberry must have forgotten. My hunting gear is inside. Give me five minutes and I'll be with you.'

She was almost as good as her word. Eight minutes later the rear of the mini-van opened and disgorged a figure very different from an East London mission priest. Heads turned.

'Right, girls,' said the Prince. 'Meet your mounts.' He signalled to a waiting groom and two horses were led forward. 'This is Fancy Nancy, Reverend. She's a beautiful creature and very surefooted. There are times when she gets a bit over-excited, but that should be no problem to an experienced horsewoman.'

'She looks marvellous, Prince.'

'And here's Clementine, Ms. Kubaka. She's a tiny bit slow, but she'll carry you all day. I would have liked to give you something faster, but there was nothing with the necessary stamina.'

Thus, diplomatically, the Prince let it be known that Araminta was just too heavy for anything normal. Clementine was huge, slow, sleepy and friendly. She ran her nose all over Araminta, seeking food.

'Why the name?'

The Prince smiled. 'It was a joke, really. It comes from the old song about a miner and his daughter – Clementine. It has the lines;

Light she was, and like a fairy, and her shoes were Number Nine.
Herring boxes without topses sandals were for Clementine'.

When the stable staff saw how large she was going to be, they got this smart idea for her name. And just look at those massive feet!'

'Well, I love her already. We're going to have a great day, Clementine, you and I.'

The time came for handing round the stirrup cup, and Fred slotted easily into his role. Simply dressed in black trousers and a white pullover, he looked fit and manly and attracted admiring glances from the women. Nshila, once the majority of people had mounted, had found herself a seat on the brick wall that surrounded a flowerbed. She watched his progress through the riders, keen to be sure that he had reached the Prince and that the Prince had drunk the potion. There were times when Fred was concealed behind a horse, and once, when she relocated him, he was standing outside the group fiddling with something on his tray. But soon after that she had a clear view of the Prince taking a glass, drinking it, and handing it back. When Fred next passed her – on the way to the bar for more supplies – she called him over and asked what had happened.

'A near-disaster. I was asked a question by one of those women who are going to keep an eye on Araminta. I was looking up at her and an arm came over my shoulder, took a glass off my tray, and a voice said, "I'll have one of those, thank you". It all happened in a second, and I was still speaking to the lady. When I looked at the tray, I realised that the mystery hand had taken the glass set aside for the Prince. I couldn't see who it was that had taken it. Luckily I had the pill bottle in my pocket. I fixed a replacement drink and the Prince took it. All's well.'

'Another thing, Nshila. The Prince is a truly evil person. He's all sweetness and goodwill towards us, but I heard him talking on his mobile. It must have been to some subordinate in his own country. He said, "If I don't call you tomorrow you can carry out the sentence. But I might easily be in touch. Two fingers is a poor punishment for that sort of crime. The whole hand might be more appropriate".'

Nshila was neither surprised nor concerned about the cruelty. But she was inclined to dispute Fred's airy statement that all was well.

'Giving the drug to an unknown body will be very bad news if it proves too strong. We may have an unwanted accident. Are you sure you don't know who took it?'

'No. They were all moving around so much. What I did notice, when the arm came over my shoulder, was that the hand had a very large ring on one of the fingers, and a green stone in it. It was certainly a woman's hand.'

'That doesn't help us much. I hope it was a big woman because the more the body-weight the less effect the drug will have.'

'There's nothing we can do now. Let's just hope for a heavy body or for the drug to be ineffective without the spell.'

Fred continued with his handing-round duties, and then hounds began to move off. He came to sit beside Nshila and they watched the field go by. As Reverend Abigail rode past, she waved her hand to them. Both of them had clear sight of a heavy gold ring with an emerald set in it.

Fred panicked. 'What can we do? What can we do?' He started to run after Abby, but the close-packed riders made it impossible. 'She's not a heavy girl. The drug may be too strong for her. We may have killed her. Think of something, Mistress. Help me. Help her. You have to. You must do. We can't endanger a lovely girl like her.'

Nshila was less worried. She thought that Abby was smart enough to recognise any lessening of her faculties and act sensibly. There was a risk, but in her view not a great one. And she had never liked panic.

'Well, Fred, you could try praying.'

'Yes. Yes. Yes. Let's both do it. But which God?'

'Hers, I suppose. The Christian God. She's on his payroll, after all.'

Fred started. It was unconventional but utterly sincere.

'Oh, God! Christian God! Yahweh or Jehovah or whatever title is right! Hear me, please, and keep her safe. It was my fault, God. I never meant to hurt her. Keep her safe. Keep her safe. She's a lovely girl and she's done nothing wrong. You're not going to hold those piddling errors in the crypt against her, are you? They never harmed anybody. The men loved it. I know it seems obscene to you and me, God, but they did. Keep her safe, God, please! She's a fine priest. Remember those uplifting sermons she gives. And she'll make a marvellous Bishop. You don't want to lose one of those do you? You don't have too many good ones. You need her. Keep her safe, God, please. And forgive my stupidity. Don't punish her because of my mistake. Please, God, please!'

When he paused, Nshila managed a friendly 'Amen' and moved her own agenda onwards.

'You go on praying, Fred, but do it in the car. We're going to that vantage point from which the Master said we would see most. I'll give you back-up support with an 'Amen' whenever you need it, but I'm more interested in the Prince.'

The viewing point was not quite what had been promised. In order to get the car off the road it was necessary to open a broken and long-neglected five-bar gate. Fred was totally committed to his prayerthon and Nshila had to do the physical work. The top part of the broken gate was not too bad. It moved, reluctantly and noisily on the hinge. The bottom half was so overgrown with grass and weeds that it seemed set in concrete. Bit by bit, Nshila tore the grass away and exposed the lowest, heavily rotted bar. Loosing patience, she drove the car into the remains and finally got through.

The result was worth it. They had a fine view of the country and several riders could be seen. The action was too fragmented for Nshila to figure out where the fox was – if they had found one – or in which direction the general affair was moving. But a succession of short scenes were acted out in front of her.

A large, middle-aged lady walked up the field towards their gate, leading a lame horse. She stopped beside the car and explained. 'Rotten luck, today. We were going like wildfire until she suddenly went lame. I'm not going to take any risks with Shiner, so it's back to a warm stable and some TLC.'

As she moved onto the road, 'By the way, that young lady you brought with you is a bit of a demon. She's tackling every hedge in sight like a bouncing ball. What a seat she has! I wish I was young and devilish and over-confident like that. I just hope she doesn't come to grief. We like our visitors to survive, if possible. I think I'll wait here for a moment in case we see her.'

That set Fred off again. 'Thank you, God. At least she was alive till a few moments ago. Take her in hand, please, God. Get some sense into her. I can't stand much more of this tension. Think what she did for you this morning, God. Up at some appalling hour to take that dawn service. And remember how well she does it, God. No mumbling at the floor like so many of your preachers. Straight honest stuff in clear forthright tones. That business of flogging the papist back at Hedgewood? You're not going to punish her for that, are you? It was a good thing to do. It helped his spirituality, God. Please, please keep her safe.'

'Amen.'

The next scene opened. Out of a wood two hundred yards in front of them, and off to their right, appeared a horse and rider, going fast. 'That's her. That's her.' The lady behind them on the road almost screamed in excitement. 'Just watch her. I never saw anything like it.'

Abby and Fancy Nancy were taking a line across a field below them, heading towards a large hedge. There was a gap in it – an easy and obvious way through – but they seemed to be ignoring it and going for the very highest part of the hedge. Abby looked briefly behind her. Why, wondered Nshila and Fred. They soon knew. Out of the same wood, riding the same line, came a tall man on a grey horse. The Prince! It had to be the Prince! Somehow or other, the two had got into competition. 'Anything you can do, I can do better.'

Fred closed his eyes, crossed his fingers and started praying again. 'Get her over, God. Please. Get her over and then make the horse lame. Just stop her, God. Please! Any way you like. Just stop her. I know there's a sadistic streak in her, but you made her, didn't you? All those men, God? Same answer. If you build a woman that way, what do you expect? Keep her safe! Keep her safe. Please.'

'Amen.'

Fancy Nancy flew gracefully over the hedge, landed safely, and the pair were off down the next field. Fred relaxed. The grey, following, took off fractionally too early, caught the top of the hedge and threw his rider. The grey landed safely but the rider lay still. Nshila clasped her hands over her head in a victory gesture.

Too soon. About a minute after the fall, the body moved. The Prince raised his head. Somehow he drew his legs under his body and was on all fours. Then he was on his knees. Finally he was on two legs and staggering very slowly along the line of the hedge towards the gap.

The final act. Nshila knew what was to happen. It was like one of the comic films of past times when a sequence is built up with such skill that the audience can see the climax coming. Nshila was well placed, of course, because she knew about her own instinctive reaction after the simulated fall in the platelayers' hut. She was totally certain when she heard a loud female voice shout, 'Tally-ho, the fox...' and saw a huge figure on a huge slow horse emerge from the wood. Neither Clementine nor Araminta had any intention of jumping obstacles. It was as if Clementine, with years of equine wisdom, had somehow communicated with Araminta:

'Look, you just sit on my back and relax. Watch the scenery and enjoy yourself. I'll look after where my feet go. That way we'll get through the day without any alarms.'

They cantered majestically towards the gap in the hedge,

Araminta surveying the world from an upright stance and shouting, at intervals, words that – she had been told - were appropriate. 'Gone away!' was her favourite. Meanwhile, the Prince - on the other side of the hedge and sheltered by it - crept painfully towards the gap.

It all happened so fast that most observers would have been unable to describe the sequence. For Nshila, it seemed to be presented in slow motion, as if the spirit was trying to point out how clever he had been. The Prince arrived at the gap just as the bulk of Clementine's forequarters filled it. The surprise called him to fall again. He fell forward into the gap and hit the ground just behind Clementine's front hooves. He almost escaped the back ones, too, but not quite. The last hoof fell fractionally in front of his neck but the backward thrust of it made contact. His neck was neatly broken and he never moved again. Araminta seemed to hesitate for a moment, as if she had spotted the riderless grey and was wondering whether she should do anything. She must have decided against it, for she shouted 'Tally ho, the fox!' and rode on. Clementine might have noticed the event, but she did nothing. Her job for the day was to take care of Araminta.

Chapter Forty-Two

Outcomes

The local GP had seen such things before. He certified the death as accidental with the minimum of fuss. The only significant witness was Nshila, for Fred had had his eyes shut in prayer and Araminta had been focused on the riderless horse. It seemed odd that the grey had landed beside the gap in the hedge, while the Prince had been found lying across it. But nobody suspected foul play, it was an accident, whatever the exact circumstances, and there was no value in starting a tedious official enquiry. Also, the MFH wanted the affair closed off as soon as possible.

The Prince was buried quickly, in accordance with his religion.

Everybody was sympathetic to Araminta, assuring her that she was in no way to blame for the death. She insisted on taking Clementine back to her stable and helping to wash her down. She told everybody what a marvellous day she had had and folded the MFH in a hearty, lengthy embrace. He seemed relieved when it was over. She dined with Nshila and Fred at the hotel, consuming huge quantities of food and alcohol. Her hosts were worn out and very abstemious.

The Reverend Alice Abigail Fordcombe said that she had ridden all day in a confused mental state and expressed amazement when people described how she had ridden. 'Did I really do that? I can't believe it.' She remembered some rivalry with Prince Thaqib, but, 'One moment he was right on my tail. The next moment I had lost him.' She rejected the invitation to dine with Nshila and Fred, saying that she had to be back in London to conduct a counselling session early next morning. Fred was quite pleased to see her go, for his relief at her survival had made him over-attentive. She had felt crowded, and been angry with him.

A minor thief in the Prince's home country was relieved to be punished only with the loss of two fingers. With the remaining two fingers, and an opposable thumb, he could still ply his trade. His wife upbraided him for being caught and urged him to plan more carefully in future. She was furious when he attempted a cheap joke about the reduced risk of finger-print identification.

Sir Barnaby Scott returned to his manor house. He asked the vicar of St Bartholomew's Parish Church to dinner – they had been friends for years. Sir Barnaby waited till they were sitting in the library over the port and then explained what he wanted.

'Eddie, I know that you want to retire. I know you find the present ecclesiastical climate objectionable. I sympathise with you. But I really would be grateful if you could hang on for another eighteen months.'

'Why, Barnaby? Till now you have been resigned to my retirement. What's changed?'

'What's changed is that I have met your replacement. I was out with the Snargate Vale yesterday and I met this outstanding woman, Reverend Fordham.'

'You know I don't like female priests.'

'Yes, I know. But times are changing and you won't be here to see it. After all, whoever we get is bound to be different. You've been here thirty years and a new person is bound to alter things. Will it matter too much if the person is a woman?'

'You must have strong reasons for wanting her.'

'I do. Firstly, she is very intelligent. Secondly she has the right social background. Thirdly, she has the most marvellous seat on a horse. She will fit in here perfectly and everybody will love her.'

'What about her churchmanship? We don't want some sectarian enthusiast who will divide the community.'

'Quite safe, Eddie. She has a broad, understanding attitude and won't rock any boats. Typical Church of England, she is. Reckons you can believe almost anything in your heart provided you never say or do anything that will seriously antagonise people.'

'If you're so convinced, Barnaby, why do you want me to hang on?'

'Because she still has to complete her curacy. She's at St Aubyn's in the City and can't reasonably leave just yet.'

'Will you be able to get her appointed? I know that you are the patron here, and at St James and St John, too. But will you be able to get the PCC to accept her, and the Bishop to approve?'

'I think so. The people on our PCC are very sound. And the bishop dines here from time to time. You know that. Do you seriously think he is going to offend half the county by being difficult?'

'I suppose not.'

Fred was totally confused. Nshila's witchcraft had achieved the death of Prince Thaqib. His prayers to the Christian God had preserved Abby. Where did power truly lie? Nshila comforted him. 'You'll never know, Fred. Nobody will ever know as long as the world lasts. Just accept that there is power beyond human understanding and that we can sometimes tap into it. All seekers have their own routes and all of them work some of the time. For the record, I am becoming influenced by Christianity myself. It's got some intellectual credibility when you get the right people presenting it.'

'What should I do?'

'For the present, stick with me. I've grown accustomed to your face and I can even see some potential in you. You'll never know the hut under the baobab tree, but I can teach you all that Kwaname taught me, and that's quite a lot. And I can teach you all that I have grafted on since. By the time you are twenty-five you will be standing where I am at thirty-five. That, of course depends on your surviving whatever graduation ritual I devise for you. And you'll have years and years to go on growing. You may even find meeting points with Christianity and the other great world religions. Perhaps they are not opposites to witchcraft at all.'

Clementine dozed comfortably in her stable, dreaming horsey dreams that were somehow pleasurable. She was dimly aware of having used muscles not often brought into play – also of a large human who seemed to love her and smelt interesting as well.

In the next box, Fancy Nancy was so exhilarated by the day that it took her ages to relax and sleep.

The Prince had been staying with an old school friend. His name was Gerald Gilliat and he owned Gilliat's Leisure and Adventure

Centre. It was he who collected the grey horse and took it home. It was he, also, who sorted through the Prince's personal effects. Since the Prince had stayed at his house many times there was more than just week-end baggage. Gerald was disturbed to find some papers that seemed to describe illegal acts, and named 'operators' who were to take part. Gerald didn't want to know about such things. But he took the papers with him when he next went to London and handed them over to another old school friend who had shadowy links to the intelligence services. A month later six arrests were made.

Jilly Jordan passed through customs at Heathrow. He passed a newsagent and a shocking headline caught his eye. This, he must see – if he had any English coins in his pocket. He didn't. Ten minutes later he had changed some money, bought three different papers, and was sitting in a café area with coffee and croissants. From the papers, he learnt of the death of Prince Thaqib. Confusion overwhelmed him. Maybe he should go right back to South America on the next flight. Life was not treating him well. Two failed attempts on the target, an abortive trip back home to neutralise a non-existent threat, and now the target removed. But wait! The death seemed to have been accidental. Could he somehow claim that he had engineered it? Perhaps he would tell his employer that he had paid an associate to drug the horse? The idea was attractive, but not really plausible. And his employer was a hard man to deceive. The best he could do, Jilly thought, was claim for expenses – which he would inflate dramatically.

Simon Trent was relieved, relaxed and happy. Prince Thaqib was dead, his principal accomplices in prison and his plot abandoned. The person he had chosen for the Anacanda expedition had brought it to an excellent conclusion and would soon be contributing to debates in the Lords. Relations with Anacanda were good, and the attitudes of the neighbouring dictator were slowly moderating. Nobody had guessed at his connection with the death.

Just one thing puzzled him. What an extraordinary coincidence that the person to be rewarded for the assassination – unknowingly – should have witnessed the death! It was extremely odd, but why should he worry? Coincidences do happen.

In a private letter to Simon's Minister, the Prime Minister wrote. 'Trent seems to be doing better than expected. He ought to be given a bit more responsibility. And perhaps you can get him to take elocution lessons. Or marry him to the right sort of woman.'

Graham Schwarz continued to visit Mistress Meg and never connected the practice with his surprising failure to win a peerage. A year later he consented to a publicity shot that required him actually to take a voyage on one of his boats. He was lost overboard in mysterious circumstances.

Nshila herself had doubts about the Prince's death, doubts that she shared only with Rasputin.

'She is a big woman, Ras, and she was sitting upright on a big horse. Is it possible that she could have seen over the hedge and been aware of the Prince staggering, bent, towards the gap?'

It had been a wide gap. Araminta could have altered her line towards the right and the Prince would have been saved. She had not done so. Was it possible that the very last contribution to the death had not been the spell, nor the drug, but a decision by Araminta that a dead Arab Prince was a small pay-back for the slave trade?

Rasputin yawned.

Chapter Forty-Three

Of Where?

Coincidences do happen. The posting of Emrys White-Walker to social services had been cancelled in favour of a stint at the section of the Cabinet Office that dealt with protocol. One morning Gillian Harker found herself staring up at a tall, gangling figure dressed in a morning coat and striped trousers.

'I don't believe it. I've strayed into a comic opera.'

'I'm sorry about the gear, look you, but this is a formal visit. Some things still have to be done in the old way. May I see Ms. Ileloka, please?'

'No. I still don't believe it. This is some crazy joke or confidence trick or marketing gimmick.'

Emrys confessed. It was indeed a joke, but primarily aimed at an old girlfriend in Wales whose ideas about London life were centuries old. He wanted a photograph of himself, thus dressed, with Nshila.

Nshila knew him at once – it was hardly possible not to. He said he had a message. 'This is formal and personal. Can we be private?'

Not a good idea, thought Nshila. The visit could be about one thing only, and keeping that quiet from Peter and Gillian was not only impossible, but rather insulting.

'No, Emrys. These are my friends.'

So Emrys worked through all the required preliminaries about the Prime Minister being 'minded to do something' that required checks and enquiries and references. Then he got to the point.

'Baroness Ileloka of Where? That's the remaining detail. Most people being elevated link themselves to some physical place that has significance for them and are styled, for instance, as Lord Littleham of Lostwithiel or such like. What will you be?'

This was not something she had thought about.

'Are there any guidelines? Surely it can't be just anywhere? I can't put a pin on the map and pick the nearest name, can I?'

'No. There are conventions, certainly. You can't choose a name already used by a peer, and you ought to have a genuine connection with the place. You can't choose a name that sounds ridiculous, and it's a mistake to choose one that's too long or is unpronounceable. If I were ever made a Lord I should like to be Lord White-Walker of Llansantffraed Cwmdeudwr, but too many people would boggle at it. Of course, some people keep it simple and use their birthplace.'

'So could I be Baroness Ileloka of Namushakende?'

'Namuwhat? Difficult to pronounce, you see, and it sounds foreign.'

'Must it be English, then?'

'We would prefer it. English or Welsh or from Northern Ireland. Scotland is a bit dodgy these days, with all the talk of independence. It would be great if you could use the place where we had that run-in with the witchdoctor, but it's as bad as Namuwhatever. Pity. Baroness Ileloka of Limalunga would sound great once one got used to it.'

Nshila was sidetracked. 'Have you heard anything from Limalunga at all? Anything about Mbangwe?'

'Yes. The government didn't want to emphasise the work of foreigners too much, so they built up his part in the affair and made him a bit of a hero. He's got a medal, and a small retainer as "Adviser to the Government on Traditional Wisdom".'

'How about that place where you fixed the weather for my wedding?' Gillian and Peter had been listening attentively and wanted a part in the discussion. 'Laxton Fen, it was called. Baroness Ileloka of Laxton Fen. How about that? It was a major triumph for you.'

'Baroness Ileloka of Bow Street? Honouring the place where you rescued me from those trumped-up charges?'

'Shut up, both of you. Look, Emrys, if it is a real place, maybe I have to ask the people who live there. They might not like it.'

'That's relevant if the place is big enough to have a proper civic body. A town council or city council. You couldn't be Baroness Ileloka of Lowestoft without asking them, for instance. Small places are usually proud to be chosen.'

'And there's one more point – you can't abbreviate. If the place you choose is, say, Trapton-by-the-trout-stream, then that's what you've got to be. You can't be just "of Trapton". Don't ask me why, it's all lost in history.'

'How long have I got?'

'I must know within a week.'

'You shall do. And you might as well have that photograph you wanted for your girl in Wales.'

Emrys unfolded himself carefully from his chair and posed with Nshila for the photo shoot, choreographed by Peter. After he left, Nshila was swamped by suggestions from Peter and Gillian, but in her mind the choice was made. On one of their long country walks, she and Mike had passed a road sign that directed them to two places with linked names like, for instance, Great Barnby and Little Barnby. Having walked for two miles in that direction and passed no habitations of any sort, no buildings at all and no side roads or tracks, they had found another sign pointing back the way they had come. It said, Great Barnby and Little Barnby. A place that didn't exist, with no population to consult. A place that had been lost for ages. As a place to be 'of' she thought it most amusing.

Four months had passed, daffodils were showing, and a dream was coming true. The vicar of St Martin's stood on the platform and addressed the village.

'Ladies and Gentleman. It's no secret that for some years we have felt ourselves to be a village in decline. We have lost the bus service. Our numbers are falling. I have buried more people than I have baptised. The Post Office is threatened with closure. The brewers would close The Goose and Gander tomorrow if Bert and Ethel were not there. When I myself retire, St. Martin's will become part of a 'Group Ministry' and all you will get is a visit once a month from a spotty adolescent, straight out of an abbreviated course at theological college.........'

'Get on with it, vicar! What's the good news?'

Peter Proctor knew he was long-winded and forgave objections.

'Alright. I'm only confirming rumours you have already heard. Ladies and Gentlemen, Rowan Hall has been bought! It has been bought by a lady with enough money to restore it properly. She will then use it as a study centre for Worldwide Open Enquiry. I'm not sure what that means, but she assures me that her students will be highly regarded experts from all over the world. Things are getting better. There will be work available in and around the hall. There will be visitors with money to spend. We shall have a patron for our cultural activities. There's even more – she is going to join our choir, and the fine young man she employs as her business manager is going to join our bell-ringers and pull the tenor bell. At Christmas we shall be ringing a full peal. It's all great news. People will soon be asking, "How do I get to this place called Fanwell St Martin?"'

'Do get on with it, vicar.'

'Very well! So, to cut the tape and open our Spring Festival, please welcome:

Baroness Nshila Ileloka of Straight and Crooked Scholey.'

Made in the USA
Charleston, SC
21 October 2011